GUNPOWDER
MOON

GUNPOWDER
MOON

DAVID
PEDREIRA

HARPER Voyager
An Imprint of HarperCollins*Publishers*

This is a work of fiction. Names, characters, places, and incidents are products of the author's imagination or are used fictitiously and are not to be construed as real. Any resemblance to actual events, locales, organizations, or persons, living or dead, is entirely coincidental.

GUNPOWDER MOON. Copyright © 2018 by David Pedreira. All rights reserved. Printed in the United States of America. No part of this book may be used or reproduced in any manner whatsoever without written permission except in the case of brief quotations embodied in critical articles and reviews. For information, address HarperCollins Publishers, 195 Broadway, New York, NY 10007.

HarperCollins books may be purchased for educational, business, or sales promotional use. For information, please email the Special Markets Department at SPsales@harpercollins.com.

Harper Voyager and design are trademarks of HarperCollins Publishers LLC.

FIRST EDITION

Designed by Paula Russell Szafranski

Frontispiece © Chris P / Shutterstock

Library of Congress Cataloging-in-Publication Data has been applied for.

ISBN 978-0-06-267608-5

17 18 19 20 21   LSC   10 9 8 7 6 5 4 3 2 1

For Lori and Madison

GUNPOWDER
MOON

1

THE MOON, MARE TRANQUILLITATIS, 2072

Dechert stood at the crater rim and looked down. Dionysius was a monster—two miles deep and wide enough to swallow the isle of Manhattan—and with the light from the setting sun coming in too shallow to illuminate its depths, it looked as black as a well. What had Fletcher told him when he was training to take over the station? Oh, yeah:

Panic will kill you—and make you look like an asshole in the process.

Bold words, but Fletcher had never strapped a six-pack of thrusters to his spacesuit and jumped into the open mouth of a crater.

No one ever had.

Dechert clenched his toes to push blood into them, but

pinpricks of frostbite continued to spider up his feet. He fiddled with his oxygen mix and stamped his legs and tried to digest the void beneath his boots.

"All right," Quarles said into his helmet.

"Shit."

"Shit what?"

"Nothing. Just warn me the next time you do that."

"Do what?"

"Talk."

"Okay. How do you want me to warn you?"

Dechert gritted his teeth. "Never mind. What do you want?"

"I was going to say things are looking good. Jets are in sync and ready to fire. Fly-by-wire and telemetry are online, angle of attack eighty-four degrees. You got your lamps on?"

"Yes." *Not like it matters.*

"Good. Let's make history. Forty seconds on my mark. And . . . mark."

Forty seconds. Dechert took a dozen clumsy steps back from the rim wall, counting off the paces. He was afraid for the first time in a long time and the sensation wasn't pleasant—a coppery taste in the mouth, a rush of awareness that reminded him of war.

"Thirty seconds."

"This better not be a feed error, Quarles. If I find that drill still eating rock down there, I'm going to throw you out of an airlock."

"Copy. Twenty seconds. Everything looks nominal."

Blood rushed through Dechert's ears. Nominal. *What the hell does that mean?* Is there a worse word in the English language? The fear held him now and he grasped for mental distractions, old pilot tricks, anything to stay focused. He skimmed the highlights of his career, checking the bullet

points of his résumé as if they were flashing across the heads
up display in his helmet: six first flights through the mountain
ranges rimming the Moon's central maria, two lunar traverse
distance records, command of a Level-1 mining station, a Silver Star for combat valor in the Bekaa Valley back on Earth.
Was this the pedigree of a coward, some Terran tenderfoot?
Could anyone doubt that he had the balls to make this jump,
whether he was huffing too hard for air or not?

And yet here he was, doubting himself.

A muted alarm beeped in his helmet and Quarles's voice
poured into his headset, coming out of the ether from five
hundred kilometers away: "Okay. Counting down from ten.
One-zero, nine, eight, seven, six, five, four, three, two, one . . .
mark. Step, and step, and firing."

He needn't have worried—as soon as Quarles said "firing,"
Dechert was taking three running hops through the Moon's
microgravity. The thrusters on his suit lifted him from the crater wall. He looked beneath his boots at the blackness and
drew his head into the back of his helmet.

"Three hundred meters and climbing," Quarles said. "Ten
seconds to apogee, twelve seconds to reverse thrust."

The last dayside views of the Sea of Tranquility appeared
as he ascended above the rimrock surrounding Dionysius.
The vertical impact cliffs of Ritter and Sabine gleamed with
ribbons of white ejecta to the southeast. The darker volcanic
flatlands of the surrounding mare stretched to the horizon like
dead African plains. He closed his eyes and waited for the heat
of the sun to be taken away from him. It was a childish thing
and he was angry as soon as he did it.

"Reverse thrust on my mark," Quarles said. "Mark."

Dechert fell. Lightness in his gut signaled the descent, a
feeling that his body was dropping while his critical organs
remained hovering above. He sucked in air and kept his eyes

shut to escape from the flight and from the Moon itself, but it only increased his feeling of disorientation. Disembodiment. He focused on the sound of his breathing, the hiss of the regulators echoing in his helmet like a scuba diver finning through a current. Quarles wouldn't need to read the biotel to know he was scared. He'd only have to listen. The Moon is soundless, and the air coming in and out of Dechert's lungs rang with evidence against him.

"How we doing?" Quarles asked.

"Not good."

"Don't throw up in your helmet."

"Good advice."

"No problem. Four-zero seconds to hop one. Still looking nominal."

"Right."

They had selected Dionysius for Drill Station 7 because it had decent water trace, but also because it was accessible. It was relatively small and uniform for a lunar impact crater, an infant cosmic bullet strike of only a billion years or so, with a floor as smooth as a North American salt flat—or so the selenologists had promised. Of course, those selenologists were reading topo-maps back in New Mexico, so Dechert wasn't overly comforted by their assurances.

He could have gone down to DS-7 in a shuttle with the extra security of a reinforced titanium seat and two tons of superalloy surrounding him, but the jetsuit had to be tested in a live mission, and he didn't like putting his crew in prototypes. Anyways, it wasn't the method that was important now. It was the mission. There was a mystery down in the crater black and a crisis that had to be resolved. The drilling station's water rover had gone silent fourteen hours ago without any warning. There was no telemetry before the crash, and no data dump to the hydrogen reduction reactor or the station's central computer. DS-7 provided a quarter of Sea of Serenity 1's fresh water and oxygen. Its failure wasn't catastrophic, but the circumstances of its demise—and more important, the timing—filled Dechert with dread. Why wasn't there any telemetry before a total blackout? Quarles couldn't figure it out and neither could Thatch, and they knew those systems better than they knew their own fingernails. The only plausible explanation was a micrometeor strike, but the chances of that happening were statistically negligible. It was as if a plug had been pulled . . . but plugs don't get pulled on the open surface of the Moon.

Cold enveloped him. He opened his eyes in Moon shadow and had to blink to make sure they weren't closed. On Earth, shadow isn't much more than shade, a patch of cool retreat from the constancy of the sun. On the Moon it's a pure black that can't be described, and at the bottom of a shadow-sided crater you might as well be at the starless edge of the universe.

The plasma lamps on his helmet cast pinpoint beams of white that did little to obliterate the nothingness. Numbers flashing on the inside of Dechert's visor told him that the crater floor was getting closer. The altimeter dialed backward like a clock flying into the past. He couldn't see anything. *I am a coward*, he thought, pushing back a wave of low-g nausea. *All the crazy shit I've done before, I was just trying to hide the goddamned truth.*

"Why do I always get the first crack at your chickenshit prototypes?" he asked Quarles, needing to break the silence even though he knew the answer that was coming.

"Because you're the only one who gets paid enough to risk explosive decompression. Also, you volunteered."

"Remind me not to do that again." Dechert looked around. "We shouldn't have tried this without infrared."

"You told me to rig the helmet without FLIR so we could

simulate blackout conditions," Quarles replied. "Look down and make sure Alpha is clear. Radar's not picking anything up, but we're gonna need at least twenty seconds to change your trajectory if there's terrain below."

Dechert craned his neck so he could see beyond the lower lip of his helmet, hoping that concentration on a task would ease the vertigo. *Pilots aren't supposed to get sick,* he thought. But pilots are usually *inside a ship,* instead of free-falling in the dark. Steam from his breath left a halo of fog on the bottom of his faceplate. His headlamps moved through the surrounding blackness as he rotated them in a slow arc, but the beams were too narrow to renew his sense of up and down. He widened the circles of illumination and saw the ground. There was only fine lunar powder in the place where he was supposed to land, regolith pounded into dust by eons of cosmic barrage.

"Looks like nothing but reg," Dechert said between breaths. "Small boulders, breccia I think, about a hundred meters to the north and a wrinkle ridge to the east, but Alpha looks clear. Remind me again what the hell I have to do on impact."

"Impact? Jeez, boss, have a little more faith. The thrusters are already slowing you down. Should be a featherbed landing. Take two steps like you're dunking a basketball and punch REENGAGE."

"How often do you think I've dunked a basketball?"

"True enough, white boy."

"Yeah, you're white, too, Quarles."

"Well, you've seen guys do it, right? Anyway, the launch sequence will start automatically and the computer will adjust the jets for orientation. We've got you set for fifteen hundred meters on the next hop. DS-7 is only two hops away after that."

"Copy."

Two hops away if something doesn't go wrong and I end up flying off into space, Dechert thought. He hated physics even when he wasn't in a panic and didn't have the mental energy needed to compute escape velocities, but he did know two things: If the minijets didn't shut down at the right moment on the way up, he could keep going into space, and if they failed to reignite on the way down, even the Moon's weak gravity had enough of a pull to make him hit like a snowball on concrete. The shutdown of DS-7 would have to be investigated by someone else.

After they collected his frozen remains.

"Two-zero seconds, reverse thrust at eighty percent, rate of descent one meter per second," Quarles said.

Dechert refocused and saw the illuminated rounds of lunar surface had grown into finer definition through his faceplate. Specks of color at the sharp edges of his field of vision had turned into ejecta boulders; hairline cracks, into deep, rocky rilles. His breathing quickened. The heads-up display flashed with numbers and a blinking quadrant of arrows pointed to the place where he would land. A muted alarm began to beep.

"Five seconds."

The steps on the powdery crater floor came quickly and with surprising anticlimax and then he was spaceborne again, climbing from Dionysius's bottomland as thrusters on his boots, shoulder harness, and backpack hissed propellant and the heads-up display in his helmet registered the ascent with a jumble of red and green numbers and attitude markers.

"One hundred meters and climbing," Dechert said, scanning the data as g-forces pushed him into the back of his suit. "Oriented at seventy degrees and in the pipe."

"Roger that, boss," Quarles replied. "Fly-by-wire is a beautiful thing. Three-zero seconds to apogee; two-six seconds to reverse thrust."

"How we looking for radiation?"

"Sun's asleep and you're shielded by angles anyways. Safe for six hours at least. Looks like a beautiful day on the Moon."

He landed at Drill Station 7 ten minutes later. It was Bible-black and cold. The water mining grid and the hydrogen reduction reactor should have been illuminated with a perimeter of blue triliptical lights. They weren't. Dechert turned up his lamps and took a few cautious steps to ease his body out of vertigo. He inched his way toward the rille, which snaked northwest across the crater floor like a finger pointing to the deadness of the Mare Vaporum. He scanned the pit's monochrome grays for several seconds before catching a flash of white.

"Okay. I'm here. I can see the sifter about twenty meters below me on the eastern wall. It's down. Doesn't look damaged. Just off-line."

"Copy. What about the command deck on the reactor?"

"Everything's off. No illumination. Making my way there now."

Dechert scrambled up the spine of the ridge to the reactor's operating shack, which looked for all the world like a telephone booth plopped down on the belly of the Moon. He could tell before he got there that nothing was on. He reached the structure and wiped a coating of dust off a hardened plasma screen. Blackness looked back at him. As he moved closer, his foot knocked into something and he glanced down at his boots.

"Jesus."

"What?"

"One of the power cells has been pulled out of the chassis. It's sitting here on the ground."

"You mean it's physically pulled out?"

"Yes."

"Which cell?"

"Hold on. A6."

"Is it damaged?"

"There's gotta be dust intrusion, but otherwise it looks okay. I'm not sure I should put it back in. Recommendations?"

Quarles was quiet for a few seconds. "Blow it out as clean as you can with compressed air and reinsert it, carefully please. We'll probably have to go back and replace the drive anyways. Let's see if that's the main issue."

"Copy. Reboot in one minute."

Dechert blew as much moondust from the triangular power cell as he could and jammed it back into the rack. He flipped the breaker and green and red dots flashed into life on the plasma screen. He could sense the xenon mining lights charging up behind him, blooming one at a time.

"She's recharging." He walked around the shack. "I don't get it, though—why didn't we receive telemetry when the cell was pulled out?"

Quarles hesitated and Dechert could almost hear him thinking. "I'm not sure. It's a variable frequency drive and it's got advanced cell bypass, meaning if one power cell fails it gets automatically isolated, and the others pick up the slack. But it also means the other cells burn out quicker."

Dechert continued to walk a widening circle around the shack. "So whoever did this knew it would slow-bleed the sifter, but we probably wouldn't be alerted?"

"That's right," Quarles said. "And they knew not to pull the cell at the star point of the configuration, which would have shut the whole thing down immediately."

"Well, whoever did it left footprints all over the place down here, and they aren't ours."

"Okay, are they alien or human?"

"I mean they aren't American, smart-ass. Treads are different, and I don't recognize them from anything I've seen on Luna. Taking pictures now. Tell Vernon or Lane to cross-reference the soles and look for a match."

Quarles was silent for several seconds. "Okay. So what the hell's going on, boss? Is this someone's idea of a prank?"

"Making us do an EVA in a shadow-sided crater is no fucking joke, Quarles. Neither is screwing with our water supply. Someone's sending a message."

"Great," Quarles said. "What language do you think it's in?"

2

Sea of Serenity 1 had been open for fourteen years, and it looked it. Buried under ten feet of lunar soil in the southern rim of Mare Serenitatis to protect the crew from radiation, the station's tunnels, modules, and decks felt more like the innards of a World War II submarine than a Level-1 lunar outpost. The cramped outer passageways stank of sweat, cigar smoke, and hydraulic fluid. Moondust, smaller than grains of sand on Earth but spiked with crystalline edges, covered everything outside of the clean rooms, burnishing the web of access tunnels in a slate-gray haze. The air filters and nano-sweeps fought a losing battle with the dust every day. It found its way into computers, processors, spacesuits, electrical systems, and purifiers, breaking them down like a cancer. The station and everything in it needed more repair work than an old army tank.

In the first decade of spaceflight, Robert Heinlein described the Moon as a harsh mistress, but Dechert always thought of her as a desert gone too far. Earth's stillborn sister, stripped of the wind, clouds, and air that could have saved her from lifelessness. He felt a connection with the Earth tribes who spent ages perfecting how to live in such desolation. The Bedouin, who handled sandstorms that could rip flesh from bone. The Inuit, who hacked out a life on frozen slabs of ice. How did they do it? After more than four years on the Moon, he was beginning to understand. They learned hard lessons the first time.

There aren't second chances in such places.

Dechert was a careful man. He always checked twice. So when he sealed the inner hatch of the airlock and checked the board for green lights after coming in from his flight at Dionysius, he punched the status button twice before fumbling with the seals on his helmet.

"You've got balls," Vernon Waters said behind him. "Not a chance in hell I'm serving as Quarles's guinea pig, especially five hundred klicks out. That boy smokes too much weed."

"It gives him creative energy," Dechert said.

He sagged onto a changing bench and pulled off his gloves. The hangover of a prolonged lunar walk seeped through him, cramping his muscles from his calves to his shoulder blades. Seven hours in the cold soak, and most of it taking two-kilometer leaps across the Tranquility basin. Way too much walk time for a man pushing forty. He wriggled his toes to get the burning sensation of bloodlessness and frostbite out of them. He kneaded his thighs with the heels of his palms and thought wistfully of his flight-training days at Pensacola, with its white beaches as long as air force runways.

"What the hell happened out there?" Vernon asked.

"Nothing good. You listen in on the com?"

"Yeah, and I've got Briggs analyzing your boot prints. But man, what the hell happened out there?"

Dechert rubbed his eyes with the backs of his fingers. "You tell me, Vernon. Clearly someone is upping the pissing match over the mineral rights in the Tranquility basin. Who signed the Altschuler Treaty? Russia, the Chinese, Brazil, India, and us. You want to take a guess?"

Vernon gripped one of the support bars above his head and swayed back and forth. "Well, it wasn't the Russians. They don't give a shit about Tranquility. They're too worried about staying alive on the far side, those crazy bastards. And the Brazilians and Indians haven't even started to grid their own He-3 deposits. They're still camping in tents."

"So, the Chinese."

"Either that or it's ghosts. No one else knows how rich those fields are—unless someone's been running test strips out there we don't know about."

Dechert puffed up his cheeks and blew out some air. He was too tired to think about the firestorm that lay ahead once he reported to Peary Crater. "Well I doubt we're talking ghosts, but here's a question for you, Vernon. If it is the Chinese, how the hell did they know exactly what power cell to pull out without immediately killing the sifter? Quarles says that if they had yanked A7 or B7 or C7, the whole thing would have gone down. Whoever did this either got real lucky or knew about the bypass system."

Vernon frowned for a second and then gave a grin. "Hell, the electronics were probably made in China. I'll have Quarles do some checking, but I doubt that power system is a state secret."

"Yeah. I guess. But have him dig around anyways. Hopefully

Lane will get some answers from those boot prints." Dechert pictured the scene at Dionysius again—how the saboteur's boot prints had gone from a landing area just west of the drill station directly to the power shack, then to the rille where the water sifter had been operating, and then back to the landing area. Like whoever it was knew the place. And whatever craft had landed on the bottom of Dionysius had left no imprint on the Moon—it had somehow been wiped clean. But how do you wipe clean the landing area of a one- or two-ton shuttle, when the guy who's flying it is back in the shuttle? The landing gear should have left clear depressions in the soft regolith. It didn't make any sense. Dechert closed his eyes and took a deep breath. The gunpowder smell of moondust filled his nostrils, and his head hurt too much to work the mystery. He didn't want to think about the Chinese or anyone else until he had taken something to kill his headache.

"What's our status at Posidonius?" he asked Vernon. "Any word from the boys?"

Two of his diggers, Benson and Thatch, were laying grids and running test bores for a new helium-3 strip mine at Crater Posidonius, and even though Dechert had received an update that morning, the mission had never left his thoughts. Posidonius was in a relatively safe part of the Serenity basin, but this was the Moon. He didn't like being hours removed from an update on a remote-site mission.

"They're good. Lane mentioned something about the comlink screwing up again, but last I heard they're still breathing air and laying spirals."

Waters smiled as he spoke, and his Louisiana drawl reminded Dechert of the last drops of bourbon falling into the bottom of a glass. It was an affectation to some degree, as his accent diminished as conversations went on. Dechert wondered if it was a subconscious thing—Vernon's way of yearning for the oxygen-rich lowlands of his youth.

Dechert rubbed the sweat out of his week-old crew cut with an open hand. He looked at a small mirror in his locker and saw the gray pressing its attack on the top of his head. It had started a few years ago, a rogue hair in one place. And then another. And then the assault had grown in silvery numbers and spread from his sideburns up to his temples, amassing like an army preparing for a siege. Age unleashed. It wasn't just his hair anymore, either. The years had burrowed into Dechert's muscles and tendons with relentless will, and now he couldn't let his face go unshaven for more than a few days without looking at gleaming white whiskers, beckoning him to the grassy hills. He was spent, and he knew the recovery from this hop would take much longer than it should—days instead of hours—limping around on bad knees in the feeble gravity of one-sixth g.

He brushed away the self-pity. It wouldn't do him any good in this colony of overworked, understimulated lunar miners. Not with the spreadsheet boys back on Earth running production variables that didn't consider downtime. They were pushing for Serenity 1 to outproduce the Chinese. Pushing hard.

"You look like hell," Waters said.

"I'm aware."

Dechert wondered for the hundredth time if the people back home had any clue what it was like to live on the Moon. There was a weatherworn old laser print that he had seen several years back at Las Cruces Spaceport. It showed three miners standing on a lunar mountaintop with helmets gleaming in the sunlight, looking like Spartan warriors in spacesuits, ready to defend the celestial passes of Thermopylae. He thought of a child looking at that ridiculous poster and dreaming about how great it would be to spend a few days on Luna digging for alien fuel to save the homeland. If only the Earthbound could see him and Vernon now, crammed into the access tunnel that led to Main Quarantine like commuters on a city bus, only with charcoal dust in their hair.

He struggled to get his right arm out of the pressure suit, but his efforts got little notice from his flight officer. Waters never moved unless there was a pressing need, saving his energy like an old lizard waiting for the sun. It was a passing annoyance. When trouble presented itself, Vernon Waters was the best man on the Moon, the most dialed-in flight officer Dechert had ever had. Waters's arms rippled as he swayed on the restraining bars and a helixed tattoo circling his black biceps moved in waves, the muscles tensing and relaxing, serpentine. Waters performed two hundred pull-ups a day in a 1-g heavysuit and he was proud of the results. He was wider than a whiskey barrel at the shoulders, and his frame had to be acrobatically realigned to make it through some of the station's smaller sub-hatches. His large-lidded eyes and Jimi Hendrix hairdo scared the hell out of anyone who didn't know him, and Dechert always wondered if the microgravity affected him as much as everyone else on the Moon. He seemed to bounce around less.

He was too damned big for the Moon, and too set in his habits, but there wasn't a man Dechert trusted more on Luna than Vernon.

Dechert powered down the jetsuit, turned off the air systems and the walk-profile computer, and locked down the propellant valves. Waters finally began to help him when he reached down to unbuckle his boots.

"Appreciate the effort," Dechert said.

"Anytime, boss."

They continued the work in silence, giving Dechert time

to mull things over. If Quarles could get these jetsuits operational, maybe it would take some of the pressure off the station. The Space Mining Administration had been screaming for greater output as it prepared for the basing of Europa. Its market analysts were getting paranoid about the success of their Chinese competitors, whose new station could reportedly convert almost twenty metric tons of helium-3 every month.

Again, it was a difference between being dirtside and being on the lunar surface. The fact was, the crew of Serenity 1 had welcomed the company when the Chinese staged New Beijing 2 from their main base at the South Pole a few years ago. The new station was only six hundred kilometers away, tucked into the lip of Archimedes Crater, and that brought them closer to Serenity than anyone else in the solar system, turning them into adopted brothers and sisters. The two stations traded seeds and flash-frozen dinners and launched homemade vodka to each other on low trajectory nano-packs. Lin Tzu, the commander of the Chinese station, had become Dechert's friend and online chess adversary. Tzu played like a mercenary, convincing Dechert he was far better as a friend than an enemy.

But the Administration hadn't adapted as well to its new neighbors. In its view, lunar competition was a violation of the company's manifest destiny—an insult to the spacefaring nation that had launched Apollo with vacuum-tubed computing more than a century ago. *The firstborn are always jealous of their siblings*, Dechert thought, and if the Chinese kept up their rate of production and found a way to keep their mining costs in control, they would be able to compete for the most lucrative terra-energy, space-tourism, and system-exploration contracts in the next bidding cycle.

And that, apparently, was his problem to solve.

"Easy on that buckle," he said. "Shit."

"Damn thing's jammed. Wiggle your foot."

"Okay, hold up. Watch the thrusters."

"Damned moondust."

Terra-energy they could have, Dechert thought. He unzipped the inner lining at his neck and scratched at the damp strip of skin that had been pressing against the suit's metal frame while Waters continued to wrestle with his boot. Terra-energy was still being subsidized by a corrupt international commission to coax the home world back from the Thermal Maximum, and the margins were lousy. Sys-ex wasn't much better. It required a lot of fuel, and governments were starting to pay decent money for it, usually on a cost-plus basis, but the demand was spotty. After the Thermal Max, scientific exploration had become something of a luxury—and entrepreneurs were only now beginning to scrape up enough capital to explore the inner system and the Asteroid Belt for new riches.

No, it was tourism that was going to command the big money. Once the icy oases of Europa and Miranda were based and miners began running helium-3 scoops into Jupiter's and Uranus's roiling atmospheres, newly minted thrill-seekers looking for a week of zero-*g* would become the Moon's core market. The deep-system crafts of the near future would pull up to Europa like it was a corner gas station, and Mars would be Mars, a forgotten way station with all the use of a played-out nickel mine. Still, the brand-new resorts orbiting Earth would need helium-3 for their fusion reactors and water and oxygen for their paying customers. The rich wouldn't suffer a Level-1 bag shower—a quart of recycled urine and a hydro-sponge. They had more refined sensibilities. *The Earth is waking up again,* Dechert thought. *Even if half the planet is hungry, the top of the food chain is back to eating well, and fed stomachs only stretch.*

"These things are a goddamned Greek tragedy waiting to happen," Waters said.

Dechert snapped back to the present and saw Waters release the dust-covered jetsuit boot from his foot and turn it in his broad hands, looking at the thrust-vectoring HEDMs soldered onto its side with eyes that flared theatrically wide. "You wanna strap me into one of these, you better shorten my hitch. I didn't sign up to be a freakin' beach ball."

"Right."

Dechert got up and unhooked a 1-g heavysuit jacket from the clothes locker, struggling to pull the weighted sleeves onto his frame as the cold air of the accessway ran across his bare shoulders. He could have given Waters a glance to show his displeasure at the feigned insubordination, but Dechert had long ago discarded the SMA manual on maintaining a chain of command. Serenity 1 was more like an oil rig than an army barracks, a place where solitude and danger melded the crew into a state of unwritten informality. You don't pull rank in a madhouse unless it's about to blow.

When it came to the crew, Dechert danced on the line between discipline and surrender. He even let Quarles grow a blend of Moroccan cannabis in the greenhouse and play classic rock to his floor-rattling content in his engineering dungeon under the science lab. All that mattered was hitting quota and keeping things at a slow simmer, especially at times when the walls felt close. Dissatisfaction among the natives is a bad thing when you're off-Earth and more than a thousand klicks from a main base, as Fletcher used to say. When things go wrong, the last thing you want to be is in charge.

Because if there's a mutiny, the guy with the most patches on his shoulder will almost certainly be the first one tossed out of an airlock.

"You're a union man," Dechert said. He took a navy blue baseball cap out of the locker and pulled it low on his head. He rubbed moondust off the epaulettes on his heavysuit jacket and made a halfhearted effort to stretch by reaching for the rubberized floor with his palms, stopping half the way down when he felt the tendons at the backs of his knees start to give. "If your rep can't short you, you damned well know I can't."

"Shit," Waters said.

Dechert straightened, patted him on the shoulder in mock sympathy, and then walked toward the clean-room hatch, eager to unfold his body and lie under the dry furnace of the decontamination blowers. The heavysuit's 650 pounds of distributed VECTRAN weighting almost made it feel like he was back on Earth, mimicking the leaden gravity of Terra as it clung to his lean frame. Only his head felt light, and that was just something you had to get used to.

"And I hate to tell you," Dechert said, looking back at his flight officer, "but you *are* going to have to climb into one of those suits once we dump the profile from this hop. As soon as Peary Crater hears about what happened down there, we'll all be taking Moonwalks. We're going to have to check all our spiral sites, water mines, and substations now to make sure the Chinese or whoever the hell else hasn't been screwing with them. And we're gonna have to go back to DS-7 to replace that drive."

He engaged the quarantine sequence and waited for the clean-room door to slide open so he could kneel down and clear the hatch. "Take it from me, Vernon. Eat light before your first hop."

3

As Dechert walked into the CORE, Lane Briggs was slouched over the communications console, her face cupped in her hands and her elbows propped on the blue composite worktop. Her ankles were coiled one around the other as she tapped a heel on the floor with rapid bursts of energy. Quarles sat at the Lunar Positioning Satellite station across the circular room, staring at her backside. The moment was almost incestuous—the two bickered like siblings stuck in a small room and Dechert could imagine no stranger scenario than finding them making out in a corner. And now that he had that image in his head, he was sorry to have even had such a thought. He rapped an open palm on the gunwale, wondering if Quarles had exceeded his virtual porn minutes. The sound reverberated like a rifle shot in the small amphitheater and they both jumped as Dechert bent low to clear the door.

"Jesus," Quarles said.

Dechert glared at him and looked back to Lane. "What do we got? Are Benson and Thatch done at Posidonius?"

She stood up and stretched, pulling her arms back to impossible angles. Quarles turned back to his station and pretended to review the incoming data stream from the Posidonius mission. The banks of polymer and holo-displays cast a green and yellow glow to the room, playing across Lane's pale face and dark copper hair, which was cut short above the neckline and moved in slow rows of color as she turned her head in the low gravity. *If you ever want to understand the beauty of a woman*, Dechert thought, *she has to be seen in less than one-sixth g*. And then he shook his head.

My God, we've been up here too long. . . .

Lane broke his reverie. "They got DS-4's converters up again and they're about to lay the test strips on the new fields," she said. "Thatch is already prepping the *Molly* for the run home. They should have her ready to move by 2230."

She checked the computer on her slim wrist, but he knew she was also watching him as he tried to maneuver his aching legs down the rubberized gangway without wincing. Her lips pulled together in a red bead and she leaned back against the console, tapping her fingers as she used her palms to support herself, her every movement a controlled outburst of energy. Dechert knew she was angry, and he knew it had to be the *Molly Hatchet*'s communications system. He waited for her to go off.

"I'll say this one last time, Commander, before I file a complaint with the SMA-holes back at Las Cruces. We're going to be walking through black water if the com keeps shitting the bed every time we run an op outside the perimeter. Someone's going to die out there, and they're gonna form a panel of the clueless back on Earth to try and figure out what I've been bitching about for six months."

She picked up a fuse cord from the worktop and pulled at it, stretching it in her hands like a garrote until he could see the veins standing out on the tops of her knuckles. Dechert grimaced as he watched the rubber stretch. Quarles moaned with feigned dismay. Chronic worry and a distrust of management were parts of Lane's ethos, spurred equally by her cynical nature and her role as the station's safety officer. If she could pile up every Space Mining Administration bureaucrat back on Earth and drop a napalm bomb into their tepid, flabby center, Dechert knew she would do it. He just wasn't sure she understood that such an action would make no difference: You can always find more drones to fill their space, and the company was probably not going to change if it meant spending more money.

"I believe 'bitching' is the key word there, boss," Quarles said.

Dechert turned and raised a finger.

"Jonathan, don't make me do something I'll regret. I was out in the cold soak too long to deal with your bullshit."

Quarles hated his first name, which is why Dechert used it. The young man turned back to the screens and pretended to review mission data. Dechert figured it was for the best; if Quarles got under Lane's fingernails, she might just kill him as a proxy for the bureaucrats. He looked again at the fuse cord in her clenched fists and admitted to himself that it would hurt on more than a professional level if she ended up in a brig at Peary Crater because of a spontaneous act of violence against his young propulsion engineer. Lane Briggs thought as he did—a cynic who left nothing to trust. She was his security blanket, the person he turned to first when he wanted to make sure he wasn't going Moon-crazy.

Dechert rubbed his temples and sat in one of the CORE's worn microsuede seats. His EVA hangover had gotten worse and he longed for Earth air, real air, not the stuff that ran through a thousand meters of carbon filter.

"Look, I've been asking the commo shop at Peary Crater to send someone over for two months. If they don't put a techie on the next resupply, I'll personally fly over there and trash some offices for you."

She grunted, disbelieving. They had run four deep-site missions in the *Molly Hatchet* in the last two months, all with a sputtering com, an aging half-track, and no reliable redundancies. Not even a satellite phone on the damned thing that worked right. *Lane is prescient*, Dechert thought. Someone *is* going to die. If the Administration doesn't grind down on the gears a notch or put a few more communications satellites in low lunar orbit in a hurry, someone is definitely going to lose a life in the name of Sino-American competition.

"What about dipshit over here?" Lane asked, pointing a finger at Quarles. "Don't they pay him to fix this stuff?"

Quarles grinned, happy to be a part of the conversation again. His desire to talk grew proportionally to Lane's anger.

"Transport, my chestnut-haired Artemis," he said. "I do transport. Communications is a more problematic beast, and I've been with the Administration long enough to know you don't break something you haven't signed for. That said, if the *Hatchet* throws a piston, I'll be happy to fix her for you."

With all the radiation damage, Dechert doubted if Quarles could fully repair the *Molly Hatchet*'s communications system anyways. A solar flare had fried most of her satellite uplinks two weeks ago when she was outside of the Bullpen during a heat/freeze check. Her systems couldn't be shielded as well as the stations', and if the *Hatchet* happened to be crawling on the surface when another flare cooked up she would be as vulnerable as an earthworm on a field of bricks. The controllers at Peary Crater had been able to only partially restore her backups, which left Cole Benson and Rick Thatcher with few options if the com failed them.

Dechert scratched his forearm, trying to wake up enough to think as the electrical systems in the CORE buzzed around him, giving the spherical room the feel of a soothing, charged cocoon. Redundancy on the Moon is as important as a tent in the Himalayan death zones, Fletcher used to say. Without it, nothing is safe. If communications failed and another flare erupted, Benson and Thatcher couldn't be warned. The *Hatchet*'s short-range sensors might not pick up the radiation wave in time, and they'd die before they could spin up their electrostatic domes and retreat to the leaden tub in the center of the crawler.

But redundancy wasn't at the top of the list at Peary Crater right now. Dechert would complain to the managers once again and they wouldn't do a damned thing—not unless they could spare the extra man-hours without losing ground to quota. They were running at 120 percent at the Moon's North Pole, just like the crew at Serenity 1 and the newly opened U.S. mining station on the southeastern rim of Tranquillitatis, and the whole machine was grinding toward a breakdown, not just the *Molly*. Dechert had done enough postmortems on disasters to realize that outsize demand was one of their greatest causes.

Unfortunately, there was absolutely nothing he could do about that.

But it wouldn't be for want of trying. "Quarles is right, it isn't his job," he said, stealing a quick look at Lane but refusing to lock eyes with her. "Look, we've got a CM at 2130. Put together one of your razor-worded dispatches for me to send over to Peary Crater, and I'll transmit it after the meeting. If those guys can get their shit together long enough to do something right, maybe we can make quota this month and keep the dogs in the kennel."

"And what about DS-7?" Lane asked. "I've run the images you sent. Those treads don't match any of the standard EVA boots currently being used on the Moon. That includes the Chinese."

"Great. Where are they from?"

"Looks like they're an older model made by Groombridge Space Systems. A bunch of countries used them in the mid-60s, including us, Russia, and China. There's no way to match a tread to a specific pair without actually inspecting the boots."

Groombridge. One of the biggest general aerospace contractors on Earth, they had been supplying missions to the Moon since the 2050s. Tracking a pair of their old boots would be like trying to pin down a particular set of Nikes in New York City.

"What about the power cells?" Dechert asked Quarles. "Should we be concerned that whoever sabotaged our water drill at Dionysius knew how to do it without us getting immediate telemetry?"

"Not necessarily," Quarles said. "The VFD in the power shack uses a pretty standard advanced cell bypass, and it's not proprietary equipment. Anyone could have dug up the topology and figured it out."

"Lovely."

"You gonna tell Yates?" Quarles asked. "Peary Crater's gonna go shit-crazy when they hear about this."

"I'll call him. Later."

He stood up to leave, not wanting to consider any more questions, mostly because he didn't have any answers. Especially to the question that had been nagging him since this first started: *What the hell was going on back on Earth that was causing everything to blow up on Luna?*

When Dechert left for the Moon in '68, much of Europe and North America were still being called the New Third World. The Thermal Maximum was an unequal dispenser of misery. Two trillion tons of methane hydrate had bubbled out of the Pacific Rim with almost no warning in the North American spring of 2058, enveloping the planet in a Venusian shroud. For the next several years, Earth was a wasteland. Epic flooding on one continent, drought on another. Superstorms. Pandemics. Fires. Biblical stuff and some things that were even worse—at least people didn't eat one another in the darker parts of the Old Testament. The midlatitudes fared the worst, and much of the industrialized world became the Third World before its overfed, upholstered residents had time to absorb the shock.

Climatologists called the catastrophe a cleansing of an overpopulated and overheated planet. Religious extremists took a bloodier route to the truth. They killed one another en masse and tried to kill everyone else in between as they wrestled over which verse of which holy text was to be taken as the literal truth and fulfilled to its conclusion. By the early 2060s, there were three billion fewer people on the planet, and a freeze on carbon-energy emissions forced the remaining civilized nations to quell the holy wars and figure out how the hell to survive.

Fusion energy sprang out of that reflexive effort, clean and powerful as the stars. But fusion reactors needed an exotic fuel, stuff not found within the womblike magnetic field of the Earth. The best thing available was helium-3, a light, nonradioactive solar isotope that could be easily contained.

An isotope that lay in abundance on the dead regolith of the Moon.

And just like that, space became important again. Lunar mining turned into a brief unifying force for a scrabbling world, a reminder that humans could control their destiny—even if they had to leave the planet to do so. It stayed that way until the late '60s when the star-burning energy the scientists created began to bring the larger economies back from their depressions. Within a year of Dechert's deployment to the Moon, common cause had been run over by a bull market.

It was once again nations instead of humanity.

"How are the Posidonius core samples looking?" Dechert asked Quarles, hoping for some good news. "Did we at least get decent He-3 trace outside of the DS-4 perimeter?"

"Not bad for a sunlit zone," Quarles said. "About thirteen parts per billion in the early runs."

"Good."

It's almost funny, Dechert thought. When helium-3 was a lifeboat keeping the drowning masses alive, lunar miners were treated like heroes. When it became a marketable commodity, they were chastised for falling behind their numbers. And now the Chinese were getting aggressive about disputed He-3 fields in the Tranquility and Crisium basins, and the Americans were pushing back hard, forcing their own diggers to double-shift to stay in competition, forcing them to dig in places that were orders of magnitude more dangerous than the diamond mines of central Africa—all with aging, vacuum-cracked equipment. Dechert had been getting desperate vibes from the managers at Las Cruces and Peary Crater in the last month, as if they were taking heat from higher sources and channeling it back toward him. Safety had always been priority one on the midlatitudes of the Moon.

Now production was.

"This is going to blow over," Dechert said aloud.

"All hail the power of wishful thinking," Lane replied, and Dechert knew that she could read the empty spaces of doubt in his eyes.

He shrugged his shoulders, too tired to give a better defense. "Wishful thinking is a command prerogative."

He pulled the brim of his baseball cap lower on his face and climbed back up the steps leading out of the CORE, wondering how much longer he would remain in control of things on his own station and how much longer it would be before a real fight broke out between the powers on the Moon.

Wondering how long he was going to be kept up thinking about it.

"I'm going to go catch a quick two hours," he said. "Wake me up if something bad happens."

4

Serenity 1's master alarm rang thirty minutes later. Dechert woke in a panic. The lights in his quarters flared to 200 percent and then dimmed to emergency status. A red strobe over the hatch brushed the tiny room with flashing crimson. Dechert slammed his shoulder against the bulkhead as he leaped from his bunk, his heart thumping with blood as he swore. The alarm had gone off only once before in his nearly four years of command. It sounded like the departure warning on a high-speed train, a low and sinister series of baritone bells. When it came on, the CORE's audio alert was no more comforting:

"Condition 1-EVA, Condition 1-EVA. Decompression alarm on Mobile Habitation Two. Location 31.1 degrees north,

29.2 degrees east, 400 meters west-southwest of Crater Posidonius. No communication from crew. Telemetry incoming."

Decompression alarm. Dechert almost didn't believe it. What the hell could cause a decompression alarm on the *Molly Hatchet?* They were on the Serenity plain, as smooth a terrain as you could hope for on the Moon. They weren't drilling and they weren't supposed to be moving for another three hours. And other than her fickle electronics, the *Hatchet* was built like a navy warship—a bulk of carbon-carbon weave wrapped over a skin of superalloy.

He didn't stop to put on his heavysuit, bolting out of his room and careening through the crew quarters passageway in an unsteady sprint, half flying through the low gravity as he used his arms to ward off the pipes and conduits that layered the white-tubed walls of the station in corded veins. He almost hit Vernon head-on as he approached the CORE's outer hatch.

"This shit real?" Vernon asked. His eyes were wide and his forehead gleamed.

Dechert barely heard him. He yanked at the CORE's hatch, almost pulling it off its moorings. Quarles was already at the telemetry station. He didn't take the time to look up.

"It's a definite decompression," he said. "I'm getting sporadic data from the low-gain antenna. They've lost pressurization in the aft section." He punched up a schematic of the *Molly Hatchet* on a stereoscopic display and finally looked at Dechert. "It's in the EVA room, boss, but the hatch is dogged. I'm reading a closed hatch."

Dechert said a quick prayer that Thatch and Benson were in the *Hatchet's* cockpit. "Can we raise them?" *Where the hell was Lane?* She must be on-station in the main hangar or Bio-Med, or she'd already be up here by now.

"Trying."

"Keep trying, and turn off master-alarm audio. Remain at condition one," Dechert said. He punched the com. "Lane, are you down there?"

"Jonathan's right, Commander," Lane said. "The beacon triggered in aft EVA. Navigation module is still pressurized, but I'm reading no primary life support in the aft section."

The emergency beacon only went off if a module lost pressure outside of the standard depressurization sequence. *Explosive* decompression.

"I'm trying cockpit and suit coms," Lane continued. "System is green but no response."

The tension in her voice filled the CORE. She left the channel open as she repeated calls to Thatch and Benson every five seconds. The static that came back across the Moon broken by her metered transmissions chilled each of them, slowing them down as they waited to hear a human voice cutting into the distortion.

"Vernon, get the shuttle ready," Dechert said finally, flipping channels on the com to see if Thatch and Cole were knocked off frequency. "Maximum velocity profile. You're flying. I'll be there in five minutes."

He gave up on the com and pulled the base phone off the wall. "Peary Crater, this is Serenity 1, Peary Crater, SOS-1. We've got a master decompression alarm on MH-2. I repeat . . ."

The landline immediately crackled to life. At least someone was working up north. "Serenity 1, Peary Crater, I copy a master alarm on mobile habitation number two. Can you confirm?"

The dispatcher's voice sounded too calm, and it made Dechert angry. The bastard probably hadn't been outside of an airlock in months. But he took a deep breath, because snapping at this com-jockey wasn't going to change anything. "Confirmed, Peary Crater, decompression alarm on MH-2.

No communications from crew. She is four-seven-zero klicks north-northeast of the station, just southwest of Posidonius. We're relaying coordinates and launching the shuttle. I'll be on open com in five minutes."

Dechert hung up the phone before hearing a reply. He knew that Commodore Yates was already stirring to action and would be looking for an immediate briefing. He didn't want to talk to him until after the launch. *Economy of motion,* he thought. *Economy of action.* What did Fletcher tell him? *Time kills on the Moon.* Have to move quickly

"Jonathan you've got the CORE. Give us telemetry updates as you get them and help Vernon upload a flight profile. We'll be on open channel."

Quarles nodded, his face fixed to the display screens and his shaven head gleaming as his hands moved across the console. Dechert lurched out of the room, sealing the hatch behind him. He ran down the launch checklist in his mind as he flew down the red-lit passageways, past the hatches for Observatory, Greenhouse, Supply, Bio-Med, and Astro-Mechanical. Launches made him nervous, even with Vernon flying. They had to stay sharp. Couldn't compound one emergency by creating another. Dechert felt the old carbonation of self-doubt bubble up inside him and tried to push it back down. His heart pounded and his mouth felt papery. He wished he had ordered Quarles to turn off the emergency lighting along with the audio.

Lane was fighting to get a pressure suit on Waters when Dechert got to the hangar. After John Ross Fletcher was killed in the Sea of Clouds crash, they didn't fly without personal life support. Neither of them spoke, barely looking up as he came into the room. Dechert went to a locker and grabbed a suit. He threw it onto a bench and picked up the flight pad.

"I've already got her sequenced," Waters said. "Tanks are stirred, electrostatic shielding coming online."

Dechert looked at Vernon and saw a thin line of wet running down one cheek into the thick, dark stubble of his beard. Lane was pale and silent, moving as fast as she could. Dechert put down the pad and attacked his suit, knowing it would take him at least three minutes to get it on and powered up.

Time kills on the Moon.

"They're probably just off-com," Dechert said, knowing how unlikely that sounded. "Concentrate on the mission. We'll get them back."

Thatcher's voice broke through a field of static when they were four hundred kilometers out. It sounded as if he was talking through a stream of running water. "Serenity, this is *Molly Hatchet*. We've got an emer . . . decompression in port EVA module. Can you hear me? Can't raise Cole. Cole is . . . outer hat . . ." He spoke in quick, confused bursts.

"We read you, *Molly Hatchet*," Dechert replied. "We're inbound shuttle, five minutes out. I repeat, ETA zero-five minutes. Uh, Thatch, give me Nav-Mod's status and repeat last on Cole."

The com popped and hissed like a blown transformer. Solar activity again, or worse. Dechert prayed Thatcher was confused about Cole Benson or that he hadn't heard him correctly. Maybe Cole was stuck in the prep module with the inner hatch sealed off, and the *Molly*'s internal communications weren't working.

Thatch's voice came through again in garbled urgency. "Explosion . . . A module. Boards green in navigation. Cole . . . EVA. I can't reach him. Do you read . . . Commander? . . . Cole."

Static washed out Thatch's last sentence, but they had heard enough. Cole was in the EVA module. Now in open space. *Was he just getting back into the crawler or prepping to go out? Please, God, let him be in a pressure suit.*

Dechert looked over at Vernon but his flight officer didn't look back. The big man kept his face forward, concentrating on flying as they skimmed over the Sea of Serenity at nearly a kilometer per second. The shuttle's multidirectional HEDM thrusters hissed with propellant bursts, keeping the scarab-shaped craft from tumbling out of control. Dechert thought he could see Posidonius in the distance, its shallow rim almost overwashed by an ancient lava flow. The crater's sloping western spine grew too slowly in the cockpit window.

"Forty klicks out, descending to one hundred meters," Vernon said. "Retracting electrostatic spheres, radiation levels in the green."

The shuttle skimmed over the northern terminus of the Dorsa Smirnov, a wrinkle ridge that snaked like a scar across the Serenity basin. "Give me ten percent continual outflow on the valve seals," Dechert said. "We don't need to be inhaling dust right now."

The ridge receded and Vernon pushed the craft lower. Dechert spotted the *Molly Hatchet* in the distance, her boxy metallic hindquarters glinting in the lowering sun. She sat just to the west of Posidonius's snowy ejecta blanket, and as they grew closer, Dechert could see a thin wisp of gas rise into the blackness from the back of the crawler. Gas rising from the surface of the Moon was never a good thing.

The *Molly Hatchet* was venting.

Vernon flew the shuttle in too fast and reversed thrust two hundred meters from the stricken craft, the g-forces from the maneuver pinning both men into their seats. Moondust billowed up as they landed.

They saw it at the same time, a speck of white against the darker hulk of the mining crawler and the ash gray of the regolith, lying just outside of the rear EVA hatch in a ring of debris. It was a pressure suit. Dechert could see the control board on the suit's midsection through the rising blanket of dust, blinking red. He looked at Vernon and didn't want to look back out the window. The suit wasn't empty. It was turned on. But there was no helmet attached to it, just a smaller object extending from the solid circular frame of the suit's neckline. The object looked extraordinary on the surface of the Moon, incomprehensible. It took Dechert a few seconds to understand why. Its exposed reaches had curly blond hair.

"Oh no, baby, no," Waters whispered. "No way. No way."

5

A YEAR AGO

"Why did you come to the Moon, Cole?"

"I don't know, boss. Boredom, I guess."

"Boredom?" Dechert asked, looking up from a Touchpad with his eyebrows raised. Cole Benson sat across from him on a 3-D–printed chair in the Astro-Mechanical lab, his knees bunched together and his shoulders tucked in toward his chest. "People go to the movies when they're bored, Cole. They don't take a spaceship a quarter-million miles up to a dead rock in the sky."

Cole fidgeted, wiping his blond hair from his eyes with the back of his hand. "I don't know what you want me to say, boss. It just got old for me down there. All of the bullshit."

"Elaborate," Dechert said. "Humor me."

"You know—the whole thing. Half the world is starving on the back end of the Max, and I'm spending my time surfing with the Safe Zone elites, those freakin' pussies. You know I was junior champion in Encinitas, and we all got waivers for international travel? I did all the big breaks from Snapper Rocks to Burleigh for a year in '66 when Australia started getting those six-month monsoons. Surfed Bells Beach just after Typhoon Andora rolled by and the wind switched offshore. Must have been twenty-foot sets that were as clean as cut glass. Everyone said it was a good diversion for the people who still had power. That's how they justified it. And we were eating like kings and getting laid. Fuckin' hell."

Dechert sat back in his chair and locked his hands behind his head. He clenched his jaws in an effort to calm down; he didn't want to give his youngest miner a lashing that he couldn't recover from. Cole had become a good digger in his first two years on the Moon, better than Dechert could have hoped for. But the kid had a flair for recklessness that bordered on self-destruction. Maybe he hadn't been close enough to death yet or the realization of the Moon's always imminent danger had yet to sink in enough for him to feel its regulating squeeze on his heart. Or maybe he just didn't care.

"So I'm guessing it was boredom that led you to build a makeshift snowboard and take it for a run down the Montes Haemus during a survey mission, when you were supposed to be covering Vernon's ass?"

Cole looked over at the laboratory equipment that sat unused on a far table, as if he were counting the test tubes and sub-A-scopes lined up there. "We were on break and the theodolites were on auto and green. I told Vernon I was gonna check something out for a few minutes. He said it was fine."

He picked at his pants leg while Dechert stared at him, keeping his face turned away from his commander's gaze.

Dechert had almost been amused at the description Vernon gave him of the incident out on the Serenity basin earlier that morning—of how Vernon had heard a scream over the com that would freeze any man's soul out on the reg—and how he had looked up into the foothills above him to see Cole Benson shooting down a steep ravine like a ground-hugging missile on what appeared to be a carbon-fiber corrugation sheet, catching twenty meters of space every time the jury-rigged snowboard hit a small bump in the microgravity.

Maybe he would have stayed amused about the whole damned thing if Cole hadn't wiped out at the bottom of his ski run and cut a small gash in his pressure suit, triggering a decompression alert that had thrown the station into a panic. Vernon had moved quickly, bounding up to Cole and spraying some quick-seal on the cut before it blew out his suit, but the alert had shaken the crew, and it was a good thing that it had taken Cole and Vernon a few hours to get back to the airlock after the accident. If they had returned sooner, Dechert might have throttled his young mining specialist with a pipe cleat.

"Cole, let me explain something to you about boredom, and residual guilt. They will get you killed up here, plain and simple. And not just you, but the ones around you."

"I realize that. I'm sorry."

"Sorry doesn't cut it, kid," Dechert said, leaning forward in his chair. "You fuck up out on the reg, and sorry won't bring back the dead."

Cole looked even worse now. His eyes were getting moist and his legs began to shake as he tapped both feet on the rubberized floor, his hands still on his knees. He was a child, Dechert realized, a curious, reckless child who pretended to be a man. And here he was at Serenity, a thousand klicks from the nearest main base and working one of the most dangerous jobs inside the Asteroid Belt.

"Boss, you know me," Cole mumbled. "I might be stupid once, but I'll never be twice. I swear to God it won't happen again."

Dechert puffed up his cheeks and let loose with a blast of air. He had put together a good team for Sea of Serenity 1, but they were too damned young. Between Cole's recklessness, Quarles's penchant for practical jokes at the most inopportune times, and Lane's inherent surliness, the trio often left him feeling more like a high school counselor than a Level-1 station chief. *But Briggs was starting to come around, and at least Waters and Thatch had some age to them*, he thought. *My rocks of Gibraltar in a stormy hormonal sea.*

"All right," Dechert said. "We'll leave it at that for now. Get your ass over to Bio-Med, and have Lane check you out for decompression sickness."

Cole looked up, hopeful but still wary. "Is that it? I mean, I'm not getting docked or anything?"

"Not right now. But don't worry, I'll find other ways to make your life a bone-sucking misery for the next few months."

"Thanks, boss," Cole said. He stood up, still not convinced that he had been temporarily spared the hangman's noose. "I promise I'll square it away. Strictly protocol from now on."

Dechert shook his head and scratched the stubble on his face, knowing that the penitence in his young miner's soul would eventually be overtaken by the testosterone coursing through his veins. Knowing he would do something ridiculous again and hoping that things wouldn't end up worse when he did. Hoping the next incident wouldn't come until at least 2072.

"Cole?"

"Yes, sir?"

"If you ever do something as cosmically stupid as that

again, at least get it on video. You'll need a keepsake of this place when I fire your ass, and nobody will ever believe this one when you get back on the beach."

Cole Benson grinned. "Right. I can't even screw up good."

"Then don't screw up at all."

6

The dead settle in our mind like cooling embers. After a time they diminish, snuffed out by the immediate, and then a puff of memory rekindles them and for a moment they are hot and near once again. The smell of cigars did it for Dechert. He had opened Cole Benson's locker and it hit him with a palpable blow, a sharp and immediate pain in the chest that replaced the numbness of the last few days and triggered his daydream of Cole's attempt to be the first snowboarder on the Moon. As the memory faded, he shook his head and stared at the small stash of cigars in the cubby.

Benson had a connection at Peary Crater who smuggled reconstituted "Thermal Max" Dominicans up through resupply, probably the same entrepreneur who ran Lane her small-batch bourbon. Their earthy smell wafted out of his locker and Dechert envisioned Cole in the crew mess, his feet up on the white basalt table, lighting a forty-gauge Churchill and describing the perfect sets that rolled in from the Pacific Ocean and broke on the sandbars of the Playa Hermosa.

"Ten hours of surfin', then ten hours of lovin'," Cole would say. "That's what Costa Rica is all about."

Dechert gathered up the cigars and put them in an evidence bag with Cole's other personal effects. He thought of giving them to Thatch, but he was in too much of a stupor now to want them. They all were. The station felt like the foyer of a funeral home, where people linger to avoid the sight of the casket but still feel its powerful presence. Quarles and Vernon and Thatch had barely said a word in two days. *But at least they had honest reasons to be depressed,* Dechert thought . . . genuine reasons to mourn. They lived and worked with Cole like brothers, risking their necks with him every day on the exposed lunar plains. Even Lane, as distant as she tried to keep herself, could mourn without any guilt. She used to muss Cole's shaggy blond hair and call him her little man. It was probably the deepest sign of affection she'd shown to anyone in her three years on Serenity.

But what about Dechert? What was he most sorry about: Cole's death or his unblemished command record vanishing in the vacuum? Dechert hadn't lost a crew member since taking over Serenity 1, and now he had and it was Cole. And in the back of his mind he would always equate his sadness over Cole's death with guilt over the notion that maybe he was sorrier for himself than he was for Cole Benson. *Even grief can be selfish,* he thought.

Or maybe it was just the rekindling of old memories that haunted him. He hadn't dealt with death in many years, but there was a time when it was a weekly visitor to the confines of his soul. What line officer didn't lose soldiers in the Bekaa Valley? A gunnery sergeant or a cherry private would be dismembered by a sonic charge or a seeking bullet, and he'd be replaced a few days later like a broken rear axle that was requisitioned, processed in triplicate, and shipped in from the States just in time for the next firefight. Dechert hadn't even learned the names of some of the kids who had died under his command. The young ones were just too goddamned ignorant to stay alive. And in the end it might not have mattered how good or bad they were as warriors. The instinctive ones had a better chance, but no one can stand up for long before the withering law of averages. People just died out there in the Bake, for no damned reason at all other than the fact that it was a war.

But this wasn't a war, and that made things worse. And Cole didn't just die—an occurrence in many ways more natural than remaining alive on the Moon. An occurrence that wouldn't have been too hard to fathom, given the young miner's reckless nature. No. Someone had killed him.

Someone *killed* Cole.

Every time the phrase entered Dechert's mind, he shook his head as if he had just walked through a cobweb. The idea seemed impossible. People kept people alive on the Moon. They didn't kill them. Accidents might be an order of magnitude more likely on Luna than they are in the most treacherous places on Earth—the exposed rocks of Mount Everest stabbing into the jet stream; the poison-filled rain forests; the scorching miles of the great deserts. But at least you can survive long enough in those places to come up with a plan. At least there is some air there, some boundary between human beings and the void of the universe.

When mishaps occur on the Moon, they degrade into catastrophes before there's time to reverse the sequence. Seven

Russians had died in their first attempt to open a permanent station on the far side in 2067 because of a few grains of moondust. The spiky chunks of anorthosite shorted a hardened circuit that shorted another hardened circuit, and—in a seemingly impossible move—the master computer opened up all of the decompression hatches on the tiny station without so much as a blinking light to warn anyone. A SAR team found the men a week later, strewn wherever they had been before the air went away and frozen so deep that they had to be thawed with handheld heaters before they could be unfolded enough to be put into bags and shipped back to Earth. One had been sitting on a toilet, an old paperback copy of Sholokhov's *And Quiet Flows the Don* in his frozen hands and his pants around his ankles.

And just last year a landslide in the Apennine Mountains had crushed four Chinese diggers. One of the men had lost his spatial reference—a common thing on the Moon's monochromatic expanse—and fallen into an unmapped rille. The others tried to recover him by lowering a cable from their rover, but the steep walls collapsed around them, crushing them inside their pressure suits.

Hell, even Fletcher had succumbed to the Moon's cold embrace. The unbreakable John Ross Fletcher. One frozen thruster and his shuttle went into a spin from which no man or machine could recover.

But no one had ever been *murdered* on the Moon, and Dechert wouldn't have thought it possible if he hadn't seen for himself the blown EVA hatch on the *Molly Hatchet*. It didn't take a forensics expert to realize it had been detonated from the outside, and that it wasn't a micrometeor or some stellar phenomenon that did the job. Someone had planted an explosive under the crawler's manual hatch release. Dechert had seen enough bombs in the Middle East to read the tapestry: black carbon-scoring, shrapnel, a four-inch circular hole gouged into the hull just under the hard seals, pointing upward. It looked like a shape charge to him, and he wondered if Thatch or Vernon had realized it as well. Probably not Thatch. He was too deep in shock when they got him out of the crawler through an umbilical airlock. But Dechert saw Waters look at the blown hatch when they had scrambled out of the shuttle to go to Cole, and then look again. And if Waters realized that Cole had been killed by a saboteur, then the rest of the crew knew it by now as well.

It doesn't matter, Dechert thought to himself, closing Cole's locker and sitting down on the cold metal bench in front of it. Peary Crater had a full forensics team working on the *Hatchet*, which had been towed to the main base by a lunar barge at no small expense—and over strong protests by Dechert, who wanted to run the investigation himself. They would know by now what had happened; Dechert was just waiting for the blowback and wondering how much access he would have to the report.

As it was, the only intel Dechert had was his own memory of the horrific scene, which tormented him with disjointed flashbacks of color, sound, and smell. The burnt cordite scent of the Moon mixing with the unmistakable smell of an explosion, which had either infiltrated his spacesuit somehow or had been some kind of olfactory hallucination triggered from his time in the war. The sight of Cole collapsed in a ring of debris only five yards from the helmet that would have saved him. Cole had tried to get to it. His right hand was dug into the regolith in front of his body, and the tracks left behind him were those of a man crawling. Thatch's voice, high-pitched and desperate from the cockpit as Dechert and Waters tried to work on Cole's body. The flotsam from the explosion, which blew equipment that wasn't locked down out of the *Molly*

Hatchet's EVA module in a concussive instant. And the emptiness inside the back of the crawler, void of oxygen and warmth, with only a few tools left to show the life that had once been there. Dechert had glanced inside just long enough to take the grim inventory: a surveying tripod latched down to the port wall; a gammon reel that had somehow managed to stay inside the tiny workroom when the air blew out; magnetic locaters clipped onto a small workbench; and Thatch's spacesuit, an eerily human-looking thing inside the blown-out module—its white gleaming hulk strapped to the bulkhead, dirtied with gray moondust on its legs and boots.

Mocking everyone, as if saying, "This one could have saved him. This one had a helmet attached to it."

Who the hell would do this? The question spun in Dechert's mind like something without weight being blown through a storm. Would the Chinese go as far as murder because of a territorial pissing match? The Russians? An American? A loner with some kind of grudge, or maybe even Moon hysteria? A kid back at Peary Crater had gone Moon-crazy last year, and it took four men to stop him from using a breccia drill to punch a six-inch hole in one of the station's central-hub portholes. He had just wanted to get a little fresh air, he explained afterward, when he was sedated and shackled to a wall.

The suspects were many; the suspects were nonexistent. This was the Moon, and none of it made any sense.

The com buzzed above Dechert's head, and he looked up with regret at the blinking control panel. It buzzed again. Dechert tried to resist the years of military conditioning that willed him to answer. Eventually, though—moving in slow motion, cursing as he did—he flipped the metal toggle and sat down on the bench again.

"Yes?"

"Commander, we just got a flash message from Peary Crater,

marked for priority," said Quarles, and he sounded no happier than Dechert felt. "It came in with a quantum encryption code. You believe that shit? They're sending a shuttle down here at 1430. We're getting a visit from the Space Mining Administration."

I bet we are, Dechert thought.

"Right. Tell Vernon to prep the hangar and turn on the basin's running lights. Get the CORE's autonomics configured for extra souls. You know where Thatch is?"

"He's in the observatory with Lane."

"Okay. I'll be there, too."

He looked at Cole's closed locker one last time and stood up, feeling old and encumbered even in the microgravity. Even his anger felt weak. Too many suspects. No suspects. Or was it really a mystery at all? The SMA and the Chinese Lunar Authority had been bickering about mineral rights for months. The U.S. and Chinese governments had entered the fray at the prodding of the bureaucrats in their mahogany-walled think tanks. A crisis waiting for a tipping point. Hadn't the same thing happened hundreds of times before—the few pushing the gullible straight toward the walls of Troy?

It almost didn't matter who killed Cole, Dechert decided. There were progressions falling into place now that seemed inevitable. He had seen them in action before in Lebanon, in the Bake back in the '60s. One tribal killing, one soldier dropped by a sniper, one bomb landing on the wrong house, and the lid had blown off. He had seen it before.

He didn't want to see it again.

7

How to explain the Moon's thunderous star field to the un-initiated? It would be like describing the yellows and reds of van Gogh's *Wheatfield with Crows* to a blind man. Even an exile like Dechert tired of Luna's gray sterility, but he never lost the wonder of her heavens. The crescent Earth was low over the Mons Argaeus and the sun still lingered in the sky on its western descent, but the observatory's reverse apertures blocked their blinding effects on the star field above Serenity 1 as Dechert walked through the hatchway. The room's nano-glass dome peered like a bulbous eye from under the blanket of regolith covering the rest of the base. It was lit by starlight; the Milky Way hung overhead like a vertical swarm of fireflies.

Thatch and Lane were at the back of the room, sitting on

the ends of two formfitting recliners. Thatch had Lane's silver flask in his hand.

Dechert walked over to them. "Bourbon, I hope?"

Thatch handed it to him without looking up. Dechert took a drink and the whiskey hit his nose and throat with the punch of wood smoke. Memories of Earth flooded back to him: the old memories of camping in the White Mountains north of the Kancamagus Highway and fishing Sawyer Pond for brown trout, of sitting with his back to a fire under the stars and drinking away the troubles that lay to the south.

"That's the good stuff," he said.

"Booker's," Lane said. "Just came up."

Dechert took another swig before handing the flask to Lane. He leaned back against one of the dome's metal reinforcing beams and looked down at them. Lane was tiny next to Thatch's big frame. Neither of them returned his gaze. Thatch's bushy brown hair was matted to his head and flecked with dust.

"The SMA's sending a team down from the North Pole. Should be here in a few hours."

They didn't respond. Dechert uncrossed his feet and then crossed them the other way. He wished he had listened when the military tried to teach him about grief counseling during the desert wars. He always figured it didn't really matter.

He wasn't sure his belief had changed, either.

"Thatch, I know you already debriefed, but I'm guessing they're going to want to go over everything again."

Thatch grunted. Lane handed him the flask and squeezed his shoulder.

"Look, Thatch, take another hit on that bourbon and go get a shower and some sleep," Dechert said. "I know you're messed up, but I'm going to need you. We're all going to need one another for the next couple of days."

Thatch looked up. His smallish eyes were red and swollen. He took another drink and nodded. "Yeah, I'll square up."

He pushed himself from the chair and handed Lane the flask and shuffled his way to the door. He turned around before he got there.

"You know it should have been me out there."

Dechert shook his head. "It could have been either of you, Thatch. It was just a short straw, long straw kind of thing. Believe me, I've been there before."

"No. It *should* have been me. I let Cole run the perimeter check and the first test strips when we got to Posidonius. It was my turn to EVA, but he was already suited up and he wanted to go back out, and I let him do it. I don't know why I let him do it."

Lane started to protest but Dechert cut her off. "Cole ran the initial perimeter check?" Usually the senior miner did the first EVA on the Moon.

"Yeah. He was all charged up and he wanted to get out there and it was the Posidonius overflow. Nice and safe, so I let him do it. But it was my turn to go out for the second walk, and I don't know why I didn't. I think maybe I was being lazy."

Dechert ran both his hands through his hair. "Thatch, you had nothing to do with Cole dying. You hear me? The kid wanted to do an extra EVA and you let him do an extra EVA. That's it. I'm sure Vernon's done the same thing a dozen times."

Thatch nodded but Dechert saw in his eyes that he would never accept the argument. "Okay I just wish it had been me. Cole, he was . . ."

He didn't finish. He opened the hatchway and left the room, and Dechert sat down on one of the recliners and let out a deep breath.

The stars cast a diamond-blue glow over the room. Dechert

looked up at the spiral arm of the galaxy rotating over the Serenity basin's ancient lava flows. A few billion years ago the entire mare had been a monstrous crater, gouged out of the Moon's belly by a protoplanet collision of unfathomable magnitude. Now it was a dead pool of basalt, old and calm. The pure constancy of the plain made him anxious.

"We're going to need him, Lane. Can you get him back in shape?"

Lane sighed and took another drink and lay down on the recliner next to him. "I think so—at least enough for him to function. I'll keep an eye on him, and so will Vernon. We'll make sure he stays busy, especially now that we're getting visitors."

Dechert leaned back, and his eyes began to shift their focus into three dimensions as he stared at the heavens, until it seemed as if he could plot the relative distance of each star above him as they flew away from the Big Bang and into the void. The constellation Leo stood out to the northwest, Regulus gleaming blue-white in the foreground like the paw of a lion running straight toward him. Denebola seemed a thousand light-years behind, flickering a dim yellow in the curling tail of the beast.

He looked over at Lane. She wasn't wearing her heavysuit, and her slender body moved lightly in the low gravity as she sank into the chair.

"You should be wearing your weights. Medical's gonna give me hell the next time they run our Bios. All of you are gonna fail."

"Yeah, I know, but the damned thing pinches."

Dechert grunted. His head spun from the whiskey and he wished for a minute of quiet, but he knew Lane was going to speak before she opened her mouth.

Sure enough, she said, "You want to fill me in on what the

hell's going on? Waters said Posidonius was no accident. What exactly does that mean?"

"I can't say, not yet. It's special access and I'm getting paranoid about chain of command stuff right now. But I'm guessing you're going to get an earful from whoever's coming down from Peary Crater."

He ran an open hand back through his hair and scratched three days of growth on his jaw and wondered if the gray stubble mixed in with the black stood out in the starlight. The alcohol seeped from his chest down to his arms and legs, warming his blood. His body was still wired with more muscle than fat and his face still held its tight lines, but he felt faded lying next to Lane. An old barn jacket left outside for too long—still useful, maybe, but not to be worn in public.

She got up on her elbows and Dechert watched the movement of her bare arms, which were lean and athletic but lacking in sharp lines. A tomboy's arms, descending to smooth, symmetrical hands. Dechert noticed her fingernails, clipped short. Lane didn't give much of a damn about her appearance, and he liked that about her. She bit a side of her lower lip.

"Fine, but I can't be a part of the solution if I don't know the problem," she said. "And I've got to tell you, Commander, I'm getting anxious about the coms coming up from New Mexico. Someone down there has a real hard-on for China, and it got a lot worse after Cole got killed. Have you been reading this stuff? They're claiming that New Beijing 2 is infringing on our He-3 rights by expanding eastward onto the edge of the Imbrium, and you know that's bullshit." She paused and curled her fingers to look at her clipped nails, and Dechert wondered if she wanted to chew on them.

Instead she asked, "How did we get primary mineral rights to the central maria, anyway? Because some thrill junkie from the Apollo days was the first to stick our flag in the reg?"

She glanced sideways to see his reaction, then pushed on when he didn't budge.

"I thought the politicians hashed all this out with the ISA Treaty. All of the Mare Imbrium was supposed to be fair game for the Chinese. We get primary rights to Tranquility and Serenity, the Chinese get the Sea of Islands and Sea of Showers, and the Russians and Indians get to split the Oceanus Procellarum. The far side's open hunting ground for anyone crazy enough to claim it. Isn't that the way it was supposed to work? And forgive me for waxing historic, but when a treaty gets torn up on Earth, doesn't a war usually follow the falling paper?"

Dechert took in the measure of her speech, closing his eyes and wondering just how intuitive Lane was. Since Cole's death, the signals from Peary Crater and Las Cruces had gone from tense to downright belligerent. He knew Lin Tzu was facing a similarly bristling posture from his minders back in Shanghai. Things were tightening up, as if some unseen force was drawing a string around parchment to see how well it would roll up or if it would crumble. The level of message control coming out of the SMA's political reengineering teams had ascended into the air of propaganda. A memorandum he had just read warned that the Chinese couldn't be relied on if an emergency threatened any crew between Serenity 1 and Mare Imbrium, whether Chinese or American. The Chinese Navy had a long history of leaving crews abandoned at sea, the memo explained with a conspicuous lack of evidence, so all SAR operations should be launched with the presumption that there would be no help from New Beijing 1 or its sibling station, NB-2.

Sweet Lord, Dechert had thought, *that shows how well on-Earth administrators understand the Moon.* Life is so tenuous on Luna's desiccated expanse that staying alive is an endeavor practiced with almost religious fervor. No one ever deserts another man on the Moon. Race, creed, religion, flag—none of that crap matters. Dechert would risk his life for any Chinese digger in distress, as long as they were within range. And he knew they would do the same for him.

At least until what happened to Cole.

He shifted his weight on the recliner and stared at the stars again, knowing they had looked pretty much the same to men in his spot for thousands of years. Whenever the wheel-spinners want to pick a fight, they use the same playbook, written before bronze and iron gave way to steel. Ramp up the rhetoric, create a crisis, and start to put the pieces in place for military action. Dechert wondered if the growing legal debate over helium 3 rights and the sudden demand for increased production were Act Two, and Cole's death was the beginning of Act Three.

He remembered spearfishing long ago in Pensacola in the blue-water deeps under an oil rig. A bull shark had climbed up from the rig's superstructure and circled him with unusual aggression in the naked expanse of midwater, agitated for some reason though the big bulls had always been calm before. The shark had literally bowed up—dorsal fin high, snout and tail low—and had swum erratically around Dechert like a gangster defending its corner of the street—a sign to be read by any creature with an understanding of the sea. *I'm about to attack you, and I will kill you if I do.* Is that what was happening now—and were he and Lane and the rest of the crew about to be caught in the middle?

"What the hell do you want me to say, Lane?" he finally asked. "You know I avoid politics whenever I can."

"You avoid anything to do with Earth, whenever you can."

"Yeah, well, when was the last time you got something done by calling the home planet?" He looked at her. "Let's focus on one thing at a time. I want to work on problems I know about, starting with Drill Station 7. Can you dig around the old manifests to see who had Groombridge boots requisitioned to them back in the day?"

She looked at him incredulously. "You mean Chinese manifests? I doubt it."

Dechert didn't look back at her. "I mean *our* manifests. Peary Crater, SOS-1. The other substations. SOT-1 while it was being built, and the Nubium."

Lane sat up. "Dechert, are you suggesting . . . ?"

"I'm not suggesting anything. I'm just checking and unchecking boxes. If I have to, I'll ask Lin Tzu about DS-7 in a private conversation. But first I want to know where those boot prints didn't come from."

"You think it's connected to what happened to Cole?"

"I think coincidence is for suckers. We have to start solving mysteries. Quietly." He looked at her again. "I don't know where to get straight answers, Lane. I'm thinking you and I are going to have to find them for ourselves."

She stood up, almost bouncing in the low gravity. "I'll poke around. I've got access into Materials and Equipment as safety officer. But I'm telling you, Dechert, if what happened to Cole is what I think happened, I'm not going to stay quiet about it for long."

Dechert nodded. "Me, either. And believe me when I say it won't just be fucking talk."

He had come to the Moon to leave that part of his life behind him, but now the old memories of war were bubbling up. The last memories. On a broiling afternoon in Lebanon seven years ago, he had stood over the body of a young Druze guerrilla he had just shot in the chest. He had watched as the kid's blood turned from red to ochre in the orange sand. He stood there and waited for the boy to die, sweating under the desert sun as his men formed a perimeter around him. There were no words spoken and they had only briefly looked at each other, the living and the dying. He swore at that moment he would never kill another person as soon as he finished his hitch in the Corps. Not for someone else's agenda. He swore he would climb off that wheel.

The boy had an RPG in his hands when Dechert brought him down, but it didn't matter. He couldn't have weighed more than ninety pounds. His leather sandals lay on the ground where he had been blown out of them and he had the feet of a peasant. Thick, calloused heels. A farmer, maybe. Twelve months of kicking in doors and flex-cuffing angry young martyrs had led up to that moment and it had sucked the war-fighting out of Dechert with a sudden force. He had left for the Moon years later with most of his men dead behind him, and Luna had become his sterile asylum, a place where people looked out for one another because the enveloping vacuum could easily take them all. A place completely unlike Terra in the very best of ways, and the very worst of ways.

Dechert looked at Lane now and held her gaze. His anger dissipated. Her face was blue with starlight, her eyes flecked with green. *If I ever had a daughter, what color eyes would she have?* he wondered.

"I've got really bad vibes about this," she said.

"You're a Thermal Max baby, Lane. You've known nothing but chaos, so that's what you always expect."

"Well, call me Cassandra, but my worst expectations are met with a disturbing regularity. I was hoping you could talk me down."

Dechert got to his feet, trying to smile, feeling worn-out once again as the alcohol toyed with his balance and pulled the blood from his head.

"Let's stick together. That's about the best I've got right now."

8

J. Booth Standard walked out of quarantine and into the main hangar of Serenity 1 like a malarial Caesar landing in Britain. What did Conrad call the station manager in *Heart of Darkness*? A papier-mâché Mephistopheles? *He must have had the Administration's man in mind*, Dechert thought. Standard's face was the color of candle wax; his shoulders were narrow and sloped, but he had a look of preternatural intelligence about him. He moved with a sense of purpose that Dechert found disquieting—a certitude with no nuance. *Nobody should believe in anything that much*, Dechert thought, *especially on the Moon. Belief gets you killed up here.*

Two men walked in a line behind Standard toward the hangar's flying deck. One wore a Peary Crater heavysuit that was too bulky around the shoulders and too long on the arms. He had wide blue eyes and the gravity-shocked gait of a man who had just blasted off-Earth a few days ago and was still adjusting to the physical and mental duress. The other was obviously a soldier—with the look of a man who'd left the regular service a long time ago to handle jobs that stay out of government paperwork. He had cropped black hair and moved with sinuous ease, a barely perceptible frown on his lips. He bore no indication of rank, only a small insignia on his shoulder depicting the solar system with a silver sword running through it. *Air & Space Marines.* Dechert knew him immediately. A killer.

"Commander," Standard said. He walked as casually as he could in the microgravity, coming up to Dechert and offering him a long-fingered hand. His grip was weak. "It's a pleasure to meet you. I offer my condolences on the loss of your man. We're certain it was through no fault of your own."

He spoke with the warmth of a casket salesman, in a metered tone that was sympathetic and mildly condescending at the same time. Dechert wondered who constituted the *we*.

"Thank you, Commissioner," he said.

Standard turned and saw Lane standing next to Dechert. He smiled unconsciously and cleared his throat and then turned his attention back to his colleagues. "This is Captain Hale of the Air & Space Corps, and . . . umm . . . Joshua Parrish, a reporter with Reuters whom we allowed to tag along—for a background briefing alone, of course."

A reporter. Lane and Dechert stole a glance at each other. Why the hell would the Administration bring a reporter here? Dechert assessed the young writer, who flinched every time the station made one of its respiratory belches and was too overwhelmed to give more than a mumbled hello. He had a small flash-recorder in his hand, and he clutched it as if it were the last flotation device on a doomed ship. For some reason, his nervousness—coupled with Standard's hesitation at Parrish's presence—made Dechert glad the reporter was here.

"Gentlemen, this is Lane Briggs, my safety officer," Dechert said, breaking the moment of silence. "That's Vernon Waters up on the flying deck, our flight officer and the pilot during the *Molly Hatchet* search-and-rescue operation."

The group traded nods. Vernon sat in the hydraulic chair up on the deck, his arms hanging over the open banister. Dechert felt no more enthusiastic, but he had inwardly pledged to be diplomatic with this odd entourage. This was not the time to make his concerns known—and he didn't want to say too much in the company of a reporter, much less an Administration bureaucrat and a marine who looked like one of the recon boys who would show up unannounced and uniformless at the forward operating bases of the Bekaa Valley, hang around quietly for a few days, then disappear into the desert like an evening shadow. He wasn't sure which of the three men he should be the most worried about. His instincts told him it was Standard, but Standard couldn't kill him with a single blow.

"All right," he said. "Well, Commissioner, gentlemen, if you'll follow me to the crew mess. It's the largest meeting room in the station and we can scrape together some food if you're hungry."

He led the group toward the main hangar hatch, with Lane at his side. *Speak only when spoken to,* he told himself, *and then not much.* He glanced over at Lane again. If she could muster a little charm, she might deflect the concentration of this trio, put them off their guard a bit, but Lane remained quiet and cold as alabaster—no surprise at all. Nor would he usually care; if he and the crew had to deal with it, so could their visitors. Still, Dechert chided himself, making a mental note to talk to her later. *Whoever finds the secret to summoning a woman's power when it's most needed will rule the universe,* he thought. And he knew it wouldn't be him.

"Commander, if I might ask," Parrish said, "why am I spending half my time on the Moon in quarantine, being sucked by particle sweeps and scorched by flash-burners? I've heard of cleanliness, but this is bordering on neurosis."

Dechert looked him over again. Parrish had scruffy brown hair and a thin goatee, and he wore the first set of eyeglasses that Dechert had seen in years. His journalistic instincts were apparently helping him recover from the flight over from Peary Crater, and even Lane smiled at the question, maybe remembering a day when she was so naïve. Or maybe she was just asking herself the same thing that Dechert was:

What the hell is this guy doing here?

"More like survival," Dechert replied as they walked toward the mess hall. "Regolith, or moondust, is as big a danger here as radiation and rapid decompression. That's why we divide our stations between clean rooms and dirty rooms, and why all shuttles have decontamination pods."

He paused at the central station hatch, which led to the heart of Serenity 1, letting the others duck through the low entrance. A pipe hissed as coolant flowed through it, and Dechert could feel the bass harmonic thrum of the fusion reactor coming up through the rubberized floor grates and into his boots. Parrish would get used to the strangeness of living on the Moon if he stayed long enough. The weeks of dull repetition followed by sudden moments of fear, the heightened sense of sound in a world of ancient silence, the preciousness of every organic material, from potting soil to urine. For now, though, the only thing Dechert needed was for him to *respect* it.

"Have you seen a piece of moondust under a microscope,

Mr. Parrish? It's not the stuff you blow off your holo-cubes back on Earth. It's spiked like a sea urchin, and it interacts very badly with any machinery or electronics it comes into contact with. It's incredibly difficult to eradicate—been a problem for all lunar settlements since the Apollo days."

"Isn't dust intrusion what killed the Russian crew on the Mare Orientale?" Captain Hale asked. Dechert had almost forgotten he was there; he had managed to slip into the back of the line, and he walked like a ghost, always outside of everyone's peripheral vision. Dechert looked back at Hale and noticed his tan, and the deep furrows and ridges along the corners of his eyes, which were set iron gray into an otherwise unlined face. This was a man who spent a lot of time in the bush, a man who hunted. Dechert wondered how long he had been with the Air & Space Marines. That group didn't usually have sun on their faces.

"That's right," he said evenly. "It's also what probably caused the crash of the *Prospector* in '68."

They continued in single file through the curved, white-walled tunnels of the station, Dechert letting the group determine for themselves what sections of Serenity 1 they were passing through. He wasn't a tour guide, and the color-coded hatches were prominent and well marked. In his glances back at the group, he noticed that Parrish took in everything—the multicolored conduits, pipes, and airshafts protruding from the spherical walls, which allowed engineers to quickly find and fix malfunctions before they became catastrophic; the sound of dripping water and controlled steam releases and machine breathing that gave the station a darkly animate quality; the confined spaces, womblike, barely wide enough for two people to walk side by side.

Hale barely reacted to his surroundings and remained in

the background, as though he already knew the specifications of the corridor he was walking through. As for Standard, he seemed too absorbed with his mission to care much about the environment. He looked at nothing, but Dechert could sense him thinking behind dark eyes that blinked too often.

It was Standard who broke through his observations. "I thought the final report on the *Prospector* crash was inconclusive," he said. "Even the early versions of the GB-4 shuttle had anticontaminant protocols."

"I said *probably*," Dechert replied. "They never found a definitive answer for why her port thrusters froze, but foreign matter intrusion was always the prime suspect. We use continual outflow valves on our shuttles now to reduce those risks. And we have redundant thrusters on all spaceborne craft."

Dechert remembered the exact moment he had heard the *Prospector* was down. He had immediately pictured Captain John Ross Fletcher emerging from the broken craft, bruised but heroically alive. He didn't find out that his boss was dead for another two hours, and he was forever grateful that he had stayed at Serenity 1 to oversee the rescue mission, rather than lead the team that sifted through the impact field for body parts.

It had taken a long time to get used to the idea that his mentor had probably died because a few rocks the size of birdshot got stuck in just the wrong place at just the wrong time. There was no heroic ending to the crash, just an arrow of scored metal and burnt circuitry that stretched in a dark line across the Moon's usually immutable surface.

"All that's to say," Dechert concluded, suddenly not wanting to discuss the topic anymore, "that it's simply station protocols, Mr. Parrish. No one ever enters a clean room without being cleared by the nano-sweeps. It's a part of life up here that you'll get accustomed to, and if you don't, you'll be heading back to Earth."

If he had to bet, he'd put money on the latter.

They reached the crew mess and Dechert let them file in. The room was small and spare, with brushed-metal cabinets and walls and a long white table surrounded by chairs that had been built by a printer. It looked more like an emergency operating room than a cafeteria, a stereoscopic telescreen and a chess set pushed to the back of one of the countertops providing the only human comfort to the place.

Dechert glared at Lane as they walked in, and she relented, helping him to get the men coffee and a tray of Louisiana-style beignets that Vernon made for the crew every Earth-Tuesday. They took their seats, and after he and Lane had put everything on the table, they ate in silence and took tentative sips of the steaming coffee, waiting for someone to begin. Dechert knew it would be Standard.

"Well gentlemen—and ma'am," the commissioner said, nodding at Lane with a self-conscious smile, "I think we all realize the unprecedented nature of this incident." He looked around the rectangular table. "I wanted to provide a little downtime before having this discussion, but Commodore Yates wants things expedited. I'd like to begin by stating, categorically, that everything spoken in this room today is classified, and I'm going to have to ask you to sign for that."

He handed a Touchpad to Lane, who crossed her legs and began to scan the Administration's confidentiality agreement, her forehead furrowing as she plumbed its bureaucratic depths. Parrish looked confused, but Standard caught him before he could protest.

"Mr. Parrish, you can use some of what I tell you today, on deep background, to write a story. But it will be vetted by me and the Earth-Media team at Peary Crater before it is trans-

mitted, and it will be embargoed for release at the appropri-
ate time. Any aberration from this protocol will be deemed a
violation of the SMA Secrecy Act, which is a class-one felony.
There will be no off-station transmissions from anybody without prior approval until this matter is concluded. And please,
nothing is to be recorded. You may take written notes."

Standard's eyes did a slow round of the table again to make
sure his words had been absorbed. He waited for everyone
to read and sign the privacy agreement, sitting at the end of
the table and drumming the fleshy parts of his fingertips on
a crossed knee. Finally the pad came back to him and he
nodded. He stood up and began to pace the length of the
table, a coffee mug in his right hand, his left hand behind
his back.

"I think you'll understand our need for strict information
control when I'm finished. It would be one thing if a faulty
valve compromised your crawler's EVA pod. Everyone under-
stands an accident, particularly on the Moon. But I'm afraid
this wasn't an accident."

He paused for effect, and Dechert realized that he had rehearsed the speech. He wanted to say to the man "no shit,"
but bit his tongue while Standard continued. "I want this to
be clear and unequivocal—the reason we're here is that we've
finished our initial forensic testing, and concluded that your
mobile habitation unit, the, umm, *Molly Hatchet*, was compromised by an explosive device. By a bomb."

He spoke the last word with a hard flourish, and looked at
the group for reaction. Dechert and Hale didn't move. Lane's
eyes glowed, and Parrish looked stunned.

"A bomb? Jesus, I thought this was a mining accident," the
young reporter said. "I thought I was sent over here to cover an
accident. I mean, you're saying someone deliberately killed an
American miner on the Moon?"

Yes, that's what he's saying, Dechert thought, *and four billion people on Earth are about to find out as well.*

"That's correct, Mr. Parrish," Standard said, sitting down again and looking around the table, his chin jutting out. "Someone killed Specialist Benson, and we're pretty sure we know who it was."

9

Standard didn't need the theatrics; he had the room. The blood in Lane's lips went away and the bow-shaped upper part of her mouth drew itself straight. Her jaw clenched tight— Dechert could see bone pressing against her smooth cheeks. Even Hale was interested and alert now. He sat up and folded his hands together and stared at Standard. Dechert poured himself another cup of coffee and took a few deep breaths, waiting for a barrage of questions from Parrish. He had some experience with reporters during the Lebanese campaign. They asked more questions than they would ever need answers for, baiting and cajoling and waiting for a slip until they finally got a response that was worthy of quotation marks.

Every story Dechert had ever read about himself seemed more interesting than the reality of the occurrence itself, and he came to the grudging conclusion that it was just the way that news-streams were sold. Hits on the headline. And now Parrish had one hell of a headline.

But it was Lane who spoke first, and her voice was low and cutting.

"Maybe you'd be kind enough to end the melodrama, Commissioner, and tell us what the hell you're talking about."

Standard fumbled with his coffee cup. Some of the hot liquid spilled onto his thumb, which he thrust into his mouth. He cleared his throat and let his eyes wander around the table for a moment. *He should see how badly Quarles gets it when she's pissed*, Dechert thought.

"Of course, Officer Briggs," Standard said, folding his hands together on the table and staring at his fingers with great concentration. "A team of explosives specialists brought in from LEO-1 earlier this week did a thorough examination of the mobile habitation unit." He glanced at Dechert and then away. "Their mission was secret, so your team wasn't alerted to the landing."

Just another violation of standard protocol, Dechert thought. The Administration was supposed to alert all Level-1 mining stations about shuttle landings on the Moon, whether at Peary Crater or anywhere else, so they could remain on standby in case they had to launch a rescue in their quadrant. Dechert wondered how many shuttles had come up from LEO-1 in the dark in the last few weeks, and what the hell their crews were doing out on the mare.

"Munitions experts they are, in part, but also very specialized investigators," Standard continued. "Captain Hale headed the team, and serves as the military liaison to the Administra-

tion for this investigation. He has . . . both military and para-
military experience in these matters."

Standard looked at Hale, silently asking him to take over
the briefing. Dechert wondered whether the commissioner
had considered when he rehearsed his speech on the shuttle
over from Peary Crater that he might be scolded by a young
female safety officer on a remote mining station. The incident
had clearly thrown him off his timing.

Not Hale—he didn't appear to notice anything amiss. He
looked at Lane and Dechert. "As miners I assume you're famil
iar with explosives?"

"Yes, but most of the helium-3 mining is done with hydraulic scoops and tillers," Lane said. "We're more like regolith
farmers than miners, Captain, although we do blast for water
ice and ilmenite in the craters and mountains. Garden variety
one- to fifty-kilo Cynex charges and Type-A blasting caps. No
digital triggers. Solar flares tend to make those go off at the
wrong time."

Hale nodded. "Yes, that sounds right for the Moon, and
that's part of the problem. Every explosive in our lunar stockpile is pretty conventional mining fare, Officer Briggs, from
organic plastics to liquid-metal polymers. The residue we
found on your mobile habitation unit was more exotic."

He looked at Standard again before continuing, and the
administrator nodded. Hale put a Touchpad in the center of
the table and typed in a command, and a shimmering orange
representation of the *Molly Hatchet* appeared over the table
like a grid-lined holographic ghost.

"We found evidence of a small shape charge under the port
clasping joint of your crawler's EVA hatch—right here." He
touched the image and it briefly shimmered. A blinking blue
dot appeared under the hatch. "Probably the size of a pill; it

couldn't be seen unless someone was looking for it. The device was very sophisticated. It had a polymeric nitrogen charge, and its triggering mechanism was designed to fire on an orbital cue."

"Someone is going to have to explain that to me," Parrish interrupted. "Starting with the poly . . . starting with the explosive."

Dechert sat up, surprised for the first time since the meeting had begun.

"Polymeric nitrogen is pretty cutting-edge stuff," he said, looking at Hale as he spoke. "It's a cubic form of nitrogen in which all the atoms are connected with single covalent bonds, like a diamond. About five times more powerful than traditional munitions. Mostly used by the militaries of large and well-financed governments, because it's hard to manufacture."

"That's right," Hale said. "It's handy in advanced urban warfare, to take down blast doors and bunkers with minimal concussion on missions where collateral damage and noise have to be contained. But that's all Earth-side. No one with a permanent station on the Moon has been known to use it up here, and it wouldn't be economically feasible to do so. Not the Russians, the Chinese, the Indians, the Brazilians, or us. As for the detonator, it was programmed to pick up open-source Lunar Positioning Satellite coordinates and detonate when the Moon was at point four-three degrees of apogee. In other words, a sophisticated way of blowing up at exactly 1900 hours, thirty seconds on December the twelfth, 2072. We have to assume that whoever set the trigger knew the *Molly Hatchet* would be out on the mare on a mining run at that time."

Standard continued to drum his fingers on his knee, more audibly now. Dechert wondered if he was tapping his feet as well. "Thank you, Captain," the commissioner said. "The important thing, of course, is the explosive charge, which is traceable through subatomic residue. Like a DNA fingerprint, if you will. We ran our forensic samples through the DOD's global intelligence database and found a signature."

He stood up and began walking broadside of the table again, his composure regained, hands behind his back.

"The explosive came from a batch of polymeric nitrogen made by the Russian military in 2062 and stored in Turkmenistan. It was stolen a year later by thieves in a raid on a remote arms depot. You can imagine how poorly those sites are guarded. One of GI-Asia's strike teams took down a weapons merchant in Indonesia three years later, one Abduran Amir Serkasa. He was fairly big game, but not very bright. He kept his bills of lading on an unencrypted Hashfile, and his shredding program proved inadequate."

Standard stopped and put his palms on the table, standing over Briggs and Parrish with the foreboding of a minister.

"Our computer forensics group restored the files. In 2066, Serkasa sold four thousand micrograms of that same polymeric nitrogen to Kowloon Pacifica, a front company run by the Guojia Anquan Bu."

"Excuse me?" Parrish asked.

"The Ministry of State Security, Mr. Parrish. Chinese Intelligence."

Dechert had sensed this was coming, but it still left him with a hole in the bottom of his stomach. The rhetorical buildup against China in the last two months had fallen into place like the last pour of cement on a foundation, and he realized that the Administration's bluster had just become weaponized. The Moon, arid and cold and devoid of the larger human sins that had taken so much from him, now felt hot and full of Earthly danger. Conflicting theories pulled at his mind. Could the Chinese really have done this? It made sense to a true believer like Standard, but blowing up a mobile habitation unit seemed too overt a move for them. *They're slicker than that,* he thought. The Chinese kill with a small blade. They don't bludgeon you with an axe. And if they really were going to take a stab at the jugular, why didn't they just snap-shot a missile at Serenity 1 and blow up the whole station?

But if not the Chinese, who? He had to give Standard credit for one thing—no other theory made sense. The Russians had their patch of the Moon on the western rim of the Mare Orientale, and they hadn't made any serious inroads on the near-side maria. They focused on ilmenite and ice mining and it was hard enough for those crazy bastards to survive over there, separated from the rest of the lunar colonies by thousands of kilometers, always facing away from the Earth and into the deep of the solar system. The Indian and Brazilian lunar programs were too nascent to even consider territorial expansion. Both nations' diggers were living in temporary inflatable bubbles and mobile mining skiffs. Only the Chinese and Americans had major settlements on the near side; only they were in international court squabbling over central maria mineral rights. Only they had the terrestrial and orbital might to stand against each other if the litigation failed to come to a satisfying conclusion and a real fight broke out.

Dechert thought of his friend, Lin Tzu, and wondered if he was now his enemy. He would need more convincing before he believed it. But he also couldn't just discount it, either, and that made him uneasy.

"Pardon me, Mr. Standard," Lane said, breaking the silence that had hung over the table, "but that's the biggest crock of Earth-shit I've heard since they started selling residential real estate near Tycho." She leaned forward and stared the commissioner down. "We've been here a little longer than you, and we know the people over there. They'd launch a rescue mission for one of us just as quickly as they would for one of their own. I'd just as soon believe my mother blew up the *Hatchet.*"

Standard looked straight back at Lane for the first time since he had arrived. She was finally treading on territory where he could gain a steady purchase—the twisted road of international politics. "Which people do you know over there, Officer Briggs? The astro-scientists and miners you trade gardening secrets and homemade hooch with? Do you think those are the people I'm talking about?"

Lane and Dechert stole a quick glance at each other to make sure Standard's words had sunk in: The Administration had been listening in on their personal communications.

"I'm sure the miners at New Beijing 2 are a friendly bunch," Standard went on, "but they aren't in control of this situation any more than you or I, and they work for a government with less than benign intentions. You aren't privy to the information I have, Officer Briggs, so I understand your skepticism. I can assure you, though, that the Chinese have both motive and intent in this matter."

He paused and lowered his voice. "I think you know things haven't been neighborly between our two countries lately, but this crisis would make more sense if you understood the full scope of the political situation back on Earth. To say it isn't good would be a gross understatement."

Dechert stared at the holographic image of the *Molly Hatchet*. His eyes focused on the blinking blue dot—the exact place where the air had rushed out of the crawler's EVA module with explosive force, leaving Cole Benson to die in space. Dechert pictured Cole trying to expel the air from his lungs so they didn't rupture as he crawled toward his helmet, desperately trying to stay conscious. He saw him pass out, his mouth and his eyes opened wide, the water in them quickly boiling in the vacuum. *That* was the part of this whole mess that wasn't good.

"One thing I don't understand," Parrish broke in. "This

man Serkasa—how is an arms merchant clumsy enough to leave behind records of his covert dealings with a state government, and how did we know the exact chemical components of this stolen batch of explosives?"

Standard turned to Parrish with a puzzled look on his face, ready for the intelligence of his question, but perhaps unprepared for who had asked it.

"Arms treaties, Mr. Parrish," he said, with a wave of his fingers. "We have a joint agreement with the Russians to track all hyperdestructives. They provided us with the trace-element profile of the polymeric nitrogen as soon as it was stolen. As for Mr. Serkasa, I don't have the inclination to delve into the mind of a man who profits on death, but I would venture to say that such people are anything but conscientious about their records."

Dechert shook his head. He had known men like Serkasa, and he couldn't disagree more. They tend to be the most meticulous of people, because death always waits for their next mistake. He looked over at Hale and the two locked eyes for a second, and Dechert knew the captain was thinking the same thing.

Which meant Standard had a poor understanding of the operational world, or he was lying. Dechert wasn't sure which one it was yet.

"Has the Chinese consulate been made aware of the fact that our government is implicating them in the explosion, Commissioner, or are the results of the investigation still a secret?" he asked.

"Captain Hale's team just finished their initial report, and we haven't received information from Earth on how they'll proceed with the diplomatic process," Standard said. He sat down again and lowered his voice. "However, Joint Space Command has received orders from the president to put contingency plans in place immediately, and that is where all of us come in. I'm afraid that life is about to change up here, for you people, for the civilian teams at Peary Crater, for all of us. Until this crisis is resolved, all U.S. mining stations on the Moon are to be, at least for the time being, militarized."

Nobody spoke. Parrish looked up from his notes. Dechert looked at Lane and smiled, apologetic. The promise he had made to her when she first came to the Moon had been rendered obsolete by a man who spent most of his life in a corner office a quarter of a million miles away.

"Captain Hale," Standard said.

Hale keyed the Touchpad again and a topographic hologram of the Moon hovered over the table. Dechert had forgotten how beautiful she looked from space, a silver and gunmetal gray marble—Earth's naked shadow. The hologram marked the positions of every main base, substation, and mining operation on the lunar surface: U.S. in blue, Chinese in red, Russian in green, Brazilian in purple, and Indian in yellow. Serenity 1 appeared as an indigo speck on the northern margins of Menelaus, dwarfed by the crater's thirty-kilometer impact basin. The southern ridgeline of the Montes Haemus rose just to the west, their humpbacked peaks climbing two kilometers above the Serenity plain. The U.S. main base at Peary Crater, near the North Pole, was well over a thousand kilometers away, the first truly permanent settlement on the Moon and one of the only places on its surface that enjoyed nearly perpetual sunlight because of Luna's unique rotational axis. It had been a while since Dechert had looked at a lunar map of this scale. *Damn, we are alone down here,* he thought, stuck in the middle of two sparring giants with little more than ten feet of topsoil to protect us.

Their closest neighbors were the Chinese. New Beijing 2 had been burrowed into the impact wall of Archimedes Crater in the Mare Imbrium, about six hundred kilometers to the west.

What were they doing over there now? Dechert wondered. Were military commanders briefing a reluctant Lin Tzu on the distinct possibility of a war with the Americans? Had they already moved weapons into place, and were some of those weapons pointed at Sea of Serenity 1? The thought of an AI seeker missile or a focused electromagnetic pulse hitting the station chilled Dechert to his spine. There wouldn't be enough time for a search-and-rescue mission from Peary Crater if Serenity were attacked. All they would find is bodies preserved by the vacuum of space. The station had no significant defense systems—she was built before governments saw enough strategic importance on the Moon to warrant fighting over it. Like so many things on this rock, that was probably shortsighted of the people on Earth.

"A squad of Air & Space Marines will be arriving here tomorrow, at 0900," Hale said. He looked almost apologetic, clasping his hands together and squeezing one thumb under the other, as if he were unsure of himself for the first time. "I want to stress that we are not cleared to take any offensive actions. We're simply putting pawns on the front row in case the politicians back on Earth can't sort this mess out."

Dechert leaned back in his chair and closed his eyes, a feeling of impatience welling through him with the power of a nicotine fit. He had to get his crew out of harm's way, and he didn't appreciate being told not to worry about a squad of marines arriving at his station. Or being called a "pawn." *No more deaths on my watch*, he thought. *I'm not going to lose control of this situation.*

"Please don't comfort me with the possibility that the politicians are on top of things, Captain," he said, and turned toward Standard. "So you're telling us that the ROC Treaty is now null and void, that we are actually militarizing the Moon? Do you understand what that means, Commissioner?"

Standard reddened. "I do, Commander, but I would point out that we aren't the ones in violation of the ROC or ISA agreements. We're the ones who got attacked, and under international law—whether it's maritime, terrestrial, or lunar—we have a right to defend ourselves. And please don't be naïve enough to think the Chinese aren't doing exactly the same thing right now."

"Maybe they are, and maybe inner-system politics isn't my specialty, but I know how these things tend to escalate," Dechert replied. He stood up but kept his hands on the table's edge. "Maybe the Chinese did do this, but I sure as hell haven't seen any proof of that yet. The evidence you've presented has an air of one-sidedness."

He looked at Lane, slowing down when he saw the warning in her eyes, lowering his voice and changing tack. "I also have to remind you that we're miners, Commissioner. *Civilians.* I don't care whether the marines are coming here to prepare for an attack or to take a few days of R&R. But my team should be evacuated to Peary Crater or maybe even to Low Lunar 1. At the very least I can stay and run the systems. . . ."

Standard started to say no, but Dechert cut him off with a raised hand.

"You're shaking your head because you're thinking of what you want to happen, not what is possible. On a practical level alone, Serenity isn't equipped to sustain the number of people you're talking about. You want a platoon of marines to bunk here; you're going to have to move some bodies around."

"We're talking about a four-man reconnaissance squad, Commander, not a battalion," Hale said. "I thought a Level-1 substation could accommodate up to fifteen souls."

"It can in a pinch, but it's built to house five or six. We'd be pushing the biofilters and the reactor to their limits, and the basin is going dark for fourteen Earth days when the sun sets at 1630 tomorrow, so solar will be gone. We'd also have to hot-bunk. We've only got eight beds. But that's not the real issue. My team . . ."

"No," Standard broke in, banging his fist on his leather valise, which dampened the effect. "Taking the mining operation off-line is out of the question. We must maintain a veneer of normalcy, Commander Dechert, for tactical reasons at least. And I'm afraid that, while your team *is* civilian, Article Four of your contract clearly states that it can be deputized and put under military leadership in a time of crisis. That's why substation commanders like you always have military backgrounds. The Guild will back us on this."

"The hell they will," Lane said.

"Yes, Officer Briggs," Standard said, "unfortunately for you, the hell they will. In fact, they already have."

He stood up and closed his leather folder, and the gesture reminded Dechert of Captain Bildad sealing the completed ledger for the *Pequod*'s final voyage.

"We can argue about this all we want, but we will still end up coming back to the same place, with the same realities. We're going to need an operational plan to quarter eleven souls . . . twelve if Mr. Parrish is asked to stay and see this story through." He took a deep breath and leaned over the table again. "You can make your grievances later, but for now this is a time for personal courage, and for sacrifice. You know how things have been going on Earth. We can't let the Moon fall to Chinese dominance if that is their ultimate intention, and we will not allow unprovoked aggression to stand, wherever it occurs."

The mess hall fell silent again and Dechert thought of Rome and Carthage and the endless Punic Wars. *Which of the two are we?* he wondered. He knew how much economic potency the United States had lost to China and India in the last fifteen years. While a wealthy minority prospered in the

U.S., more than fifty million people faced a daily struggle to find enough bread for their tables. Of all the continents, North America and Europe had been hit the hardest by the Thermal Max, Earth's punishment for their centuries of dominance, perhaps. Within a year of the methane eruptions, half of North America's coastal cities were under water. The corn and wheat belts fell to drought. The manufacturing that had once been the backbone of these countries had fled decades before, leaving no infrastructure to rapidly rebuild. Pandemics and religious upheaval did the rest of the damage.

Maybe now that the United States was regaining her footing—thanks in large part to helium-3 mining on the Moon—her leaders were ready to retake their rightful place in the world. At the very least, a war would give the masses something to cheer for, a distraction from their hunger and a villain to blame. It was good politics, if nothing else. And if the Chinese perceived such a growing threat, would they allow it to fester? Or worse yet, because such a fact would make the situation irreversible, were the Chinese the aggressors to begin with? And that's what Dechert kept tripping over: that it *had* to be them. Who else could have sabotaged Drill Station 7?

Who else could have killed Cole?

Dechert looked over to Briggs. She opened her mouth, probably to question Standard's definition of unprovoked aggression, but Dechert warned her off with a shake of his head. This wasn't the time or place.

"Good," Standard said. "I guess that will do for now. I know we all have things to manage. Mr. Parrish, I expect you'll have a story drafted in the near term? We've notified Specialist Benson's next of kin on the circumstances of his death. We're prepared to allow a controlled leak of our findings after certain diplomatic functions are completed. Probably in the next two days."

Parrish looked up from his notes and blew air from his lungs. He played with his goatee, stroking the whiskers in a downward motion. "I have about a hundred more questions, Commissioner, and I'm going to need to speak to my editors as soon as possible. This is historic stuff we're talking about. Crazy, but epic."

"Of course. We'll set up a secure channel for you once the embargo is cleared, and you and I can speak in private in the meantime to fill in any gaps." Standard turned toward the hatch, and then realized he had no place to go.

"Umm, Mr. Dechert, I'd like to meet with you privately to discuss the logistics of setting up an operations center in the station. Perhaps after you've arranged for our quarters?"

"That may take a while. I've got a command meeting with my crew in an hour and I'm due for an on-site at Spiral 6, one of our near-station helium-3 sites, before the day is out. We can't put it off. It's a reactor and systems check."

Dechert looked at Standard's angular frame in the hatchway. He had manicured nails, he noticed, and his hands were ivory white.

"Maybe you'd like to take a ride on the Moon with me, Commissioner? I'll need my crew to remain here to get things ready for the marines, and we require two men for all off-grid rover missions."

Standard was surprised by the invitation, and hesitant. He looked at Lane, maybe self-conscious about turning down a potentially dangerous mission in front of a woman, and then back at Dechert, finally nodding his head. "Yes, I'd like that, Commander. I've never seen the mining operations in person."

No, Dechert thought, *I'm sure that you haven't.*

10

They met in the greenhouse. Dechert didn't want the formality of the CORE, where they usually held command meetings, and he couldn't take the chance that they would be overheard by anyone outside of the crew. This was as close to an off-site location as there was in the station. They sat in a small circle among perfectly manicured parallel rows of vegetables in the vibration pod, which served as a pollinator for the tomatoes, squash, and other heterosexual species that had a hard time procreating in microgravity. Quarles had turned down the light concentrators, and the low whir of the ventilators muffled their voices and gave the room a hypnotic buzz. Dechert wondered where Quarles had hidden his marijuana plants. They mysteriously disappeared from a corner of the

greenhouse when Standard and his small team arrived, and
Quarles looked distinctly unhappy, fidgeting with his fingers
and tapping his feet on the floor as he sat on an upside-down
planter.

They all looked unhappy. Dechert had briefed Thatch,
Waters, and Quarles on the meeting with Standard in the
mess hall, and the implications of a murdered friend and a
militarized Moon were beginning to sink in.

"So much for the Sea of Serenity," Quarles said. "Can we
call it the Sea of Impending Doom now?"

"No shit," said Waters. "You sure we gotta accept this, boss?
Nobody told us anything about fighting a damned war when
we signed up to be diggers. I didn't even read my Guild contract. Damned thing was longer than the Old Testament."

"Amen to that," Quarles said.

Thatch grunted. He slouched on a folding chair between
two rows of germinating Hubbard squash, his meaty forearms
resting on his knees. Droplets of water from a condensing
filter above his head fell onto his shoulder. Dechert watched
the beads of liquid bulge, reach their tipping point, and fall.
Thatch didn't move when they hit his heavysuit, which had
a dark blue stain of wet that was expanding down toward the
center of his chest. Out of the entire team, Dechert was most
interested in his response to the news and his state of mind
since their talk in the observatory. Thatch had moved silently
through the station since then, almost unseen, but his body
radiated a cold fury.

"That's what you all are worried about?" Thatch finally
asked. His teeth were clenched together so tightly it was a
surprise he could speak. "Those sons of bitches killed Cole.
I never thought I'd say this, but I'll be happy to pull the trigger if we get the say-so. They won't have to pay me a fucking
dollar to do it."

Dechert nodded at Thatch, but didn't speak. The big man ran a thick hand through his curly hair and exhaled. He hadn't shaved, but that wasn't unusual. His eyes were still red-rimmed with fatigue, and his heavysuit looked a size too tight. An old forty-niner who came up to the Moon to hit the big lode and lost his partner to a bomb on the lunar mare. *I can't blame him for wanting a reckoning,* Dechert thought.

Lane patted Thatch's wide knee. Her eyes had been creased in thought since the meeting began, and when she spoke, it was in a low, calming voice.

"We're all pissed about Cole, and I'll be just as happy as you to kill the bastards who did it, but let's make sure we're not punching the innocent kid standing next to the bully." She looked around the room at each of them. "Does anyone here really think the Chinese did this? It doesn't make any sense; they're running at full capacity and they haven't tapped a fraction of their He-3 deposits. They could stay west of the Apennines and have enough dirt to mine for the next fifteen years."

She turned to Dechert. "And even if their government did go insane, what business do we have being in the middle of this? I *did* read my Guild contract. It said we could be deputized in the case of a mining emergency or a natural disaster. It didn't say anything about fighting a war."

"I'm sure the SMA lawyers have found a way to parse that," Dechert said. "It wouldn't be the first time civilians got caught in the cross fire, Lane, and according to our pay stubs, we *are* technically an extended arm of the government."

"Fuck the technicalities."

"I wish we could. But I don't think we're going to get out of this. And at least from a tactical standpoint, I can see where Standard is coming from in wanting to keep the mining operations up and running. We shut things down and bug out and the Chinese will know about it in six hours."

He sat with his legs crossed and his fingers tucked into the neckline of his heavysuit, scratching his jaw with a free index finger.

"I feel almost as bad for our friends at NB-2 as I do for us, and I'll make every argument I can to get out of this, but we can't lose focus. We have some serious problems to address, right here and now. Nothing's going to be off-limits if this thing spins out of control, and our first concern has to be station security. We need to assess our vulnerabilities."

"Our vulnerabilities?" Quarles asked. "How about 'we're on the freakin' Moon?' Jesus, if someone started shooting at us, we'd be like a baby on a mountaintop. We have trouble enough dealing with solar flares. If someone shot a focused EMP our way, I couldn't microwave you a pizza after it hit. It would fry everything we got. Coms. Life support. Transport. Everything."

"The kid's right," Vernon said. "Our shielding is designed for naturally occurring radiation bursts. There aren't supposed to be any damned weapons on the Moon. A strong enough EMP would probably take down the reactor, even if it's encased in its second shield. And a missile or laser shot would do worse. They could kill us a dozen different ways."

Dechert tried a grim smile. "I'm sure the marines are working all this out for us. They'll probably be bringing some kind of perimeter defenses over with them from Peary Crater, but I doubt their idea of acceptable losses will mesh with ours. So let's hear some options."

They all shifted in their seats. "We need an evacuation plan, obviously," Lane said. "No more than five minutes from warning to bugout, and it would have to be in a MOHAB. We can't walk out of here."

"But what if they hit us with an EMP from low orbit?" Thatch asked. "There's no warning for that. It would knock out all of our transport capability for at least a day, maybe longer,

and we might not even last that long. All the CORE's autonomics would go down, including life support."

Dechert nodded, thinking it through. Thatch was probably right. Even if the fusion reactor did somehow survive the
pulse and stay online, it would be a heart pumping blood to
a dead body. All the circuits in the station would be blown.
They might not even be able to open a sealed hatch without
one hell of an effort. And that was if the Chinese hit them
with just an EMP. If it was a missile or laser strike, this was all
probably moot.

"All right," he said, looking up at them, "how about this?
We move the *Aerosmith* down the Menelaus Road tomorrow,
somewhere inside the impact basin, to serve as a lifeboat.
She'll need an overhaul, but it looks like we won't have to use
her as a mining platform anytime soon. The crater should protect her from an electromagnetic pulse or anything else flying
this way from the Mare Imbrium or the South Pole. I'm sure
I can get Hale to convince Standard it's the smart play. He'll
like the redundancy."

The *Aerosmith*, like the *Molly Hatchet*, had been named by
Quarles, who swore that no music made after 2020 was worth
listening to. The Administration had grudgingly accepted the
breach of naming protocol for its mining crawlers as a minor
annoyance, but those were happier days—and the *Aerosmith*
was in much better shape back then. She hadn't been out on
the lunar surface for more than six months, and Dechert could
see that that scared all of them. God only knows how much
moondust had crept into her innards or how the extended hi-
bernation in the cold soak of the Bullpen had brittled everything from her wiring to her half-tracks. Dormant machinery
doesn't do well on the Moon.

Lane must have been thinking the same thing. "Even if
we can get the *Aerosmith* running and down into Menelaus—

and that's a big if," she said, glaring at Quarles to express her doubt in his ability to pull off such a feat, "how are we going to get to her if there's an attack? The rovers would probably be down, and an EMP would fry the walk-profile computers in the suits."

"Can't we run a bypass on the WPCs, so the suits can be run manually if need be?" Dechert asked. "I'm talking twentieth-century stuff here—just set them up for basic life support with no auto-regs or navigation. It's a four-hour walk, but it's doable with a map and a compass."

Quarles thought for a few seconds. "I could rig the suits so the rebreathers are manually controlled, I guess, but we'd have to be careful about the gas mixes. We'd also need to keep an eye on one another while we're out there." He looked over at Lane. "And I can't promise that her suit will work if she keeps denigrating my skills. It ruins my concentration."

"All right, let's get it done," Dechert said, brushing past the two before they could begin to snipe again. "Lane, you work out an evacuation plan. Quarles will handle the suits and help Vernon with refitting the *Aerosmith*. Thatch, get to work on a run into Menelaus. Pull the maps and figure out a safe place to stash her, and check the latest low-orbit shots to make sure the road hasn't been compromised. I'll find out from Standard and Hale what kind of defensive countermeasures the marines have planned in case things get worse than they already are."

"They'll probably just sing 'God Bless America' as the freakin' missiles fall," Thatch said. He liked bureaucrats and soldiers even less than Lane did, and it had taken him more than a year to warm to Dechert once he realized his boss had been in the service. Something about a bar brawl in Portland a long time ago that had landed him in jail for the weekend. Thatch shifted his large bulk, and it seemed the chair he was in might

remain glued to his thighs when he stood up. "How much
warning would we have if they did launch on us?"

"You mean missiles?" Waters asked. "Figure seven thousand kilometers an hour from a range of six hundred klicks . . .
maybe four minutes once we catch sight of them. Just enough
time to shit our pants but not enough to clean up. I don't know
if we'll be able to bug out. We might get our suits on, but getting clear of the station is another thing." He smiled his big
Vernon Waters smile. "I think I'll just head down to Jonathan's
office in the Hole, for a last-second toke of his hydro-mania."

"I'll have the vape packed and hot, my brother," Quarles
said. "We'll die high, and live on with the gods."

Dechert grimaced. "That's deep, Jonathan. Did you get it
from Led Zeppelin?"

They all joined in laughter, but it sounded hollow in the
cavernous room, unlike the real laughs they had shared together in the past.

"Okay—let's just focus on an evacuation plan and make
sure we have it dialed in tight," Dechert said. "Vernon, run the
numbers and figure out our margin for error, down to plus or
minus ten seconds. I want this thing locked down."

Dechert stood up and turned to Thatch. "You're also going
to have to rig one of the rovers with a plow for the descent into
Menelaus, and bring some Cynex and blasting caps. We'll need
you and Vernon riding shotgun out in front of the *Aerosmith*."

He looked at his team and nodded his head. They acknowledged him but none of them spoke. Waters slapped Thatch on
the back and the two turned to leave.

"Lane, Jonathan—hang around for a minute," Dechert said.
"I want coms in the *Aerosmith* to be off-line from the Peary
communications hub, and I've got a couple of ideas I want to
throw by you."

He waited until the three of them were alone and then signaled Briggs and Quarles to follow him. It was an uneasy gesture, and not just because of its conspiratorial nature. Dechert had made tough decisions before. He had lost four men trying to save one soldier who was bleeding out in a bomb-gutted shack in Aanjar during the worst of the Lebanese insurrection, but he kept ordering them back in because you didn't leave a guy behind. He had ignored orders that didn't make sense, or at least pretended not to receive them until they became irrelevant. But the responsibility for those decisions always fell on him. This time, he couldn't do what was needed alone. At the very least, he needed Lane and Jonathan to help him, and the cost would have to be dealt with later, even if it was too high.

He took them to the quarantine module, where infected plants were separated from the rest of the greenhouse. They squeezed inside the white sphere and closed the hatch. There was barely enough room for all of them to stand without touching one another in the smooth-walled pod. A nectarine tree with citrus canker on its trunk poked at Lane's leg and they all leaned forward to avoid the sloping walls overhead.

"This is nice," Quarles said. "Lane, maybe we should try this sometime when the commander's not around."

Lane smirked but didn't say anything. She looked at Dechert in anticipation, as though she had hoped this conversation would happen but didn't want to initiate it. Dechert had always rebuffed her wild theories about the government and its Machiavellian plottings. Now he had them clustered in a plant hibernator so their SMA and federal minders couldn't hear them talk. He clenched his teeth and began.

"I'm not going to try and sweeten this up, so I'll give it to you straight. We're going to lose the Moon if things keep going down this path." He paused and looked both of them in the eyes. "If that happens, I want you to think about the consequences. They're more important than our little station out here on the Serenitatis."

He breathed in, keeping his head down. Giving speeches had never been his thing; he used to let the sergeants do it for him back in the Bake.

"Do you follow me? Colonizing the Moon has been one of the few real achievements our back-assed species has been able to pull off in the last thirty years. And it's been done the right way. It might not be perfect up here, but it's remained a common cause for the most part. If we let this thing happen, if we start arming the forts and the Chinese do the same, the Moon and everything else from the Asteroid Belt out to Europa will become just like Earth

"The war-gamers back home won't just be drawing up plans for a Hong Kong Variant or a European Heavy anymore. The next battles will be fought in space. The one place where every other consideration has been superseded by the right to survive since the days of Mercury and Vostok will be gone. A hundred years of peace in space—gone. And it will never come back."

They both stared at him, too surprised to say anything. Dechert had shown passion before, about blasting for ice in the Moon's subterranean lava pipes or flying a shuttle on the deck in a tight-walled rille, but he had never expressed any emotion other than dull cynicism about the state of the human condition, and he had never discussed politics. They respected him for that, had accepted the fact that he was diligent to the extreme about his command but detached and apolitical about most everything else. And now he was talking like a twentieth-century peace activist in the longest-winded speech he had ever given in their presence.

"It might be too late to do anything," he concluded, embarrassed by the fact that he was still the only one speaking. "Hell, it might have been too late when they declared the Moon a commercial zone in 2051, before the Max. And Standard could be right as well, that the Chinese are starting something that can't be stopped, but I need to know for sure if that's the case. If we're going to go the way of Earth, I want to know why the hell it's happening, and who the hell is doing it."

"So what do you want us to do, boss?" Quarles asked. He looked over at Lane, his eyebrows raised. "I mean I'm with you, you know, but it's not like we can take a shuttle down to the Mining Guild and ask them to open an independent investigation."

Dechert straightened his back, watching the ceiling so he wouldn't bang his head. "No . . . I want to open one myself. We need information and we can't get it through the conventional channels. I need both of you for that—but I want you to realize that if you help me, you're jeopardizing your careers at the very least, and maybe a lot more. It's probably in your best interest to say no, and I won't hold it against you if you do."

"You already know where I stand," Lane said. "I don't care whether *their* dumb-ass bureaucrats or *our* dumb-ass bureaucrats are picking this fight; I just want to stop it. I didn't come up here so I could hang out with a bunch of unshaven men for three years. It was supposed to mean something."

Dechert looked at her and nodded, a small smile on his lips. He wanted to squeeze her arm but resisted, looking instead at Quarles. "Jonathan? You can bail out now, and no hard feelings."

Quarles looked at Lane and then Dechert. He plucked a leaf off the nectarine tree and began folding it into careful halves and then quarters, his eyes lowered in concentration. "Well, I'm all about self-preservation, but I can't stand the thought of those assholes frying all my toys up here so they can turn a quicker dollar. I've got patents to consider." He tossed the folded leaf into the planter, keeping his eyes down. "I hate the Earth anyway, minus a few of its bacchanalian pleasures."

Dechert nodded. Quarles rarely spoke about his life back on Terra. His family had died in a flu pandemic after the Thermal Maximum, and Dechert had always sensed a seething anger that lay hidden under his juvenile demeanor. He blamed Earth for what it had done to him, and the people on it for being too stupid and shortsighted to prevent it. For Quarles, ignorance was the deadliest sin.

"For God's sake, Jonathan, is that a yes or a no?" Lane asked.

He looked up at her and smiled. "It's a yes, my quick-tempered Artemis. I'll risk premature death if it means I get to bask in the warm glow of your presence for a few more weeks."

Dechert crossed his arms, still unsure of himself, and then nodded his head.

"All right. What I need is a way to communicate outside of the pipe, totally clear of any spies at Peary Crater or Las Cruces. And I need some intelligence from Earth, from within the Administration. We have to find out everything they know about the *Molly Hatchet*, and if they've gathered any additional intelligence on the sabotage of DS-7 that Standard isn't sharing with us."

Jonathan calculated for a moment. Nobody on Earth or the Moon knew the stream better than he. "If you're talking about using the stream, I've got an idea. I could run a piggyback program and have a message dispatched to a DRP on Earth, but I'd need a little time and a lot of privacy."

Lane closed her eyes and set her jaw. "Put that in English, please."

"A piggyback's a kind of worm that lets you insert and retrieve data streams in a private pouch at the tail end of open i mail or message threads, without having to implant an executable file. Like a secret compartment in a briefcase. Once the briefcase hits the flash-servers on Earth, the piggyback links itself to a dynamic routing program—a DRP. You could send encrypted messages to whomever you wanted, and no one would even know that they came from the Moon. You could even run some basic queries and pull data directly off the stream. Problem is, you can only communicate with the servers when legitimate messages are coming up and down the pipe. In other words, you wouldn't get your responses until a real message came back from a different, legitimate source."

"But it would be completely untraceable?" Lane asked. "Even if someone was looking?"

"Yeah, it should be. I'm a bit out-of-date on the government's tracking spiders, but the last time I checked, they were two years behind the curve. NSA's snoops all got wait-listed by MIT." He smiled. "You know the government techies—they're the second string."

Dechert thought about that. He didn't like the idea of bouncing stream messages off an unknown cloud server on Earth, but the risk would have to be taken. "All right, but can the messages be routed down to Terra and then back up to the Moon, to another station?"

Jonathan looked at Dechert, then Lane, and pulled at his ear. "I suppose. Hell, no one uses traditional i-mail anymore except you dinosaurs, so it probably isn't being watched as closely as the holos and the virts. Who are you planning on talking to? You have a secret friend over at Peary Crater?"

"No. New Beijing 2."

Both of their eyes widened. "Jesus. Lin Tzu?" Quarles asked. "I mean, couldn't they hang you for that?"

"I doubt there's a yardarm at Peary Crater," Dechert said, "but, yes, it wouldn't go over very well if they found out." He put his hand on Quarles's shoulder. "Look, I'm not going to talk to Tzu until the story about Cole hits the wire, and I'm not planning on giving up any state secrets. But we have to know what he knows, and I trust him to keep our confidence. He likes his government about as much as we like ours. More important, he respects the Moon more than anyone on Earth does."

Lane looked troubled. "But what about his minders at the South Pole? Don't you think they'll be watching his traffic?"

"I'm sure they will, but we've already worked out a little code for emergency situations, to get around that. I think we can keep their spies from getting suspicious, at least long enough to set up another channel of communications."

Lane and Quarles looked at each other, surprised once again at the conspiratorial streak they had never seen before in their boss. "All right," Lane said. "What about the intelligence side of things?"

Dechert hesitated, knowing how angry she would be. The one thing Lane had always demanded as a woman on a Moon full of men was her privacy, and he couldn't begrudge her that. She had been living in an underground cocoon with a bunch of alpha males for more than three years. The problem was that, in all that time, she had never fully realized the lack of privacy that came with being a member of the Space Mining Administration.

"I'll work on the *Molly Hatchet*," Dechert said to her, "but I need you to keep digging on those boot prints at DS-7. Find me every damned pair of Groombridge boots requisitioned to the Moon in the last ten years and see if you can get into the corporate files on Earth relating to sales to us, China, and whoever. And . . ." He paused. This was where he might lose her. "And I need you to reach out to your friend at the Administration's public affairs office, in New Mexico."

She looked at him, not understanding, and then her face turned red. She clenched her jaws and he could see the bones pushing out of the sides of her cheeks and then retreating again. One of her hands slid off the sloping module wall and found its way to her hip. "*What* friend?"

"Sheldon Starks."

Her mouth opened and then closed, and Dechert thought she might slap him. Quarles looked on, intrigued, as though hoping she'd slap him.

When she didn't say anything, Dechert said, "The Administration runs thorough background checks on everyone doing extended lunar tours, Lane; you know that. I was under orders to read everyone's private file before clearing them for Serenity. I'm sorry."

Without her personnel jacket, Dechert wouldn't have been able to say for certain if Lane even liked men—or women, for that matter. She had kept her personal life too closely guarded on the station. But Lane's dossier had painted in the colors of her sexuality that she had tried to blur with protocol, describing in detail her brief and reportedly electric affair with Starks, the public relations chief at Las Cruces. She had met him on a layover after off-Earth mining school in Arizona, and they were together for at least four months before she got shipped to Serenity 1. The dossier said she had broken it off, apparently unable to accept an ultimatum from the young mining executive. They traded i-mails and virt messages for a few months after she got to the station, as lovers do until the realization sets in that things are really over, but she had never mentioned Starks to the crew.

"Goddammit," Lane said. She lowered her head, too furious to even look at Dechert. "I knew those bastards were thorough, but I didn't know they were fucking spying on us when we were off duty."

She remained silent for a moment, her hands gripping her hips, and when she finally looked up at Dechert he could see the glassiness in her eyes and the loss of trust. He had become part of the system to her. A lesser evil than the SMA, perhaps, but a part of the system nonetheless.

"All right. I can send him a message on his private account. But I don't know how willing he'll be to respond. You're asking me to risk his neck as well—and at least *he's* never betrayed my trust."

Dechert breathed out between pursed lips. He felt cold, and spoke quickly. "I know. Just act like you're scared and you want to know what's going on down there. Make it sound as innocent as possible and unsolicited, so he can say it was unprovoked if someone's listening in. We'll gauge how far he's willing to go by his response."

"I'm not sure how far *I'm* willing to go." She had turned from enthusiastic to arctic in an instant, and it felt as if all the blood in the room had pooled on the floor. Even Quarles kept silent, his eyes avoiding hers. "I'm beginning to think that there's no one I can trust."

You can trust me, Dechert wanted to say. *You know I wouldn't have violated your privacy if those psych-assholes at New Mexico and Peary Crater didn't force station commanders to review the mental profiles of their crews as though they were specimens in bottles. You know I would never do anything to hurt any of you.*

"You're right, Lane," was all he could muster out loud, talking to her back as she turned to put her hand on the latch. "There probably isn't anyone you can trust."

11

The shield doors opened on a darkening Moon. In an hour the sun would set, and it wouldn't rise again over the Acherusian headlands for fourteen days. Roughly a fortnight of darkness, the Sea of Serenity embraced by space. Already the solar disc receded to the west, its lower half obscured by the crumbling flanks of the Montes Haemus. Still a brilliant white, its light shafted and split into rays as moondust rose from the Serenity basin like an alien fog. Dechert heard Standard gasp as he watched the billions of particles climb at the terminus of the light, enshrouding the landscape in a thin, opaque cloud. The commissioner's gloved hands gripped the rover's roll bars.

"It's okay, Standard, you're not hallucinating," Dechert said.

"Those are Moon fountains. Dust streaming up from the surface to meet the sunset."

"It's . . . unbelievable," Standard said. He breathed in quick, shallow bursts as though he were sucking air through a pipe as he watched the phenomenon, which reminded Dechert of a sandstorm rising in the Lebanese desert at dusk. "What causes it?"

Dechert cranked the rover into low gear and drove out of the subterranean hangar, checking over the sides to make sure the wheels gained traction.

"The dayside of the Moon is positively charged, the nightside negatively, and that creates an electrostatic field at the terminator, or the boundary between dark and light. Remember as a kid, when you used to rub a balloon on your head and watch your hair stand on end as you pulled it away? It's the same concept here—the particles in the light rise up to meet the ones in the dark."

"This is a little more spectacular," Standard said with his polarized faceplate fixed on the setting sun and the rising wall of silver before it. "I didn't realize the Moon was so active."

"Everything's active in space, Commissioner. We just aren't able to see most of it."

The rover spun its rear wheels despite the low gear as it crossed the boundary from the hangar to the soft lunar regolith, struggling to gain footing in the microgravity and the chalky blanket of soil. Pulverized dust and tiny pieces of basalt flew into the air and settled behind them in slow-motion circles as the airlock closed. Dechert rolled the rover into the open and stopped to run a system check. They had a five-kilometer drive to Spiral 6, and they would be going from light to darkness, from a slow-cooking 260 degrees Fahrenheit to minus 290.

"Vernon, I'm at the foot of the Haemus Road. Boards are

green, radiation looks nominal. Batteries one and two at a hundred percent, EVA suits and coms are in line. Requesting clearance for Spiral 6."

The com barely sputtered this close to the base and Vernon's voice came back with little distortion. "Looks five-by-five from here, boss. We've got a good uplink and your transponder's got a heartbeat—you're a go for Spiral 6. How's the view out there?"

"There's Moon fountains, Vernon. Quarles will be jealous."

"Roger that. He's chopping up nanotubes in the *Aerosmith*. I'll let him know what he's missing."

Dechert put his boot on the accelerator and pulled onto the Haemus Road, which took a northwesterly route into the lower expanse of the Serenity plain. The road was marked with flashing blue triliptical lights staked into the ground every ten meters like an airport runway back on Earth, only this runway cut its way across an alien and desiccated landscape. The lights turned on automatically as they fell into shadow, and Dechert and Standard could see them glowing in the patches of blackness ahead, popping to life as the sun continued its descent behind the mountains.

The view was truly unearthly, and Dechert figured if ever there was a chance to get honest answers from Standard, this was it. Fletcher had taught him the trick years ago. Put a man in a completely alien environment, in a place where his mind tells him he has no business being, and his shocked system will react in a consistent fashion. He'll become a lemming, latching on to anyone with more experience than him as a lost man does to God. And in his effort to remain alive—to not make any mistakes that could lead to an unnatural death—he'll forget the tendency to say only the things that are in his best interest. He'll be scared into candor.

But Standard was a unique challenge. He was the consummate bureaucrat, trained to speak with precision and then only to advance the causes of the Space Mining Administration and its fiduciary patriarch—the United States government. He would be difficult to unpeel. The solar system would be fully inhabited by now if we had thrown politicians and their bureaucratic lackeys into the sea a few centuries ago, Dechert thought. True believers. History is littered with their flotsam back on Earth and now one of them is here on the Moon, the sound of his lungs erratic and loud in the lunar dusk. *I could end his life out here on the reg and not a soul would know,* Dechert mused. *Just a simple malfunction in his EVA suit, all for the common good . . .*

"Try breathing normally, Commissioner," he said aloud, shaking off the fantasy. "Your suit will adjust the air mix to keep you from hyperventilating, but it's best to focus on taking regular, steady breaths."

"Thank you, Commander. I'll try."

"You're doing fine. We're four kilometers from Spiral 6. Should be there in about ten minutes."

"That soon?" Standard asked. He put his hands on the rover's roll bars again. "I didn't think we could drive that fast."

Dechert chuckled under his breath and pushed down on the accelerator.

"We keep it below thirty kilometers per hour on unmarked terrain because spatial reference is so difficult on the Moon. But we can do up to sixty on the lit roads. Only thing we have to worry about is a new impact crater or a washout from rover traffic, and I haven't seen one of those in a few weeks."

Standard kept his grip on the rover's titanium frame. They crossed into permanent shadow, and even in the suits they could feel the sudden drop in temperature, as if they had just jumped from the midday desert to a frozen massif in Antarctica. The sunlit plains were yards away, but the areas of shadow were almost black, touched only by Earthshine. The sweat in Dechert's hair and on the back of his neck turned clammy and he shivered, waiting for the auto-heaters in his suit to take effect. The blue beacons of the Haemus Road flashed brilliantly now, casting long shadows in the darker gray mare surrounding them as they blinked in descending unison.

"I guess this is better than taking one of your jetsuits," Standard said, relaxing his grip but keeping his boots wedged against the floorboards. "I wouldn't sign up for that mission anytime soon."

"It's a . . . unique experience. Not for someone who hates negative g's."

Dechert thought of his free fall into the pit of Crater Dionysius and the sense of powerlessness it had given him as he stared into the void below. How would a roach feel if it had sentience and a fear of heights, as it was being picked up by a human hand and thrown into a toilet? Something like the way Dechert had felt that day as the thrusters on his jetsuit pushed him down toward the black mouth of the crater, he was sure.

"When will all the suits go online, and what benefits have you calculated?" Standard asked. He sounded steadier as he focused his attention on the firmer footing of lunar economics— quarterly revenues and cost benefits a tonic for his unsettled stomach.

"We've got three suits built but I've only taken one out for an extended hop. The others have been short-flighted on the Serenity grid. Once they're fully online—maybe in a few weeks if there isn't a war—they'll increase ice and ilmenite production by as much as thirty percent. They'll have a smaller impact on our He-3 operations."

"Why is that?"

"Because the helium-3 sites are more accessible. They

won't benefit as much from terrain flexibility. Like Spiral 6, they're mostly on the flatlands of the mare. The ilmenite and ice sites, however, are in craters or lava tubes or on the shadow sides of mountains, so the jetsuits will provide their greatest benefit there."

Dechert stopped talking for a second to navigate a notch in the road that ran along the rim of a deep rille, watching for signs of erosion. Once he was convinced they were all good, he continued. "And besides, most of the He-3 fields are automated now. The only human attention they need is an initial survey, the gridding, and routine checks like the one we're doing today—or a MOHAB run to pick up the He-3 casks for orbital ejection."

He drove them into a white ejecta field, its contrast from the darker lava flows of the mare stark even in the weak light of the road beacons. It looked like Vermont snow, but was instead a blanket of pulverized material spewed out of the Menelaus Crater hundreds of millions of years ago and unchanged ever since—the last signature of a catastrophic collision that occurred long before vertebrates could warm their blood. Except now a road ran through it, and the two men could sense their intrusion on its ancient power.

"Well, any little bit will help," Standard said after a few minutes of awed silence. "I don't need to tell you how necessary a production increase is at this point. We have to retain our tourism and sys-ex franchises when the next open bids are complete. Any Chinese increase in market share would be devastating, and I'm not privy to all the talk on the top floor, but I know there's a lot of concern that we're falling behind."

Dechert imagined he heard Standard click his tongue inside his helmet—the first Moonwalking accountant. The commissioner was talking at ease now, forgetting the fact that he was only a pressure suit away from the vacuum of space. Even as they ventured deeper into the cold of the darkness, he was warming up.

"The Moon helped pull us out of the worst crisis in our history, Commander. If we lose even twenty percent of our space mining revenues, it will stunt the recovery and force us to reallocate some of the power subsidies we've used to shore up the economy."

Dechert shook his head. He never understood how bureaucrats were so blind to the irony of their actions. They would say something that directly contradicted their own stated intentions and be ignorant of the fact that they had just done so. Wasn't that the definition of madness?

He couldn't help himself. "Then why the hell are we spoiling for a fight with the Chinese?" he asked. "I might be politically naïve, Standard, but I don't see much sense in messing with a good thing. You're getting energy for the masses and money for the government troughs. What the hell else do you want? Because I have to tell you, a war isn't gonna get you there."

Standard sighed loudly enough to be heard through the com. "You're thinking like a commander, Dechert. Short-term and tactical. If you were a general, or even better, a president, you'd have a wider perspective."

"Such as?"

"Such as the long-term strategic viability of our astro-economic programs. We've lost our dominance of the Pacific Rim and with it the world economy. The Thermal Max pushed us back twenty years, and India and China have leaped that much ahead. Our terrestrial output is still down across the board—agriculture, heavy industry, technology, you name it. And if you're about to say we should have been prepared for the disaster, just look at Canada and Western Europe." He paused and tried to shake his head in the bulky suit, but his helmet barely moved. Dechert wondered how many times Standard had given this speech.

"Asteroid collisions you can prepare for, carbon emissions you can legislate against, but who expected a subsea methane eruption would plunge us back into the Dark Ages for more than a decade?"

Dechert had to concentrate to not look over at Standard. It was a difficult thing to get used to, not looking at the person you're talking to, but he had learned long ago to never take his eyes off the lunar surface when he was driving.

"I understand what the Thermal Maximum did, Commissioner, and I seem to recall the scientists deciding we played a role in the melt. But that doesn't explain the *present* crisis. Why don't we send negotiators to China or the ISA to sort this out instead of putting the pieces in place to jeopardize everything we've gained up here? You want greater production? Send more miners, not soldiers. Remember: Mining won't be easy if missiles start flying around the mare."

"Well, for one thing . . ." Standard said, and then he screamed as a green flash ripped across the top of their field of vision.

Dechert looked up in time to see a massive ball of flame rocketing over their heads toward the Haemus Mountains. Standard flung his left arm toward the sky as if to ward off the flying object. He hit Dechert's shoulder, throwing the rover into a half spin. Dechert slammed on the brakes and the vehicle skidded violently, its starboard wheels coming off the ground for more than a second before succumbing again to the Moon's weak gravity. They slid to a rest perpendicular to the road, the rover's rear wheel spinning into one of the light footers that lined its margins.

Dechert watched the projectile cross the horizon without

a sound, a glowing specter casting an emerald shadow on the Moon's dark surface. He took his clenched hands off the steering column and waited for his pulse to slow and the plume of dust around the rover to settle. He could hear his heart beating inside his suit and Standard's raspy breathing over the com. His ears rang with adrenaline.

"What the hell was that?" Standard asked.

"The first thing was a meteor," Dechert said, taking several deep breaths of his own to calm down. "The second thing was very nearly a bad accident. You hit my arm."

Standard didn't answer for a long moment and then looked over. "What? I'm sorry. That thing . . . it didn't make any noise."

Dechert pulled the rover forward a few feet and parked it, loosening his restraints and getting out on wobbly legs to check the titanium-cleated tire and the roadway marker. He bounced lightly on his feet, getting used to the microgravity and the bulk of the suit. Both the tire and the light appeared to be in working order. *Jesus Christ*, he thought, looking down into a ravine off the side of the road that he had missed by no more than three meters. *A few more degrees of turn and we'd be sliding back-assward down that gully. Or worse.*

"Tenuous as it may be, the Moon has an atmosphere," Dechert said. He grunted as he pushed the triliptical light back into its metal footer, sticking his boot under the side of the rover for leverage. "If a big enough meteor enters at a high enough speed, it'll light up." He finished the job and stood up. "Interesting fact: We've increased the Moon's atmosphere by seven hundred percent since we've been here, just through the gas emissions of our stations and propellant-driven craft."

Dechert walked around the rover for a final check and got back in, fumbling with his restraints, which he couldn't see beneath his helmet. He figured them out and clicked on the motor, flaring up the rover's system consoles and running lights, and checked all the onboard systems. Green lights everywhere. He put the vehicle in gear and they started down the road again in silence, emerging from a shimmering ring of dust.

"Not my best moment," Standard said, his voice more subdued. "I suppose I'm better suited for an office than a shotgun ride on the Moon."

"Don't worry about it. That thing gave me a jolt, too. That's the Moon, Commissioner: hours of boredom followed by a few seconds of terror. You just have to remember to make small movements out here, even when you're scared. The low gravity exaggerates everything you do."

Standard laid his helmet back on the headrest and laughed. It was a strange laugh, thin and self-conscious. A tax collector's laugh. "Right. Well, I'll remember that the next time I see a flaming ball of iron flying over our heads."

"Like I said, don't worry about it."

"Thanks." Standard readjusted himself in his seat and grabbed the roll bar again. "Shall we resume our debate, then, as it might keep my mind off of throwing up?"

"Good idea, as you definitely don't want to spend the next half hour or so with vomit in your suit. I think you were about to explain how we could maintain our production numbers while being shot at by the Chinese."

Standard tried to suppress a grunt.

"I was about to say that diplomacy is a two-way road, Commander. I don't think you realize how bad things have gotten between our two countries." He paused, perhaps considering how much he should tell Dechert. "The newsfeeds on the stream don't give the full scope of the crisis. Your miner isn't the only recent casualty."

"You mean on the Moon or on Earth?"

"On Earth." Standard lowered his voice as if he could be overheard on the empty mare. "I'm not authorized to tell you this and I probably shouldn't, but I understand your need to know after what happened to your man at Posidonius."

"I appreciate that."

"Okay then. I'll tell you what I can." The man was actually whispering, as if someone was pointing a directional mike at him out here on the surface. Dechert just kept quiet, though— this was what he was waiting for.

"An American nuclear submarine collided with a Chinese boomer in the South China Sea three weeks ago, just south of Macau. Chinese territorial waters. Unbelievable, really, given our advanced systems. She was in stealth mode, running on biodrive, and our captain seems to have gotten too aggressive or too close. The Chinese sub did a crash stop and turned to starboard, probably to check her baffles for trailers, and our boat cracked her in the stern. The accident killed sixteen Chinese sailors, Commander, and they almost lost the boat. Their reaction was quite negative."

"I bet."

"Yes. And it occurred just as our lawyers were fighting at The Hague over the Altschuler and ISA Treaty interpretations of central mare mineral rights and production reports, and certain economic disputes in the Pacific Rim back on Earth. A few days after the incident, the Chinese ambassador advised us that they would fire on any U.S. vessel or craft that strayed within two hundred kilometers of their territory, either terrestrial or lunar. Then he left Washington with the entire consular staff."

Dechert slammed his foot on the brakes. Blood pumped into his neck as he fought to hold his anger in check. He turned his head toward Standard, squeezing the steering column as tightly as he could.

"Why the hell wasn't I told about that?"

"Because it shouldn't have been an issue. We don't have any mining operations that close to the Mare Imbrium. Your mobile habitation unit was on the east side of the Serenity basin when the explosion occurred, Commander, a full seven hundred kilometers from Chinese-claimed mineral rights. We had no reason to believe you would be in jeopardy."

Dechert suppressed the urge to launch a stream of profanity at the lunar heavens, grab Standard by the shoulders, and slam his helmet onto the roll bar in front of him until it cracked open like a nut, exposing his bureaucratic lungs to the vacuum.

"You had *no reason* to believe we'd be in jeopardy? We've had a good chunk of our water and air supply sabotaged, and I've got a dead miner in the fucking freezer at Peary Crater, Standard. What do you call that? Safety first?"

He let the anger radiate through his body as Standard sat next to him, immobile. After a minute he took several deep breaths and shifted the rover back into gear.

"Unbelievable," he said into the quiet.

They crawled their way up an eroded plateau, Dechert concentrating on the vibration of the low gears and leaning over the side to see if the wheels were holding their traction. Both men could feel the uncertain purchase of the rover's wheels on the regolith. The craft started to sideslip on the hill. Dechert threw the all-wheel drive onto its lowest setting and released stabilizers from all six tires, which pushed out from the inner wheel wells and dug into the lunar regolith like tiny, spiked training wheels. The added traction helped, and they continued to push up the hummock. The heads-up monitor showed the grade lessening from thirty-two degrees to twenty, and then to twelve. Both men exhaled.

"What the hell else haven't we been warned about, seeing

as how we're not in any jeopardy?" Dechert asked when they reached the top.

"Nothing I can think of."

"Great. And since you've brought up the *Molly Hatchet*, maybe you could answer a few nagging questions. For starters, how the hell did the Chinese plant the explosive on her hull? My sources at Peary Crater tell me there wasn't any forensic evidence at the Posidonius site. No tracks or footprints. No sign of intrusion. So where was the bomb planted, and how?"

"Your 'sources' at Peary Crater? And who might they be?"

"You shouldn't ask questions you won't get an answer to, Standard. It makes you look like a fool."

Standard threw up a hand. "Fine—I guess the exchange of information is to be strictly one-sided. I don't know how the Chinese pulled it off. I've read the full report and there are no definitive conclusions. The charge may have been set when the rover was at Drill Station 3 near the Montes Caucasus. That's less than three hundred kilometers from Archimedes, and Captain Hale said the device was placed in a recess under the EVA hatch, where it wouldn't be noticed or get in the way."

Dechert considered this. New Beijing 2 was nestled inside the Archimedes Crater on the Mare Imbrium. It was the first substation built inside a lunar crater, on the premise that the impact walls would provide extra radiation shielding and allow it to be buried more shallowly in the regolith. But the *Molly Hatchet* hadn't been near the Montes Caucasus in over a month, and Dechert had a hard time believing someone would plant a bomb and set it to go off thirty days later, especially on the Moon, where temperature changes and radiation spikes wreak havoc on even the hardiest systems. Nor would they put it in a place where a misguided boot or a gloved hand could knock it loose. At the very least, it wasn't a response to the South China Sea incident, which according to Standard had happened after the Caucasus mission.

How the hell can I get my hands on the classified version of that report, he asked himself. He didn't find a ready answer. He had already called in all his markers at Peary Crater, and the few people who still owed him weren't stupid enough to go digging through the SMA's black files.

"So the bomb was stuck to the side of the *Hatchet* for more than a month before it went off?" he finally said aloud. "And it was set to be triggered by an orbital cue? Do you know how twitchy those Lunar Positioning Satellite uplinks are, especially when you're out on the mare? I wouldn't trust them to turn on a microwave at lunchtime, much less trigger a bomb, and I know a lot of people who would agree with me. Until someone comes up with a better theory, you've got a pretty lousy case against the Chinese."

"What do you mean? We have the explosive itself."

Dechert laughed. "God knows how many times that stuff changed hands before it got up to the Moon. You don't think Chinese Intelligence sells stuff on the black market?"

"Well, who else do you intend to implicate, Commander?" Standard asked, and he swept his arm lengthwise across the black lunar field. "The last time I checked there weren't a whole lot of suspects in the neighborhood. There aren't any Brazilian rebels running around on the Moon, and no one else up here is angry with us."

Anger isn't the only reason people kill, Dechert thought, *and not even the most frequent.*

The rover reached the top of the plateau and Dechert parked it, retracting the stabilizers and dimming the display lights. The road twisted downward through a decaying box canyon and ran north onto an open plain, a glowing blue serpent that appeared to end at a point of nothingness in the dark.

It was black here. They were close enough to the southern spur of the Montes Haemus to be fully in nightside. Dechert clicked on his com as he looked into the void; the features a few feet to each side of the road were indiscernible, and the feeling of emptiness was disorienting.

"Vernon, we're at the Fletcher Promontory. Light her up for us, please."

The com popped and hissed and Vernon's voice came through, distorted this time by the distance.

"Lights coming online, boss. Cycle 3, solar reserves."

They watched in silence as the dark plain below flared with red and yellow lights popping on in a domino-like succession until the blackness was replaced by an arc of light that stretched across ten acres of lunar lowland. Dechert could see the main power station in the center, a fixed point at the end of the Haemus Road, its cylindrical structure bristling with the four giant silos that converted processed lunar soil into liquid helium-3. The mining field radiated out in a giant circle like a pushed-over Ferris wheel on the dark center of the Moon, lights marking the areas where more than a meter of regolith had been tilled and sifted for the solar isotope.

All of this engineering, Dechert thought, *just to pick up moondust*.

"The power of the stars," he said, "everywhere under our feet."

Standard nodded, enraptured by the shimmering valley. "Now that's a sight that makes you believe in the glory of God."

Or at least the glory of gold, Dechert thought, but he was entranced as well. Damned if it wasn't beautiful, even after all this time. He started the rover again, and they drove the final leg of the Haemus Road toward the mining platform's central hub, down into a sea of lights.

12

The mine ran in silence. If a comet slammed into it with all the power of a fusion bomb, they wouldn't hear a sound before they died. Dechert always marveled at this. The only sounds on the Moon's surface existed inside their spacesuits. The exaggerated thrum of the rebreathers. The scrape of an arm hitting the inner insulating layers. Hair brushing against the top of the helmet or the soft whir of the walk-profile computer. But outside, a tapestry of total blackout. No wind, no air, no noise. The telescoping arm of the spiral mine should be popping as its aluminum skin contracts in the newly supercooled air. The roving platform should be whining like an industrial vacuum as it sucks in regolith and runs it through the heaters. The processed *fine* should be pattering like rain on a window as it rushes back to the power station and blasts into the containment silos for liquefaction. Instead there was nothing. *No one knows what true isolation is until they've been in space,* Dechert thought. Even when you're sitting next to someone, you're completely and utterly self-contained. *Alone.*

Standard could sense it, too. It's one thing to ride across the mute expanse of the Moon. It's still essentially an off-road car trip, when you get right down to it. But it's entirely another to watch heavy industry take place in silence. *We're the aliens here,* Dechert thought, *and we always will be.*

"Quite a remarkable thing," Standard said, forgetting their argument for the moment.

"Yes."

"And you only come here once a month?"

Dechert pulled onto the grid road leading to the power station and dimmed his visor to cut the glare from the minefield lights. "Usually two or three times a month. Once or twice for a site check when we're in the neighborhood, and once with a MOHAB and trailer to load the He-3 casks for orbital ejection back at Serenity."

He stole a quick look at Standard without moving his helmet. The commissioner knew this had been a sore point with the Mining Guild and an even greater source of anger for the diggers themselves.

"It's a shame we couldn't build a mobile launcher or finish the fixed ejectors at each of the main spiral mines," Standard said, hearing the passive-aggressive complaint. "The cost structure just didn't work out." He looked back at Dechert and waited for a response. He was clearly used to affirmation after he spoke, and not getting it seemed to irritate him.

"There are times, Commander, when I get the sense that you don't approve of anything the Administration does up here."

Dechert laughed. "What the hell do you want me to say, Standard? That I don't mind the added danger of an extra mission every month because your accountants couldn't stomach finishing a rail launcher? You're right. I don't like my crew being put in jeopardy so the SMA can turn an extra two-percent margin, and I don't like the Moon becoming a playground for men who've never heard the sound of a bullet cracking the air over their head."

Standard stiffened. "I'll forgive the inference, Dechert, but I won't be laughed at. We all serve in our own way, and sometimes you have to stand for what is right, whether you've worn the uniform or not." He looked Dechert over again, carefully this time. "You do believe we're right, don't you? Will you at least concede that we're the good guys in this? That's your man who died out there at Posidonius, for God's sake."

"There's only one 'right' up here, and that's staying alive. Dying is the wrong, no matter how the hell it happens."

It was Standard's turn to laugh. "No, Commander, that's too easy. I can't let you get away with that. If you believe such an ordered simplicity can endure among men, I suggest you take a closer look at Earth out of your observatory window. Look at how China turned her back on her starving neighbors during the height of the Thermal Max and did everything to shore up her own power. Or maybe you should read the Old Testament—the parts about the righteous and the wicked. That may sound ridiculous to you, up here in your underground station where you have the luxury of disregarding nasty things like politics, but what about back on Earth? Do you think the Chinese are raising a finger to protect anything other than their interests? And do you really think they're an honest broker here on the Moon?"

They reached the silo, its bank of clear yellow lights casting a long shadow behind the rover as they flashed in unison.

Dechert parked, and both of them craned their necks to look up at the looming platform. It stood as the central spoke of the spiral mine, which stretched across the regolith farther than they could see. A half-built rail launcher—an electromagnetic gun that would have shot helium-3 casks into low-lunar orbit by sending a massive jolt of electricity through two conducting rails—sat like an abandoned artillery piece a few yards from the silo.

"I didn't realize our government considered altruism one of its core competencies," Dechert finally replied. "Is that why we're dropping a treaty that provides free helium-3 for the New Third World?" He started to unstrap his restraints. "I thought it was so we could prove to the orbital executives that we can keep up with their production demands."

"Touché, Commander. But generosity can only stand so much abuse." Standard continued to gawk at the platform as he tried to undo his belt, struggling with the five-point buckle on his chest harness. "Half the power we give away as charity is being stolen by the warlords in Africa and Northern Europe, and what's supposed to be allocated for the needy is wasted like so much wheat left on the docks."

Dechert reached over to help him, pushing Standard's hand away so he could get at the restraint system. "So when the power is cut off, will you just blame the warlords and read a Psalm for those left in the dark?"

"Maybe," Standard said, climbing from his seat to test the lunar soil with the toe of his boot. He looked over at Dechert. "It seems your cynicism is boundless, Dechert, reaching as it does even to heaven. Can you witness mankind's handiwork in this splendid wasteland and still mock his Creator? Do you really think such a spark of genius had its infancy in the random explosion of a star a few billion years ago?"

He said it lightly, but Dechert knew Standard was testing him. The Administration didn't like atheists. That attitude probably had something to do with their sudden hawkish posturing. When you're always in a foxhole, there's no room for nonbelievers. Dechert shuffled around the rover to the commissioner's side, ready to help him if he stumbled in his first few steps in the spacesuit.

"I was mocking us, not the Almighty. And I do believe in a higher power. I'm just not presumptuous enough to believe it's on my side."

"Ahh, a deist. That's even worse."

Standard took an abbreviated step, accepting Dechert's assistance. They walked to the side of the power station and looked up again, arching their necks as far back as they could to view the towering building. The thirty-meter silos looked like solid rocket boosters framed against the stars, ready to be launched to the edge of the solar system. But these were going nowhere. They remained fixed to the lunar dirt as cooling gas spilled from vents along their vertical processors. Dechert tapped Standard on his faceplate to get his attention and led him to a small hatch under the number-three processor. He unclipped a thin aluminum rod from his belt and inserted it into a rectangular slot and the rod turned clockwise, grooves snapping into place to open a tiny console. Dechert punched the command code onto a small alphanumeric keypad. The hatch opened and gas escaped from the control shack and into the Moon's tenuous atmosphere. A small piece of refuse—maybe a crumpled shipping cover for one of the plasma screens—shot between their helmets, rising above the surface as if in a stiff leeward breeze and then disappearing into the darkness.

"Let's put aside the theological debate for now, Commissioner," Dechert said. "There's limited space in the control shack. Be careful what you brush against, and please don't touch anything without asking."

They turned on their lamps and entered a dark chamber the size of a coatroom, a bank of telemetry monitors and freeze-hardened polymer displays on the aft wall. Dechert went to the mine's central server. A glaze of dust and ice coated the display, so thick that he couldn't see the information on the screen. He frowned. This much dust intrusion in a few short weeks? Just one more thing to worry about as everything under his command seemed to be breaking down around him. He brushed away the grime and punched a code into the oversize keyboard. He pressed ENTER.

"We get limited real-time telemetry back at Serenity, mostly power-critical data from the silos and LPS coordinates for the roving miners." He watched as a series of numbers scrolled across the screen. "Everything else is stored here and sent back to the CORE in a data dump once a day."

"What about production numbers?"

"Also stored here, along with selenology, yield percentages, and mining anomalies."

Standard stared at the stereoscopic display, and Dechert could see the man being mesmerized by the data that he was used to reading on the first Tuesday of every month back on Earth, probably while sitting in his tower office with his feet up on his desk and a cup of tea in his hand. Standard was clearly impressed.

"The next-generation systems will be far more efficient, you know," he said. "The new algorithms are incredible, quantum factoring and DNA sequencing—we're talking additional zetta-bytes of data processing. And they will be fully self-sustaining."

"Yes, I've heard," Dechert said, not wanting to get into *that* argument. He had read the papers from quantum comput-ing experts who predicted that the full automation of space-mining was only a generation away. They had said the same thing about fighter pilots sixty years ago when the first Predator drones patrolled the battlefield skies of the Middle East and Asia. But most ships, airborne or spaceborne, were still manned, and Dechert didn't think that would ever change, any more so than the colonization of the Moon by living, breathing people would ever slow down. *Humans don't like giving up too much control to the inanimate,* he thought. *One of our more admirable qualities.*

Dechert snapped back to the present and frowned again as he looked down at the data flashing to the front of the display. Several rows of numbers didn't make any sense. The telemetry he had scanned yesterday in the CORE had changed, which was as statistically likely as a cheetah bounding across the lunar flatlands just outside the control shack. He ran a query to make sure he hadn't missed something. The data came back the same. He checked the storage manifest and got the same reading. Standard was right about one thing—the computer's algorithmic processors never got things wrong.

He clicked on the com. "Vernon, this is Spiral 6."

The transmission popped and hissed. "Yeah, I'm here."

"What was our manifest on the last He-3 haul?"

Vernon took a few seconds to respond. "Looks like fourteen casks on dayside eleven, boss, or November the twenty-first. I repeat, one-four casks on eleven twenty-one."

"Copy. Now check yesterday's data dump for storage numbers so far this cycle."

"Got it," Vernon said. "Eleven casks, on target for ninety-eight percent production this month. Freakin' FMO set us back a bit."

"Say again."

"That's one-one casks. There a problem?"

Dechert looked over at Standard and then left the control

shack, shuffling to the back side of the silo where the massive helium-3 casks were stored in locked-down vertical containment racks.

"Yes, there is," he said, looking up at the car-size barrels.

"What is it?" Standard asked.

"The mine has processed eleven He-3 casks so far this cycle, and put them into the orbital ejection holding rack to be brought back to Serenity."

"So?"

"Start counting, Mr. Standard."

He stared at Standard as the Administration's man began to add up the casks by pointing a gloved finger at each of them, one at a time.

"Four casks are missing," Standard said.

"Yeah."

"Well, that's not good."

"No, it's not good at all."

Dechert wondered how much worse the week could get.

13

"What the hell is going on, Caden?"

Lane looked like she hadn't slept in a week. Her eyelids were rimmed with gray, and Dechert realized that she had used his given name for the first time since they'd known each other. He closed the hangar hatch, heard the reassuring sound of the elastomer seals expanding into place, and motioned her to follow. The station felt different than it had just a few weeks ago—more closed in. He had once considered Serenity's cramped quarters womblike and embracing, almost motherly, but now the station's close confines felt incarcerating. Dechert remembered an SMA seminar from years back on the early warning signs of remote-station stress: *If any of your crew exhibits signs of claustrophobia, if they complain in*

their weekly psych evals of the station appearing smaller or am-
bient noises appearing louder, administer forty milligrams of
Dopodran orally twice a day. If symptoms persist, transfer to a
main base, Low-Earth-Orbit station, or preferably, temporary
duty back on Earth.

This was said in monotone by a psychologist with bad posture who looked like he'd never get closer to space than the
top of a New Mexico hill, and all the mission commanders in
the room had laughed. Stress was for Earthbound bureaucrats,
not astro-miners.

Now Dechert couldn't put the psychologist's words out of
his mind. Especially with new personnel coming soon.

He walked to his quarters with Lane in tow. Waters and
Thatch were prepping the hangar for the marine squad's ar-
rival, and things were about to get complex. Eleven souls in
a Level-1 mining station. Christ. All of them on edge, and a
good percentage of them armed to the teeth. Waiting for the
next crisis; the next master alarm. At least Parrish would be
leaving with the next supply shuttle, which was bringing as
many weapons as rations with it. Dechert didn't need a reporter on site to add to the volatile mix—or sucking up their
air—but he realized it may have been a good thing that the
young journalist had come over with Standard in the first
place. If he could find out what really happened on the *Molly
Hatchet* in the next few days, maybe he could leak something
to Parrish that would defuse the situation back on Earth. A
reverse Gulf of Tonkin incident. It might cost him his career
with the SMA, but Dechert was rapidly becoming less concerned about his employment.

He popped the hatch to his cabin and stood to the side,
ushering Lane in with an extended arm. A metal plaque
read COMMANDER next to the door. Dechert grimaced at it

and walked into his Spartan quarters. The room was white-walled, like all of Serenity 1's personal habitation modules, and sparsely furnished, with a tiny bunk bed that folded up into the bulkhead and a black swivel chair that tucked under a thin-framed carbon desk. Tall, narrow recessed doors hid clothes lockers. The lavatory was no larger than a missile tube and had to be entered with one's arms tucked to the side. A single picture hung over the desk: his father in a flight suit on the tarmac at Nellis Air Force Base in Nevada, a helmet tucked under his arm and a half smile of contentment on his face.

Dechert knew the smile, that feeling of tired satisfaction after a successful flight, and it always drew him closer to his father. He stared at the picture often, amazed at how connected he felt to a man he had barely known. He recalled a letter Colonel Philip Dechert had written to his mother long ago, a year before he had died in a suborbital flight over the Indian Ocean. Dechert had found it in an old wooden cigar box in her Victorian farmhouse back in Maryland, and he remembered with clarity the musty smell of that cedar box and one passage in the creased, yellowing letter: "There are only two things that make me happy in life, Molly. Being with you and the kids, and flying. I hope you'll forgive the latter as a tragic character flaw."

Unlike his father, Dechert never had children. He had thought of the men and women he commanded in the Bekaa Valley as his surrogate kids, but most of them were long dead. His crew on Serenity 1 became their emotional replacements, and now he was no longer certain he could protect them, either. That left flying as the only link he had to his father, and for the first time in his life, it no longer felt strong enough.

"You look whipped," Lane said.

"So do you."

She slid the chair out from under the desk and melted into it, her legs spread out in front of her and her body slouched like a man's. It wasn't a posture Dechert was used to seeing from his safety officer.

"I spent my last off duty staring at the emergency decompression sequence on top of my bunk," she said. "You know I can't take those damned REM pills."

Dechert nodded. He never took the sleep pills, either—they left a hangover worse than bourbon—and he often stared at the emergency decompression sequence himself. Some masochistic bastard from habitat engineering had emblazoned it above all of the station's bunks on placards set with threadless screws, so that they couldn't be easily removed. The last thing you saw before you fell to sleep, and the first thing you saw when the alarm went off awakening you for your next shift, was:

IN CASE OF EMERGENCY DECOMPRESSION . . .

It reminded Dechert of the pamphlets they used to put on commercial airliners explaining what to do in the event of a water landing, with pictures of serene cartoon people bobbing in calm water. *False comfort in process*, he thought, *for a crisis that would probably result in a slow-motion death*.

"I'm going to make a command decision about those plaques at some point," he said. "Maybe I'll just have Thatch melt them with a welding torch."

"That would be nice."

He pulled the bunk bed down from the wall and sat on its cushioned edge. "You heard about the He-3 casks?"

"Yeah. The latest scene in a show I'm getting tired of watching."

"Standard's got visions running through his head of Ninjas creeping around the Serenity basin, planting bombs."

"Weren't the Ninjas Japanese?"

"Whatever. Chinese monks in spacesuits. Any news on the boots?"

"Great news if you like Easter egg hunts," Lane said. "Groombridge has sold forty-eight pairs of boots to go with their EVA suits on Luna since 2062. That's the earliest date I could find a requisition on. No sales since 2070. All treads are the same and they can be used with our newer suits with a little tinkering." She ran her hands through her hair. "They're spread out all over the place. Peary Crater, Tranquility 1, a few pairs were requisitioned here on Serenity five years ago. Even the Chinese and Brazilians bought a few pairs."

"Any way to track them?" Dechert asked.

"Not really. Hell, there could still be a pair here on the station for all I know, although we've been using nothing but Procyon boots since '68. You realize this was pretty much the Wild West in the mid-2060s? Trying to find out what happened to old equipment is like looking for one specific tire in a junkyard. I mean, think about the equipment locker down in the Bullpen. I doubt even Thatch and Waters know half of the crap piled up in the back of that thing."

Another dead end, Dechert thought. *Nothing but dead ends.* Even with his own inquiries. "I tried to dig into solo flight records to figure out who from our side could have gone to DS-7 without being traced," he said. "That didn't go much better. There have been thirty-seven solos launched from Peary Crater, SOT-1, SOS-1, and our other subbases in the last three weeks. You can look at the logs, but there's no way to track flight telemetries. We just don't store that stuff and it gets erased with new mission inputs." He grimaced. "Hell, I did a solo last week up near Bessel, and Waters has three solos this month. Thatch has one, too, out to Spiral 5 and Spiral 6 for site checks at the end of November. But we don't save profiles on routine hops unless there's a reason for it. So I guess each of us could be suspects."

"Maybe you," Lane said, "but not Thatch or Waters. When they go out on the mare, they don't have time to jerk around."

"Nice," Dechert said. "Has Starks gotten back to you?" he asked quickly, because he didn't know how else to broach the subject.

Lane swiveled the chair around and stared at the picture of Dechert's father above the desk, her back turned to him. "Yes. He wasn't all roses and chocolates."

Dechert wanted to apologize again about delving into the blue-tabbed sections of Lane's personnel file, but he knew it wouldn't do any good. Just the mention of Starks's name, and she closed up like a damned oyster. Dechert wondered again if Lane thought of him as worse than the bureaucrats back on Earth. At least she knew what to expect from them. His betrayal of her trust was less expected, and her discomfort in his presence was now a living thing that made the room feel even smaller.

"Can you elaborate?" he asked after a few seconds, annoyed at the entire situation and too exhausted to try to fix it. He cursed to himself. *Does she think it's my damned fault that the SMA spied on her?*

Lane unzipped the breast pocket on her heavysuit and pulled out a small piece of folded paper, handing it to Dechert without looking at him.

"Don't worry. I deleted the chat with one of Quarles's washing programs. If his techno-gadgets work, it wasn't tracked from our end. Whether our government minders are watching Starks's account or not, who the hell knows?"

Dechert nodded, unfolding the paper and scanning it, finding Lane's original message at the bottom of the string. It was brief and antiseptic.

*Sheldon, I know it's been a long time and I apologize for
not communicating. Things have been worse than crazy
up here. You met Cole Benson at Las Cruces, didn't you?
We're all shell-shocked. Does the Administration really
think the Chinese are behind this? Because I have my
doubts. Can't really give you a SITREP, but we're all
worried about what's coming next. We've been goddamned
deputized—do you believe that—and didn't the deputies
always die in the westerns? Any insight you can give me
would be greatly appreciated. How's Milo?*

Yours, Lane.

He read the letter twice, going back over the lines that
hinted at intimacy. They seemed foreign to him. Starks's response was also short, his effort in brevity obvious enough to
be contrived. Dechert wondered how the man had restrained
himself not to write more. If he had spent a week with a lover
on a sloop off the coast of Cozumel only to have her blast
off Earth and rarely correspond again, he would have been
tempted to ask a few more questions.

*Lane, it's good to hear from you. I've been worried sick, but
I'm too stubborn to be the first one to write. I can't discuss
operational stuff or intelligence, you know that, but I'd feel
better if you were off the Moon. Can you request temporary
duty on LEO-1? Things are busy here and tense. Milo is
well, still fat and eating too much, and will barely chase
a thrown stick. Not that I've been able to take him to the
Crossings lately. Too jammed up. Do you remember the
day we dove the Santa Rosa Wall? You quoted Nietzsche
and I asked how you could after swimming through those
pillars of coral. I told you Erasmus was as cynical as I
would get. I still like Erasmus, but you know I'm a sucker*

*for satire. Have to go. Stay safe, and consider what I've said
about temporary duty. You're due for some R&R and the
Moon must be getting old.*

Yours, Sheldon.

Dechert frowned and read the response again. "I take it
Milo is his dog and the references to philosophy are some
sort of code?" *Crude code,* he thought. Does he really think
if this gets intercepted by the SMA—or even worse, Military
Intelligence—he won't catch a twelve-hour interrogation in
a windowless room?

"Yeah," Lane said, twisting a lock of her hair in a finger,
her eyes on the ceiling. "But it wasn't from the day we were
diving. We were talking about the Administration right before I shipped out from New Mexico and he told me he was
worried that the SMA brass were getting pushed by the Feds
to get overly aggressive on lunar mineral rights—to essentially cheat on the Altschuler Treaty and hide it from the ISA.
Said the government minders ran their production numbers
a few years out and things didn't look good for the long-term
helium-3 franchises." She looked up. "He tried to get me to
quit my contract."

"What does any of that have to do with Nietzsche or Erasmus?"

Lane stopped playing with her hair and gripped her knees.
Her hands were white from the lack of sun and perfectly
formed. *Like the hands on a Greek statue,* Dechert thought.
He wondered if Starks had gotten over their relationship yet,
and guessed the answer was no.

"He's referring to what he said that day before I left. He was
predicting we'd get into a shooting war with China over the
Moon in the next five years. Said the government would do
whatever necessary to protect U.S. interests in space. Then he
started muttering Latin. He was a real sucker for the classical

stuff, and he knew it annoyed me. He said '*Dulce bellum inex-pertis*,' and I asked him what the hell that meant."

"Go on. My knowledge of Latin doesn't go past '*Et tu, Brute.*'"

"Yeah. Well, it's a quote 'from Pindar by way of Erasmus,' as he put it, an ancient Greek translated by some old Dutch writer, if you'd like the scholarly description. It means 'War is sweet to those with no experience of it.'"

Dechert sat up from the bunk and leaned back against the bulkhead. They looked at each other in silence. He felt a grudging respect for Starks. *For a man who had never been in battle to say something like that . . .*

"He's pretty wise for a bureaucrat. You think he's referring to the U.S., though, or the Chinese?"

"I think he's referring to us, or maybe both sides to some extent, but mostly to us."

"You do?"

"Yes, that was the context of our conversation. He was railing about the government bureaucrats stepping on the SMA when he started spouting Latin; he wasn't bitching about the Chinese."

Dechert rubbed the stubble on his face and scratched the back of his head. He was tired, not thinking clearly. Would the U.S. really be insane enough to start an armed conflict on the Moon? Insane enough to plant a bomb on one of its own mining skiffs? Would they kill off one of their own just because their long-term production numbers didn't work out with the Chinese in the mix? And how the hell could they have pulled it off? There was no way someone from Peary Crater could have gotten to the *Molly Hatchet* without Dechert knowing about it. But then, neither could the Chinese. No ships or rovers had been within eight hundred klicks of Serenity 1 in the last thirty days. And how could either side steal a shipment of He-3 casks from a remote spiral mine and leave no trace in the regolith, or pull the plug on the water mine in Crater Dionysius? There wasn't even a foreign footprint to find at Posidonius or Spiral 6, and footprints don't go away on the Moon.

Waves of conspiracy theories ran through Dechert's mind and crashed against a stone wall, and he wished, not for the first time, that he had a more analytical mind. But a thought began to take shape, and it made him feel sick as it tied itself together.

"Lane, how good are our portable foreign-material sensors?"

"You mean here on Serenity? Pretty good for hazardous materials and the full spectra of interstellar radiation, but shit for everything else."

"How about exotic explosive compounds?"

"Are you serious?"

"Very."

Lane thought for a few seconds as she looked into Dechert's eyes. "I'd have to check. I know they'd pick up the usual mining stuff, but I've never looked for traces of an exotic before. I don't even know the chemical compounds I'd be searching for."

"Cross-check the SMA library for polymeric nitrogen and get started on it—quietly. They should have the molecular structure listed for their micromining sites. Then run a scan on the entire hangar bay and all the dirty rooms and subgarages. And remember, if there is a trace, it could be a few months old, so take into account atomic decay."

Lane pursed her lips. "Our best bet for preserved traces would be out in the vacuum. I'll sweep the Bullpen, if I can figure out what the hell I'm looking for."

It was a good idea on Lane's part. The Bullpen, the unpressurized hangar where the mobile habitation crawlers and the reserve shuttle were docked, wasn't quality-controlled as strictly as the pressurized areas of the station. It would be the one place where an explosive like polymeric nitrogen could be hidden.

Dechert nodded again. "And use Quarles's Touchpad on the *Aerosmith* for your search. He's got it encrypted."

They didn't speak for a minute, each considering the implications of their line of thinking. Could the bomb have been planted here, inside Serenity 1? When was the last time a supply crew came over? More than a month ago? Dechert had a hard time believing someone could get into a pressure suit and spend an hour in the Bullpen without being noticed. But it was the only explanation that he could come up with, and it left him with a question that clattered in his head like a wind chime: Is everyone on Serenity a suspect now?

Even the members of my crew?

Dechert pushed his shoulders off the wall and stood up straight. He would at least have to trust Lane and Quarles or he wouldn't have a chance to find out what was going on. And he couldn't bear the thought of either of them as suspects. Hell, he couldn't stand the thought of anyone on Serenity 1 as suspects. Because that meant one of them *killed* Cole. Jesus . . .

One thing at a time, Caden.

"Okay, I'm going to find Quarles and see about our message to Lin Tzu. Why don't you try and get a manifest of our visitors for the last six months? And—of course—let's keep this between us."

Lane looked like she wanted to say something more, but she just nodded and walked to the hatch. Dechert had hoped for a fleeting second that their sharing of a secret would help seal the wound, but she remained detached and cold. He shook his head, angry at himself. He was thinking like a child. Lane keeping her emotional distance was definitely for the better right now.

"And Lane?"

"Yes, Commander?" she asked, stressing the formality of her reply as she leaned down to clear the hatch and half-turned her body to look back at him.

"What about the reference to Nietzsche?"

She gave him a small smile. "Oh, he was referring to one of my favorite quotes. It used to piss him off when I said it."

"What was it?"

"'God is dead,'" she said, and stepped out of the room.

14

Quarles disappeared into the Hole whenever he needed soli-tude. Engineers had built it as an emergency shelter for a hundred-year solar storm—an eruption of plasma from the sun that would tear into Mare Serenitatis with the destruc-tive force of a nuclear airburst. Even solar scientists couldn't predict if Serenity 1's canopy of moon soil and emergency shielding would protect the station from a coronal mass ejec-tion, so the lunar architects had wedged a leaden bathtub into the bowels of the station just under the Level-2 Astro-Science Lab. A hideaway of last resort for the crew, complete with a retractable lead roof and a one-week cache of water and meals ready-to-eat. Quarles had converted the sunken bunker into his own personal workshop, filled it with mock-ups of his latest engineering and propulsion experiments, and then bored a direct patch into the CORE's flash-servers so he could run diagnostics on his latest monstrosities. He also equipped the room with a holistic-wave stereo that poured out bass from a pair of thick, black, custom-built subwoofers, enough to shake the sublevel floors from the Bullpen to the storage shed. Dechert could feel the heavy thrum of the music in his feet even before he got to the science lab's access door. It felt like reggae this time, no . . . blues. He turned the corner and J. J. Cale's rootsy voice floated out of the subterranean chamber, swelling ever louder as Dechert entered the lab and approached the Hole. Dechert would have put his hands to his ears if he didn't need them to climb down the ladder, wondering all the way down how Quarles could still hear as well as he did. Cale sang away, his fingerpicking on an old Harmony guitar scorching a smoky background into the song as the sound system picked up the slight, rapid squeak of his left hand sliding up and down the fretboard.

The song, unbelievably, was about the Moon.

Dechert let slip a tight smile, his first in what felt like days. *Quarles.* An astro-engineering genius with the frail psyche of a middle schooler and enough contraband marijuana to put everyone in the station into a ten-hour coma. The idea of Quarles being a murder suspect felt like a paranoid mirage to Dechert, and he tried to shake it off. Dechert had hand-picked the kid from all the propulsion engineers loafing around LEO-1 three years ago, after he heard him debate an MIT grad student about the feasibility of extracting propellant from the methane expelled in human gas and using it to fuel the micromachines that lubricated and cleaned the roving mine platforms out on the lunar surface. Crude and laden with sophomoric language as his argument was, Dechert was intrigued by the fact that when the debate turned technical,

Quarles had driven the MIT kid straight into the floor, leaving him in a state of depression and self-doubt that forced him to retreat back to Earth. He later read Quarles's personnel jacket and learned that his IQ was somewhere north of 160. Einstein, Kepler, and Vorgmann territory.

But large frontal lobes don't always contain the stuff of seriousness, and as intelligent as Quarles was, his childlike sense of reality made him a young ward for everyone on Serenity 1. To Vernon he was the kid brother who always wanted to play. To Lane he was the kid brother who always wanted to pester. To Thatch he was the kid brother who always wanted to impress. And to Dechert? An adopted son, maybe, as far as he would allow that to go.

Quarles sat at his workstation with a microsoldering gun in one hand and a bundle of carbon nanotubes in the other, his back turned to the ladder. Dechert swung down, avoiding a clutter of boxes and tools on the floor as he maneuvered to the sterco. He turned the smooth, circular dial counterclockwise and Quarles spun around, lifting a magnifying visor from his eyes.

"Aww, you can't turn down J. J. Cale. There's something wrong with that."

"There's something wrong with you, Quarles," Dechert said, struggling to make his way back to the workbench. "What's the word on the *Aerosmith*?"

Quarles put down the gun, pulled the visor off of his head, and cracked his knuckles. "She's been a bad-tempered girl, boss, but we're getting there. I had to change out one of her trannies and strip half the wiring out of her subsystem processors. It looked like a dish of bad pasta down there. She's been in the cold soak for almost seven months, you know."

"Yeah, I know. Will she be ready?"

"Ready enough. Thatch is plotting the route into Menelaus

as we speak, and we're taking her through a wet check at
seventeen-hundred."

Dechert found the correct path through the flotsam of
tools, pipes, and disgorged circuitry on the floor and sat down
at the bench opposite Quarles. The kid had shaved his head
a few months ago, and it made him look even younger, like a
precocious child-monk with a teenager's lanky body. Nothing
Quarles wore ever fit; even his heavysuit hung on his spindly
frame like a flight suit on a coat hanger, and it was supposed
to be a custom fit.

"You guys did a good job getting her ready, Jonathan."

Dechert clasped his hands behind his head and leaned
forward, resting his elbows on the workbench. He closed his
eyes for a few seconds and enjoyed the darkness. Cale's wist-
ful tones washed through him. A white Oklahoman singing
black Delta blues. Singing about getting away to the Moon.
How the hell had he pulled that off? The feelings of guilt came
back to Dechert then, and he wondered if anyone on the station would be alive to see the next lunar sunrise. Dechert had
wanted nothing more than to get away from the military and
the Air Service and the desk generals four years ago, and he
did, all the way up to the Moon, and he slowly assembled a
crew that reminded him of the grunts he had once led into
war. And he promised to take care of them, because this time,
he had thought he would actually be able to.

"I bet you're real happy you took my advice and came up
to this rock."

"What do you mean?" Quarles asked.

Dechert opened his eyes and looked up at him. "I mean
you could be on LEO-1 right now, drinking beer with the other
nerds and debating dark energy."

"Gee, thanks for lumping me in with the nerds. But you
know I wouldn't want to be anyplace else right now."

"Are you serious?"

Quarles tapped his foot on the bottom of the stool. He never could sit still. "Yeah, I mean, I'd make the run out to Europa if they ever get the *Magellan* finished, but why do you think I'd want to bail on Serenity? It's the best thing going in space."

"I don't know, Jonathan, maybe because you could get killed sometime in the next few days."

"Yeah and I could get hit by a bus in Baltimore." He paused and held Dechert's eyes, which was a thing he usually didn't do. "Why do you think we're up here, anyways? I mean, I know you're on a walkabout from the wars and Lane is on some kind of weird, masochistic, man-hating immersion trip, but me and Vernon and Cole and Thatch, we came up here for the audacity of it."

"Say again?"

Quarles kept Dechert's eyes and stressed each word. "The sheer, freakin' audacity of it. I mean, people living on the Moon? Jesus. Just fifty feet away from us it's two hundred and eighty below zero in the shade and pure vacuum, enough to boil the water out of your body before you get the chance to freeze. We have no business being here, boss, and that's a beautiful thing."

Dechert smiled. The kid definitely smoked too much weed. But isn't that how he had felt the first time he took a rover out on the Serenity basin? That he was a second from death and it was the most liberating, exhilarating feeling he'd had in years? No enemies. No guns. Just the thin margin of human existence inside a pressurized spacesuit. Dechert recalculated his view of Quarles. The kid was a knucklehead, but he had some explorer in him, and regardless of his other weaknesses, that made him a person to be reckoned with.

"Besides," Quarles said in a more serious tone, "I'm not about to bail on Serenity after what happened to Cole. Not until we know what happened. I couldn't meet him in the next life, walking away like that."

"Amen."

They sat in silence for a few seconds as the song faded in the background. After a few pops of static, Cale came back with a new, faster riff. More city blues than Delta. Singing about traveling. Traveling light.

Dechert waited about half a minute and turned the stereo off. "I like the choice of tunes today, Jonathan, but let's save it for the next time we drink one together. I have a call to make."

Quarles nodded his head and cleared enough equipment to put a Touchpad down in the center of his workbench. His fingers struck the pad with a stenographer's precision, light but fast.

"Right. I just hope that Lin Tzu's techies are as good as they appear to be."

Dechert leaned over, trying to get a glimpse of the complex code Quarles was punching into the stream, and he looked up with alarm as he absorbed what Quarles had said.

"Wait a second—you don't think the connection will be secure?"

Quarles typed in some more code and the message from Lin Tzu hovered over the table, opaque but readable from all sides. It contained a string of instructions for linking into a virtual meeting, a connection that couldn't be tracked by the Space Mining Administration or the Chinese Lunar Authority or anybody else, and the link was supposed to be made at 1240 hours, in less than five minutes.

Quarles shrugged. "I don't know; the data packets are supposedly getting broken up and bounced off a few commercial satellites before being reorganized at secure remote servers on Earth, kinda like the piggyback we ran for Lane's message to her ex, but this is a full-on hologram call. Much more complex. Seems like a pretty heavy data packet to not get noticed by anyone."

Dechert hated the ambivalence of technicians. They were never a hundred percent certain of anything, and for a moment, his earlier good feelings toward Quarles evaporated in a haze of frustration. He took a deep breath to calm himself.

"I need a yes or no answer, Jonathan. Is this thing going to be tracked or not?"

"Umm, no. I don't think so."

Curse words ran through Dechert's head with marine fury, and he bit his lip so he wouldn't yell at his young technician.

"All right, just make the damned connection."

Lin Tzu's upper body appeared in three dimensions of high definition above the crowded workbench, hovering with spectral precision. Only an occasional scattered ion broke the illusion that he was there with them in the Hole, just a few feet away. Tzu sat with perfect posture behind a plain white desk. He wore a chalk gray uniform with a circular tan collar, and a thin smile etched itself across the even line of his mouth when he saw Dechert. The Chinese commander looked impeccable, as always, his short black hair combed and parted to the side, his lean face clean-shaven and scrubbed. Even his fingernails, on placidly folded hands, were polished and trimmed. Dechert thought of his own stubbled face and his frayed and faded heavysuit, and he cursed inwardly. *If this was a battle of appearances, we'd lose the war hands down,* he thought. Lin looked like the owner of a five-star casino, and Dechert looked like the just-fired kitchen help.

"Lin, if I didn't know better, after seeing you, I'd say the Moon's a happy place."

"Dechert," Lin said with a softness that bordered on affectation, nodding his head in acknowledgment. "You know what my ancestor said about the necessity of deceiving your enemies. I look better than I feel."

If Tzu allowed any element of narcissism in his life, it came from the fact that he traced his lineage, generation to generation, directly back to Sun Tzu, the Chinese general whose words were still read with reverence by military commanders at every compass point on Earth, more than twenty-five hundred years after he had written them.

"Yes, you rarely fail to remind me," Dechert said. "I also remember what he wrote about maintaining the element of surprise."

They assessed each other for a moment without speaking. Dechert had never known a man who thought more like he did, or commanded more like he did. They came from worlds that couldn't be more different, worked for governments that couldn't begin to understand each other, and yet the two finished each other's sentences with uncanny ability. Dechert knew that Tzu was waiting for him to ask the first question.

"I need to know something, Lin, and I don't have time to be diplomatic about it. Did your government hit our crawler at Posidonius?"

Tzu shifted in his seat, a barely discernible movement that could have been discomfort with the question, but his eyes didn't blink as they remained focused on Dechert.

"I don't think so. But of course, I'm not able to say for certain. My leaders—like yours, I assume—haven't been very open with me about their recent actions or their future intentions." He leaned back, unclasping his hands and laying his palms on the table. "Still, it does not seem to me an action that they would take. It is—how would you say it in English—too aggressive a move at this juncture?"

"I've heard some very aggressive things have been happening back on Earth, Lin. Maybe you're looking at it from the wrong frame of reference?"

"Perhaps." Tzu sat still for a second, as if reconsidering the question. He never answered quickly, which is why Dechert had confidence in what he said. "But still, I don't think so. I'm a student of my people, Commander. An inveterate Sinophile. We're a country that has existed for more than four thousand years and we've learned to move with more caution than you. Your country is still, how should I say this without offending, bristling with the overconfidence and energy of youth?"

Dechert rubbed the stubble on his chin and wished he had shaved. He didn't have time to pursue Tzu's five second psychoanalysis of the immaturity of America or to give his opinion about the cultural and psychological shortcomings of the mainland Chinese as a rebuttal.

"Okay. So who the hell planted a bomb on my crawler?"

"That's a question we both have to answer, Dechert, before it doesn't matter anymore. But if I may be bold, I think you agree that it didn't come from my government, at least not at the official level. There is always the chance that it might have happened in this way, but neither of us thinks it is so."

The hologram buzzed in the background. Neither man spoke. Dechert could hear Quarles tapping his foot. Crazy as their government may be, blaming the Chinese for the *Molly Hatchet* never felt right, and Dechert had a keen instinct for such things. Fighting a guerrilla war in the Bekaa Valley had honed his senses for treachery. Every time an attack happened in that godforsaken place, eight different groups could have been guilty, and each of them blamed another one. Druze. Shiite. Sunni. Christian. Unraveling the truth among them was like watching loose tea settle in the bottom of a cup and hoping for a recognizable shape to appear.

"I agree that it would be out of character for the Party, at least at the Committee level, but what about a rogue element?"

"That scenario would be much more likely," Tzu agreed.

"And yesterday we discovered that a good chunk of helium-3 has gone missing from one of our spiral mines. Do you think the Space Mining Administration is stealing its own gold as well?"

"No, that would be more in my government's province. I think they would describe such a thing as a proportional response."

"Proportional to what?"

Tzu paused, and then he sighed. "I'm going to trust in our relationship enough to believe that you're not feigning ignorance, Commander, much as you must put your trust in me about the destruction of your crawler and the loss of your man. But our grid mine in the Sinus Lunicus was disabled four days ago. It appears that an EMP microburst caused the damage and that the blast came from orbit. One of our crew lost power in his suit and had to perform a few miracles to keep his oxygen supply running. He nearly died before we reached him."

Dammit, Dechert thought. *How many times am I going to be blindsided by my own people?*

Tzu nodded as if he heard Dechert's thoughts. "Yes, Commander. Whoever is responsible for these acts, it seems clear to me that the progression is logical and aimed at an unavoidable outcome. Consider for a moment: The escalation has been slow but steady over the last six months. I'm sure your internal propaganda is just as stimulating as ours and just as bent toward conflict. I know you've been finding it harder to communicate openly with the outside, just as we have."

He leaned forward. "Think about it, Dechert. We're being slowly shut off, isolated like two scorpions placed in a bowl for rich men to gamble on. I know about your water mine being disabled in Dionysius. And then your crawler is sabotaged. A few days later, our grid mine is hit. And then some of your helium-3 is stolen. Why? I think it's because powerful people in our two countries are starting to see limits to what they once considered a limitless resource. And limits frighten them."

"You think they'll risk war after everything that's happened on Earth?"

Tzu shrugged. "Maybe they don't think the war will involve Earth. Isn't that how most conflicts start? With a gross miscalculation of the possibilities of escalation? A village first, then a peninsula, and then a continent? It is cold up here, Commander. Cold and distant. Just a point in space from their viewpoint—valuable, but aesthetically detached."

Tzu exhaled again and sat back in his chair. It was the most emotion Dechert had ever seen him display.

"Look beneath your feet the next time you go for a Moonwalk, Dechert, and tell me what you see. I see the Ghawar oil fields and the Kovykta gas reserves all rolled into one and multiplied by a billion. Pure energy. Enough energy to control the planet for a thousand years. Enough energy to base Jupiter and Uranus and begin building for the trips beyond the heliopause. Consider *that* for a second. Control of Earth has been the dream of emperors and tyrants for millennia. Now imagine the temptation of controlling the solar system and the systems that lie beyond. Think of how much bigger the hoard of treasure has become."

Dechert shook his head, seeing the logic in Tzu's words but still wanting to deny them. How many treaties had been signed since 1967, guaranteeing free access to the lunar surface for all nations? Six? Seven? He wasn't so naïve to believe that treaties couldn't be abrogated, but . . . he had *hoped*. Maybe still hoped.

"The Moon was supposed to be different, Lin. It was supposed to be demilitarized. It was supposed to be shared."

"Nothing so valuable ever is."

Quarles fidgeted in his seat and rapped his knuckles on the table. "Two more minutes," he whispered. "No more."

Dechert nodded. "We don't have much time, Lin, so I'll dispense with the utopian bullshit. I agree with you, but I also know we've got to figure out a way to gain some sort of a tactical edge here. I might die on the mare, but it's not going to be as a goddamned sheep walking into the corridors of steel."

"That's why I like you, Dechert," Lin said, smiling. "Such unbridled enthusiasm for a man of your age."

"Yes. Which leaves us one option—finding out who's behind the sabotage of the *Molly Hatchet*, and exposing it before this thing becomes fully developed. Can we sign our own treaty right now? Just the two of us? No knowledge shared between us in regards to the *Molly Hatchet* goes to our respective governments until that knowledge can prevent a war?"

"I can agree to that."

"Good. Then I'll go first. The explosive that opened up the *Hatchet* was polymeric nitrogen, pretty exotic stuff, and my government claims it was last in the hands of Chinese Intelligence, sold to them by an Indonesian arms merchant in 2066. Name of Serkasa. Can you do some digging on that?"

"I'll make a few inquiries."

Dechert stood up. "Okay, and on my end I'll try finding out what happened to your mine at the Sinus Lunicus and where that order came from."

Quarles tapped on the table again. "Thirty seconds."

Would it be the last thirty seconds that they would ever speak to each other?

"That's it then, Lin. We try and stop it, as best we can."

They looked at each other, knowing what had been left unspoken. They were friends but their governments were fast becoming enemies, and neither of them felt comfortable with this clandestine maneuvering. Dechert waited for Tzu to broach the subject, knowing he would.

"I'm no traitor, Dechert, and neither are you. And that is our quandary. How do we warn each other if an attack is imminent, and is it something we should even consider? Trading state secrets on the underpinnings of war is bad enough; giving warning of an impending strike is quite another matter."

"I've been asking myself that question a lot lately, Lin. I didn't spend ten years in the service to turn my back on my country. I propose that we warn each other only if an attack is pending against Serenity 1 or New Beijing 2. Peary Crater and your leaders at the South Pole will have to fend for themselves. Five-minute alert and we use the Solar Flare Warning System as a trip wire. No one else will know what it means, but it may give our crews enough time to bug out."

Tzu thought about this, nodded, and stood up. "Very well then, I agree," he said. "We risk treason."

"This is the Moon, Lin. As far as I'm concerned, the first rule is still safety for all."

Tzu's image began to distort, his face pulling in two directions for a second before coming together again as the link began to degrade.

"I hope you remain safe, Dechert," Tzu said. "If I contact you again, it will be in a different manner."

"Good luck, Lin."

Dechert stared at Tzu as his image continued to fade and saw him flash a wry smile before he disappeared into the ether. Tzu didn't believe in luck any more than he did. They both believed in probabilities, and the cold math that they contained didn't hold any comfort for either of them.

15

The marines arrived at Sea of Serenity 1 the way marines always arrive: with grim faces and an array of weaponry. They lumbered down the gangway of their long-hop shuttle and emerged into the warm dock carrying coffin-shaped olive chests with white lettering stenciled on the sides. *Weapons on Serenity 1.* Dechert had a 10mm semiautomatic locked away in a safe in his quarters, partly because an old Moon-hand had recommended it in case one of the crew got space-crazy, and partly because he couldn't scrub the lingering feelings of nakedness when he didn't have a weapon nearby. But that was a twentieth-century handgun. These were real weapons coming into his hangar bay. Electromagnetic rail guns, probably, with a horrific muzzle velocity of more than three thousand meters per second, enough to punch a projectile through a line of twenty men standing front to back. Smart antimissile arrays and liquid lasers to blunt the impact of a concentrated cruise missile strike on the station, and maybe even micro-EMPs, which could be shoulder-fired at incoming shuttles to fry their electrical systems. Dechert pictured the same scenario playing out on New Beijing 2—a somber-looking bunch of Chinese commandos unloading their arsenal in a cold and dusty hangar with Lin Tzu standing by and observing, as Dechert was now.

Standard and Hale were with him near the sub-hangar hatch, watching the marines disembark as venting gas hissed out of the shuttle's conical engines and a blue strobe flashed and dimmed over the main hangar doors. Standard had a gleam in his eye, the excitement of the uninitiated. Or maybe he was just happy to have people on the station who didn't cast dark glances at him in passing. Either way, Dechert wanted to wipe that look away with his fist.

The look on Hale's face, on the other hand, was inscrutable, like a shark swimming in the ocean. Anyone who got to Hale's level in the Air & Space Marines had to be a realist or a true believer. Dechert thought Hale was the former—that he could be bargained with because he knew that the enemy can come from within as well as without. He would consider his options before acting. Dechert was a realist himself, which is why he wasn't completely upset about the marine arsenal being off-loaded onto Serenity 1. *If things really do come unhinged*, he thought, *at least we'll have a fighting chance to defend the station*. Still, he didn't have to like it.

As if reading Dechert's mind, Hale said, "This is not my choice, Commander. The last thing I want is a gunfight. We haven't even war-gamed the lunar theater yet, and my troopers are fresh off bioquarantine patrol on LEO-1."

Standard looked over, surprised that Hale would announce

any reservations about his mission, or maybe disappointed to hear that Air & Space Marines spent some of their time serving as customs cops, making sure that exotic minerals and microorganisms weren't smuggled from a low-orbit station down to Earth. He started to speak and then stopped.

Dechert said, "I remember complaining about escalation when I was in the service as well, Captain. I don't remember if it made me feel any better when the shooting started."

Hale grunted and turned to walk down the rubber-padded stairs to greet his fighters. Vernon and Lane stood on the flying deck together, looking down at the spectacle with their elbows on the guardrail as Thatch paced back and forth in front of the shuttle, directing the soldiers with broad waves of his arms on where to put their cargo before finally grabbing a handle on one of the big green boxes to drag it to a recessed storage rack himself. Thatch knew where everything went on the station, hoarder that he was. Out of all of the crew, only he seemed enthusiastic about the marine landing, an odd thing considering his dislike for the military. He lumbered around the hangar like an old harpooner preparing to go to sea to avenge a bitter loss. One of Cole's cigars extended from his clenched lips like a cold, unlit missile. He wanted this fight to come, and Dechert still hadn't found a way to confront him about that.

Dechert turned back to Standard. "I've got secure data feeds set up in the crew mess for the 1530 briefing. Hard lines only, per your instructions, with AI encryptions. The CORE was too small to fit everyone in."

"Everyone?" Standard asked. "This is a special access briefing, Commander, well above the classified level. How many people did you invite?"

"Just the ones who understand how to run complex operations on the Moon, Commissioner. That would be Quarles for Propulsion. Waters for Flight. Thatch for EVA, and Briggs for

Mission Safety." He paused. "I think that's just about all the people I have left."

Standard shook his head. "I'll have to ask Commodore Yates about that. He wanted this briefing to be compartmentalized. Most of the people at Peary Crater don't even know what's going on yet, just that we're on alert. That's why I'm getting Parrish out of here."

"Don't ask Yates about it, tell him," Dechert said, pointing a stiff finger at Standard's chest, "and if he objects, have him check Section Nine in the Planetary Mining Code. These marines may be good at what they do, but they don't know shit about operations on the mare. You run a mission out of my station and I've got oversight authority, even in a military emergency."

Dechert didn't wait for a reply, brushing past Standard and shuffling down the steps to help Thatch lug another of the weapon crates into a holding rack. One of the marines, who looked no older than Quarles but had arms that rippled and curved like the thick stretches of a restricting python, sang under his breath as he maneuvered what must have been a thousand-pound chest of equipment down the shuttle gangplank, bouncing it along with microgravity's help. Dechert listened closely and realized it was a song he knew from his youth, when life's worries amounted to finding beer for the weekend and fumbling with the snaps and clips that covered his girlfriend. He could almost hear a mandolin intertwining itself with the background noise of hissing gas as the marine sang on, something about the pain of war, and how it could not exceed the woe of aftermath.

The crew mess was cramped and warm. Serenity 1's air conduction system tried to keep up with the overflow of people now on the station, but like a frantic host with double the expected guests arriving for a party, the CORE's flash-servers still hadn't found their rhythm. Eight people sat around the narrow white table waiting for the briefing to begin, fanning themselves or fidgeting in the torpid air.

Quarles: tapping his feet at the general lack of motion and sound in the room and stretching the sweat-stained collar of his heavysuit with a thumb and forefinger.

Lane: leaning forward in her chair with her smooth hands folded and her lips bitten inward, ignoring the young marine who stole looks at her as he plugged a cable into the power deck under the table.

Waters: punching numbers into a Touchpad as he rehearsed the *Aerosmith's* upcoming run into Menelaus Crater, mulling every contingency Thatch had given him, memorizing coordinates for the major contours of the road, gauging potential hazards.

Hale: perched like a stone monolith near the hologram port, not looking at anybody, staring at the drab bulkhead across the room with eyes that seldom blinked even as sweat ran down into their corners.

Standard: mumbling a planned introduction under his breath as he waited for his boss to appear before them.

Thatch: silent and moody.

A young woman wearing a marine dress uniform, who must have been Hale's lieutenant: sitting quietly, unmoving.

And Dechert at the other end of the table from Hale, observing all. Always a damned observer. Even when he was in action—flying the supply hop from Peary Crater to LEO-1 or jumping into the open mouth of a crater in a prototype jetsuit or firing at guerrillas in the orange streets of a sandblasted desert town—he always had the sensation that he was observing the event rather than participating in it. It was this way even when he had killed men, the act itself only vaguely registering as something he was doing in the present. He fired his weapon as if from behind a lens, looking down at himself, creating photographic evidence to be exposed and analyzed later on.

Dechert had been blamed for detachment before. By his mother after his father's funeral, when he had sat in an old-fashioned wool suit and eclipse sunglasses a few feet apart from his family and refused to cry or shake hands with the mourners or even acknowledge the priest, who explained his father's flat spin into the Indian Ocean as part of God's plan. And by old lovers who saw his passion turn into accommodation at the onset of dawn. Even his friends saw the distance he kept; his roommate at flight school, with a dark smile that showed he was only half joking, had once summed Dechert up as a "cold bastard."

Maybe that was why Lane was so surprised when he told her that he would fight any effort by the U.S. government or the Chinese or anyone else to start a shooting war on the Moon. She had never seen him champion a cause before, not like this, and he was still wondering whether it was hubris to think he could make a difference.

The hologram popped and buzzed, and the apparition of Commodore Yates appeared before them. He was a gaunt man, with cheeks that pinched inward and sank into gray in the hollows above his jaw. His eyes were of a blue that barely counted as a color, and his thick white eyebrows permanently arched toward the top of his skull so that he looked to be in a constant state of displeasure—which, given his job, he probably was. The crow's-feet at the corners of his eyes were chiseled by skepticism rather than laughter, and even his thin, curved nose looked haughtily Roman. Dechert always respected Yates's cold efficiency, but there was little else to like in the man.

"A crowded room," Yates said with annoyance, looking

poisonously at the young Air & Space Marine who had just popped his head above the table, and keeping his eyes fixed on him as the flustered soldier made a retreat from the mess. Nobody spoke—what were they supposed to say to that?—so Yates hunched his shoulders forward, squeezed his hands together, and continued.

"I'm sure Commissioner Standard had a prepared introduction for us, but new events have unfolded that demand brevity." He cocked a quick, mocking glance at Standard and then surveyed the room again. "The president has authorized DEFCON-2 for all terrestrial and space commands and has fully militarized Low Earth Orbit 1, Low Lunar Orbit 1, and the Moon itself. This happened two hours ago, after the Chinese broke off emergency talks and one of our LLO satellites picked up activity in the Montes Apenninus, outside the accepted perimeter of Chinese operations. General Trayborr is transferring his flag to Peary Crater; he should be arriving at 1100 Earthtime tomorrow. The SMA is rendering full authority over to the military and placing all of its assets at their disposal."

He paused, looking around the table yet again, this time catching the eyes of every person seated there. "All of its assets, ladies and gentlemen, which would include each of you. I know some of you aren't prepared for this, and frankly neither am I, but I can't help with that. It's a little too late to ask for a week off."

Yates rubbed his hollow cheeks with a wrinkled hand, making a sound like sandpaper being pulled over a pine bole. He sighed, and Dechert couldn't tell if he was trying to appear tired or sympathetic.

"Only the dead have seen the end of war, Santayana once said. Unfortunately for us, I think the Chinese are trying to prove him right."

The buzz and pop of the hologram heightened the human silence after he spoke, giving the room an electric tension. Standard cleared his throat after a few moments and straightened the Touchpad in front of him as the rest of them looked at one another in differing states of disbelief or resignation.

"Thank you for the update, sir, and rightly said."

He looked around the room and up again at the image of Yates and coughed into a closed fist. "As the Commodore has mentioned, our satellite detected heat blooms in the Apennine Mountains, most likely from mobile fusion reactors powering a temporary outpost. They're in a gap just northwest of Crater Conon." He looked around the table. "That's little more than four hundred kilometers from Serenity 1."

Standard typed a command into his Touchpad and a topographical map sprung up from the small computer and hovered in ashen gray over the dining table next to Yates, the image zooming in and out until it showed on a wide scale the world inhabited by Chinese and American miners along the Moon's lava-darkened belly. The Mare Imbrium, or Sea of Showers, appeared as a bruise just north of the equator on the Moon's near-side face. Its scarlike ridge of mountains, the Apennines, spiked the southeastern edge of the mare with rounded, Rockies-size peaks and a jumble of deep ravines and canyons. Imbrium's great craters—Archimedes, Autolycus, Aristillus, and Timocharis—stood out in relief, scattered across her basaltic plains like wounds from the blast of an enormous shotgun. New Beijing 2, the home of their fellow central-Moon miners and now perhaps their enemies, appeared as a red dot within Archimedes. The heat blooms in the mountain range were shown as ominously blinking orange dots. And just east of the mountains lay the Imbrium's equally dead lunar sister, the Sea of Serenity. Menelaus Crater pitted Serenity's southernmost shore, thirty kilometers wide, rimmed and ribboned with fields of white ejecta. Tucked into a cranny along the crater's northern impact wall was the station in which they sat.

"We didn't retask the satellite for a closer look because we didn't want to tip off the Chinese, but we must assume the worst," Standard said, pointing at the two small dots in the Montes Apenninus. "A mobile launching platform, maybe, or at least a forward observation post from which they can easily conduct reconnaissance or strike missions into the Mare Serenitatis. Whatever their purpose, they shouldn't be there, especially not with the very large power supply they brought with them."

Lane leaned forward to look over the topographic hologram. "They could be running test bores for an ilmenite mine. The deposits are pretty rich up there, and that's close to where their cave-in occurred last year." She looked over at Standard before he could respond. "I'm not suggesting that's what they're doing, Commissioner, I'm just saying it's possible that they could be there for reasons that aren't hostile."

"You may be right, Officer Briggs," Yates interrupted, glaring down at her as he said it. "They might think they are there for legitimate reasons, but our government doesn't agree with them. And we can't afford to hope their intentions are benign. The military has looked this over and they want to send in a reconnaissance shuttle. Trayborr himself gave the order, and that's where the marines come in."

Dechert looked over at Hale. If the Chinese were setting up a military outpost, a shuttle mission to reconnoiter their position would pose a number of extreme dangers, including the most obvious one of being shot out of the sky by a missile, laser, or electromagnetic burst.

"Why not just retask the satellite and take pictures from orbit? Or use a drone?"

Yates shook his head. "As Mr. Standard has said, Dechert, we don't want to tip off the Chinese that we've spotted them. This has to be a covert job. Satellite retask would be noticed, and a drone would have to fly within line of sight of their outpost. Only a shuttle can come in from behind the mountains at low altitude, land, and allow an EVA team to do a proper reconnaissance."

Everyone at the table looked over to Hale. He stood up and walked over to the hologram, extending an old-fashioned telescoping pointer, much like one that a high school physics teacher might have used in the twentieth century. "We're planning to go in at 2200 hours tomorrow, so we need an ingress point that is under their radar dome, assuming they have one set up, and a landing area that would give our team access to an observation point, preferably a high but ascendable peak."

He traced a line with the pointer along the southern edge of the topographic map. "Option one, as far as distance is concerned, would take us in over the Mare Vaporum, up through the southern range of the Apennine Mountains, skimming the mountains and staying on the deck to avoid detection, and then landing somewhere southwest of Crater Conon. Zoom in, if you please, Mr. Standard." Hale tapped on a point in the mountains just below the Chinese heat blooms. "There are a few peaks here that would provide enough cover and field of vision to do the job."

Standard ran his finger over the Touchpad, and the mountain range and surrounding canyonlands zoomed into greater definition. *A true run through hell,* Dechert thought. Crumbling peaks. Giant boulders tossed up by ancient eruptions and meteor strikes. Ravines and gullies that would turn into sheer walls and then drop again into fissures or box canyons. *And they're going to navigate that mess in a shuttle on a blackout run, flying on the deck in full nightside?* Jesus. Dechert wouldn't want to fly that mission himself, and other than Waters, he was the best pilot on the Moon. He looked over at Waters and Thatch, and both men shook their heads.

"Looks great on a topo-map, Captain, but that's some alien terrain to be flying in nightside," Thatch said. He leaned his bulk over the table and the seams of his heavysuit strained under the armpits as he waved a hand across the lower edge of the hologram. "Things might have changed since the last time that area was laser-mapped—peaks might have collapsed, and new craters could have been made. We haven't flown the southern Apennine in more than a year, and now you're going to have a squad of marines go in at low altitude on infrared, in blackout conditions? That's like running through a minefield and hoping to keep your legs."

Hale looked at Thatch and swung the pointer up onto his shoulder. After a long silence he nodded toward the young officer sitting next to him.

"Lieutenant Cabrera will be flying the mission, and I don't see many other options. We come in from the south or from the north, but either way, we'll be flying on the deck in blackout conditions. FLIR and passive radar only."

"Shoot," Waters said, stirring beside Thatch and putting his hand on his shoulder, "if you have to do it, at least come in from the north." He got up and walked around the table, past Hale, until he hovered over the map, casting a shadow that slightly distorted the hologram. "It'll take you closer to Archimedes and New Beijing 2, but at least it's terrain we're familiar with."

"Go on," Hale said, stepping back even as Cabrera leaned forward to pay attention.

"All right. You fly north-northwest over the heart of the Serenity basin, and do a near-one-eighty just east of Mons Hadley, near the Apollo 15 landing site." He traced a thick finger above the hologram. "Bring her in over Crater Aratus, and drop into this box canyon just south of the Hadley peaks, here. Zoom that in. There, that would give you a vantage point on those blooms you're tracking. We drilled some test bores in the area last year. I can dig up telemetry on the shuttle run." He looked back at Cabrera skeptically. "To be clear, though, we did the mission when the sun was high in the sky, and I wasn't worried about getting shot out of space by some damned Chinaman toting a handheld."

Hale rubbed his chin and looked at Vernon and Thatch, and then Cabrera, who nodded. "Okay, give us your data and we'll look it over. What's the total distance on the run?"

"Maybe twelve hundred klicks."

Yates cleared his throat and everyone looked up at him. "I'll leave the mission planning to Captain Hale and Lieutenant Cabrera, but I want a full briefing before launch. We'll tap in on the low-gain antenna so we can get a live feed, if my communications people say it won't be detected."

Dechert looked up and saw Yates glaring at him, then turned his head to Lane and raised his eyebrows. "Officer Briggs, mission safety?"

"I'll coordinate with Captain Hale and the lieutenant on a SAR plan," Lane said, nodding to Cabrera. Yates frowned at the mention of a search-and-rescue, but she went on. "This operation is outside our standard safety envelope. I'm going to need your data on Chinese radar domes, and I don't think we even have specs for a nightside run through the mountains."

"Work with the lieutenant to draw up new ones then, Officer Briggs," Yates said. "And get used to improvisation. If this conflict expands, a great number of things will be done for the first time on the Moon."

"Jonathan . . . propulsion?" Dechert asked.

Quarles was slouching with a somewhat awed look on his face. He sat up straight. "Um, I'm going to have to look over the marine shuttle. I can probably add a few maneuvering thrusters and plug all of them into the fly-by-wire hardware." He looked over at Cabrera. "We can definitely give you some redundancy and maybe even strengthen the airframe. I'm going to need a crew count and full mission weight, including equipment."

"No problem," she said. "Let's go down to the hangar and look her over after the meeting. I'll take any edge you can give me."

Hale nodded, but no one spoke. The room was frozen for an enduring moment in a trancelike state, the light staccato popping of the hologram the only sound to reach their ears as they all remained locked in their own thoughts. Dechert closed his eyes. Had it been this way throughout history? A group of people sitting around a table, planning the first mission that might lead to the first battle and finally to open war, having their talk about tactics and contingencies, and then mulling the consequences of that discussion in reverent silence? And at that final moment, before the council's break, whether it was Pericles or Westmoreland leading the proceedings, did that silence have any meaning, or was it just a momentary lack of noise?

"That's it, then, ladies and gentlemen," Yates said. "Keep me apprised of the planning, and remember, we are in full communications blackout." He paused and put his hands on the desk in front of him. "Captain Hale, I'd like a secondary briefing at 0900 tomorrow. And, Commander Dechert, would you stay for a moment? I'd like to speak to you alone."

All eyes turned to Dechert, who nodded. "Of course," he said.

Standard started to speak but stopped. He rose and left the table, his shoulders tense despite the lack of gravity. Dechert continued to look straight ahead, a disinterested look on his face that didn't quite reflect what he felt inside, while the others retreated from the room. He could hear Lane and Cabrera talking to each other as they departed, and he realized it was the first time he'd heard two women speaking to each other in more than three years. *What a godforsaken place this is!*

When the hard seals snapped into place on the pressure door, Yates sighed and leaned back in his chair. He rolled an old-fashioned gold pen through his fingers like a tiny general's baton. "Standard told me you had concerns that you wanted to address with both of us, but I assume you'd rather speak directly to me. I'm a busy man and I'm getting busier, Commander, so let's hear it."

"Yes, Commodore," Dechert said. He rubbed the back of his crew cut with an open hand and leaned forward. "As you probably know, I object to my crew being used for what is becoming a military intervention. I think they should be pulled out as soon as the preparations for the shuttle run are complete. I can stay in the CORE and help Hale run the mission." He looked up into Yates's eyes, undeterred by a gaze that bordered on the predatory. "I'm the only one with military training. You don't need the others here."

Yates held the staring match for a second and then squinted in annoyance and shook his head, putting the pen down on his obsidian desktop. "Your people knew the hazards when they signed up for off-Earth mining, and they knew that they could be deputized. This is a quasi-governmental program, Commander. Your title alone should remind you of that."

"We can be deputized for an emergency, yes, but this is looking like a goddamned war." Dechert stood and paced behind the table before gripping the back of his chair. "They aren't soldiers, Commodore. They could do more harm than good."

Yates clenched his jaw until the bones protruded from his face and his cheeks sank inward even farther. He leaned into the holo-cam and his face filled the screen. Dechert could see the red capillaries in his eyes and almost imagine the smell of whiskey on his breath—Yates was rumored to be a drinker.

"We don't have the time or the assets to pull your team out, Mr. Dechert. I'd like to evacuate my people as well, you know, but that has become impossible. And they wouldn't be a whole lot safer at the North Pole anyway."

Dechert ran through his mind how far he wanted to go with Yates. He didn't have enough evidence yet, not enough of a hand to put everything on the table. Should he tell the commodore of his suspicions?

And there was more than that, something deeper that scratched at Dechert's skin like an old scab. *Wasn't he still a soldier, for Christ's sake?* If a fight was inevitable, didn't he have a duty to see it through, to help the grunts who would be flying a shuttle into a nightmare they couldn't possibly imagine? Their chances of remaining alive would be greatly increased if his whole team helped to run the operation. Nobody knew that terrain better than Waters and Thatch, and nobody was better on mission safety than Lane. By asking for them to be removed from duty, wasn't he risking a disaster for the marines?

Dechert shook off his doubts. The marines weren't his problem, not anymore. Lane, Thatch, Quarles, and Waters were. He *did* have a duty, and it was to them. And that meant he had to try to get them the hell off of the Moon.

"Commodore, I'll speak plainly. I'm not convinced that this is a justifiable action. I haven't seen anything stronger than circumstantial evidence that the Chinese hit the *Molly Hatchet*, and I know those people over there." He paused, looking into Yates's eyes, which had narrowed to the point where only black pupils could be seen. "*We* know them. They're pawns in this, just like us. I'm not sure my team will be able to take an order that involves killing them."

Yates's eyelids opened and he smiled at the subtle hint of mutiny; Dechert was surprised at how white the old man's teeth were.

"Yes, that's what I thought this was about. I should have reprimanded you a long time ago for continuing to socialize with Tzu and his team after the communication blackout was put in place." Yates raised his eyebrows. "Oh, you didn't know that I read the monthly com logs, including the supposedly secret ones that are redirected through black-market Earth-servers? You don't think I know when your safety officer is trading gardening secrets with her Chinese opposite, or your young engineer is smuggling in booze from NB-2? There may be a few things I'm unaware of on the Moon, Mr. Dechert, but I wouldn't count on many." He pulled back from the holo-cam for a moment and frowned, looking over his shoulder at something Dechert couldn't see, holding up a finger as if telling someone to wait, and then he leaned back in.

"Listen. I'm a businessman. I don't like this any more than you. It leads to the one thing I can't abide and that's lower revenues. The status quo would have suited me just fine." He stood up from his desk. "Unfortunately, someone on Earth doesn't feel the same way, and to be honest with you, I'm not in a position to question them. Do you get what I'm saying? There is only one fact that's relevant to me right now: I'm allowed to mine on this rock just as long as the United States government gives me an operating license to do so. And they don't give operating licenses to people who question the judgment of the president."

He held Dechert's stare, straightening his back and arching his shoulders as if the gravity at Peary Crater were equal to that of Earth. An old man who was too clever to resist even minimal forces.

"I've got nothing against the miners on New Beijing 2 and

I hope we don't have to send them into the next reality. But if we do, we do. This thing runs deeper than either of us can know, and even if you're right, there's nothing I can do about it—unless you hand me the smoking gun of all smoking guns in the next twenty-four hours."

"Are you telling me to dig deeper?" Dechert asked.

"I'm telling you I'm a businessman, Dechert. You can poke around all you want as long as it doesn't hinder tomorrow's launch. Just don't expect me to intervene if you have anything short of the holy-shit truth. I hope you understand."

Yates straightened the bottom of his jacket and pushed his chair under the black desk, a sign that the meeting was over.

"Yes," Dechert said. "I understand."

16

It felt like old times, mining times, when they had bounced around the Moon's bloodless surface with the enthusiasm of old prospectors digging for the next lode, the next vein of gold that would make all of them rich. When everyone had looked after one another—Chinese, Russian, American, Indian—and traded tall tales and radiation warnings and wagered vacuum-sealed rib eyes on who would tap the first high-yield ilmenite field or discover the next cache of water frozen in the permanent shadow of a crater. Back when there was supposedly enough helium-3 on the maria to fuel the Earth and every other human endeavor taking place within the Asteroid Belt, and like dolphins feeding on a baitball, they would simply line up and wait their turn.

All before their leaders in Beijing and Washington began to look at long-term productivity curves and burn rates and question the wisdom of equal portioning. Before life began turning back to normal on Earth, and the politicians called their generals.

Dechert smiled, forgetting for a second the bastards back on Earth and recalling those early days on the Moon when his handlers at Peary Crater and New Mexico communicated with Serenity 1 only after the monthly output numbers were finalized and illustrated on a bar chart. *God, how incredible it would have been to be here back in '58, when Fletcher first opened the station*, he thought. That was deep blue frontier stuff, the kind of adventure that would scrub all the other thoughts from your head.

He looked over at Lane and Quarles, who sat in the Environmental and Propulsion stations of the cocoonlike cockpit in the *Aerosmith*, as the big crawler ground its tracked wheels into the regolith and rumbled into the open pit of Menelaus Crater like a migrating beast. All three of them wore pressure suits and helmets, new rules that served as a cold testament to Cole Benson's death in the wastelands near Posidonius. Thatch and Waters drove the rover just ahead of them, marking uneven terrain along the traverse with blue strobes and updating the old topographic maps of the Menelaus Road with laser range finders. The *Aerosmith's* running lights illuminated the black nightside of the crater, and the moondust kicked up by the churning machines cast the descent in a brume of translucent light. Everything moved in slow motion as the two vehicles slogged down the switchback road at less than a kilometer per hour.

"Feels good to be back out on the reg," Thatch said over the com. "Even if Vernon is shit for company."

"I'm just busy watching your backside, baby," Waters replied. "I'm a crater-crawlin', mother-lovin' sonofabitch. Your mother, in case you didn't know."

"Kiss my ass, Vernon," Thatch said. "Boss, we got a grade change coming up in twenty meters, nine degrees down-angle, two degrees to starboard. Looks like an eighty-meter leg."

"Roger that," Dechert replied. "Map it. Slope to nine-down, two degrees starboard in two-zero meters."

He punched the numbers into the *Aerosmith*'s navigation computer and stole another glance over at Lane and Quarles as the processors worked on a course correction. They had their polarized lenses turned off, and he could see them both smiling at the banter between Thatch and Waters. Dechert wished they could all stay down in the crater until it was over. His earlier hopes about stopping the iron wheel that had been put into motion had diminished in the last two days. How were they going to find out what happened to the *Molly Hatchet* in time to prevent what now seemed inevitable? And even if they did find the truth, would it matter? The politicians would be slow to believe it, and the soldiers would consider it of secondary importance. Dechert took no comfort from his time in the military. Captains may occasionally disobey orders in the field, but generals never did in the command bunker. The civilian leadership had always been a joke—and it was always affirmed with a stiff salute by the men with stars on their collars. *That was the irony,* Dechert thought. The ones who knew the most about the nightmare that was coming were the least likely to prevent it. And he knew the Chinese generals would be no different.

And his crew, who were now more his family than anyone back on Earth, would be the ones caught on the killing field. Quarles, just a kid with a hard on for soldering together dust-broken and cold-soaked spaceships so that they would work for one more day. Lane, who he was grooming for future command, even if she didn't know it. Sometimes she let the darker realities of life brew within her while Dechert chilled his demons with fatalism, but Lane still managed to stand on the right side of things in just about every situation they had been in together. The good side of things. Vernon, his old warhorse. Isn't that what General Lee had called Longstreet? The one who was always there, ready to rescue him from a bad decision or bring calm to a moment of chaos. Thatch, the lumberjack, who looked more out of place on the Moon than an oak tree on Mars, but ran a mining operation out on the regolith better than anyone Dechert had ever met.

And Cole. *Can't forget Cole.* Dead now, lying in a deoxygenated freezer back at Peary Crater, waiting for the next LEO-1 shuttle to take him to Earth-orbit and then to the alkaline soil of Southern California, where people Dechert had never met would mourn as they buried him. Cole, he feared, was just the first innocent to die; the early symptom of a fatal disease.

"Coming up on waypoint forty-two," Quarles said. "Slowing to point-three kph."

"Okay," Dechert said. "Taking her back into first, readying stabilizers and emergency braking."

The *Aerosmith* pitched and Dechert's ears caught the subtle sound of her downshifting gears, grinding as they prepared the massive crawler for the downhill jog. The cockpit jolted twice as the MOHAB slowed down, churning up even more regolith until the rover driven by Thatch and Vernon could barely be seen just fifty yards ahead of them. Even with his helmet on, Dechert smelled gunpowder. It always smelled like gunpowder out on the reg. Neil Armstrong noticed it first, and every Moonwalker since came to know what he described. The cordite smell of war in a barren land.

"I'd feel better if this bucket of nuts hadn't been patched

together by the boy wonder here," Lane said, and Dechert knew she had that half smirk on her face as her helmet turned toward Quarles. "Visibility down to four-zero meters, going to infrared, secondary."

"Aww, come on Briggs," Quarles replied, "you know you've always wanted to take a nightside ride on the Moon with me."

Dechert suppressed a grin of his own. "Let's get through this leg and then you can rip each other out of your suits if you want." He clicked the com back to open channel to cut Lane off before she could retort.

"How we looking, Thatch?"

"Five-by-five from here, boss. Just keep hugging the left wall. We're about sixty meters to the midslope, keeping eyes on."

"Roger that. Vernon?"

"Looks good so far. I'm gonna egress to get a look at waypoint forty-three. Should have a solution for you in five minutes, give or take."

In the fog ahead, Dechert could see Thatch stop the rover. Vernon unclipped from his safety harness, climbed out of the vehicle, and bounded down the narrow crater road, fading into the haze of moondust and the bordering wall of darkness. Dechert refocused on the road and the heads-up display in front of him, pulling slightly on his control stick's left-hand toggle as the telemetry ordered him to turn one degree to port. The rippled crater floor lay a vertical mile below and Dechert could sense the open void just a few meters from their starboard half-track, where the edge of the road dropped into nothingness. Happily, they wouldn't be going to the bottom, stopping instead at Hawking's Rim, one of the many terraced inner ledges that gave Menelaus its distinctive personality.

Every crater is different, Fletcher used to say. Some are new and sharp-edged like Menelaus, a cosmic baby of only a few hundred million years or so, still scarred with rilles on its belly and steep, angry impact walls protecting a series of inner ridges on its ribs. Others are ancient ghosts, like the crumbling Posidonius or the even more ruinous Schiller Annular Plain, which stretches across the Moon's southern hemisphere like a poorly rolled cigar, wider than the borders of the Rocky Mountains and desiccated by nearly three billion years of stellar decay.

Menelaus was the perfect crater to hide in, much better shielded from an EMP blast or a missile launch than the older impact basins and easier to traverse than the smaller, steeper cosmic bullet holes that poxed the lunar surface. *For all the asinine things the Space Mining Administration had done in the last fifteen years, at least they picked the right location for Sea of Serenity 1,* Dechert thought. And Hawking's Rim was only a klick or so ahead. They could reach it in two hours barring any significant setbacks, prepare the *Aerosmith* for an extended cold soak, and get back to the station in time for a late meal. A last supper, maybe, as the marines were scheduled to make their reconnaissance run into the Montes Apenninus in less than a day. Dechert felt a tightening in the center of his chest every time he thought about it.

"Uh, boss, we got a little problem here." Vernon's voice came into the crawler distorted, broken up by charged particles in the crater's exosphere. "Small washout of the road on ingress to waypoint forty-three . . . looks like a rim wall collapse."

Shit. "Roger that, Vernon. Can we get around it?"

"Not without pushing some rocks out of the way or taking a tumble down the crater wall. Should take us twenty minutes or so to clean it up. I'm heading back to the rover. Thatch, warm up the plow."

"That's a roger. Turning on the heaters now."

Twenty minutes. That wasn't as bad as it could be. Dechert had counted on a few delays; no lunar mission is without them.

And it would give him the time he needed to attend to the underlying business of the Menelaus run. He had to know where things stood with his makeshift investigation, and whether a war could be prevented. And he needed to find out here, out on the reg, because he could no longer trust in the isolation of Serenity 1. By now, the SMA and the Feds were probably monitoring every channel on the station with authoritarian precision, an irony that made Dechert sick. The first Level-1 base built on the Moon after the Thermal Maximum had been named Unity, and both America and China had pledged their cooperative mining efforts would be aimed at ending the dark age of the mid-twenty-first century—the poverty and famine that had struck Earth with an apocalyptic shudder. And now here they were, Dechert and Lin Tzu sneaking around like rebels in a warring banana republic, trying to figure out ways to keep from killing each other while their masters dusted for their fingerprints.

"Rover, we're going to power down and park this girl when we hit the midslope, as soon as we have your wall collapse under our lamps." Dechert turned back to Lane. "How we looking for radiation?"

"Pretty good. Sun's napping and nightside's helping. They've got at least seven more hours of EVA time if they need it, and a little extra for the ride back."

"Grade starting to come back up," Quarles said. "Four degrees down-angle, lessening to three. Increase speed to point-six kph."

The *Aerosmith* settled back on her haunches and churned onto the even section of road. The three of them watched Waters climb back into the rover and buckle up and Thatch pull away around the bend. The Menelaus Road narrowed here. It dropped off into space less than three meters off the right side of the crawler, as a sheer cliff in the crater wall fell down to the next terraced ledge. A *half-mile drop*, Dechert thought, in the slow-motion nightmare of microgravity. *We'd have plenty of time to know we're dying.*

He brushed off the image but continued to hug the rim wall, turning the *Aerosmith* to maneuver around a slight notch in the passageway as he felt the sweat collect in his gloves. The collapse lay just ahead now, a small washout of breccia and basalt that could have been caused by erosion from the solar winds or even a meteorite. They watched as Thatch raised and lowered the plow on the front of the rover to warm its frozen hydraulic joints.

"Extending the vertical lamps," Lane said. Dechert pulled the crawler to within a few meters of the collapse and parked it as the illumination from the *Aerosmith*'s overhead lanterns bloomed, washing the site in artificial daylight. Dust hung in the air like morning fog, raining down in a small circle around them.

"All right, people," Dechert said, looking with concern at the rising cloud. "Let's go to ten percent continual on the outflow valves on all systems. I don't want to be sucking in too much powder."

"Ten percent, roger that," said Quarles. "Powering down the reactor. I'll keep her breathing for the restart."

Dechert sat back in the pilot's chair and pushed his knees out, stretching his cramped body and feeling the blood seep back into his legs. His feet were cold and his head felt wet and clammy. "Vernon, we're going to go off personal life support while you guys clean up. We'll keep you on com, so let us know if you need anything."

"Yeah," Vernon said, "you guys just relax in there."

Lane punched up the cockpit's atmospherics on a small touchscreen above her head and boosted the oxygen flow, and the lights on the plasma readout blinked from the orange of

Minimal Sustaining to green, illuminating her faceplate with an emerald glow.

"We're good," she said.

The three of them unlocked the seals on the sides of their helmets and pulled them off to the sound of escaping gas. It was cold; Dechert could see steam coming off of the top of Quarles's bald head and feel the chill on the back of his own sweaty neck.

"Jesus," Quarles said. "Can we turn up the heaters a little?"

"In a second, you big baby," Lane said, but even as she did, she ran a finger across another touchscreen, and a blast of warm, dry air pushed down from the vents above them.

Dechert rubbed his damp head with a gloved hand, frowned, and took the glove off. "Don't get used to being off primary support. We just need some time off-com."

"Yeah—Big Brother, Big Sister, and every other lunatic on this rock is probably pointing directionals at any spurt of static they can pick up right now," Quarles said. He took off his gloves as well and turned his chair toward the center of the cockpit. "And I've got some pretty heavy stuff to lay on you guys, so it's best that no one's listening."

Dechert looked over at Lane and then back to Quarles. "All right, Jonathan, you go first, but curb your instinct to wax poetic. We only have a few minutes."

"Yes, please," Lane said.

Quarles clicked his tongue to show he was underappreciated, but pulled a small metal briefcase from under his seat, unlocking the clasps with a dramatic click of his thumbs. "I've taken all of this off the stream and scrubbed the servers—it's really too unbelievable to put your mind around." He looked up. "I'm telling you I had to smoke a joint after seeing this stuff."

Dechert nodded but didn't say anything, thinking of the

warning Yates had given him about trying to keep anything hidden from the all-seeing eye.

"Okay," Quarles continued, "we received a transmission from New Beijing 2 this morning, on the open channel, which initially freaked me out until I realized it was a routine astroscience bulletin on a meteorite hit near T. Mayer A, in the Montes Carpatus a few days ago. Only the telemetry seemed to be a little off, so I ran it through the Quantum on the *Aerosmith*—off-channel, of course—and I discovered that our Chinese friends had added extra numbers into the coordinates and trajectory of the strike." He looked up. "Are you following me here?"

"A code?" Lane asked.

"Yeah, a code. Just twelve letters and numbers in variable sequence, but they formed a stream address."

Dechert looked back at Vernon and Thatch, who were making the first run with the plow through the rock washout, trying to get traction against the slide as the rear wheels of the rover spun in slow motion. Both of their white spacesuits were already gray with moondust. "Any chance anyone else could have picked up on it?" he asked, keeping his eyes on the two working outside. "I'm sure Peary Crater gave it a good scan."

"Doubt it. It was pretty ingenious, but then so am I. Who's going to take the time to run telemetry from a routine meteor impact through a quantum computer?" He grinned. "And who else could notice offhand a few degrees in variation on the declination of a cosmic bullet strike? Luckily, the powers that be are still letting impact reports and solar bulletins come through the open pipe."

Lane shook her head again, already losing her patience. "All right, all right, we're duly impressed with your intellect. Now what the hell was at the end of the address?"

Quarles typed with two index fingers on the port inside his

briefcase, and then turned it to Lane and Dechert with a flourish. "A message. And a video that you have to see. It was placed
on the back end of a discrete server somewhere in China, near
Shanghai I think. Probably a black-market gambling box, or
maybe a porn aggregator. As soon as I downloaded the file, it
self-immolated on the back end." He looked over at Dechert.
"Your friend Commander Tzu is very clever."

They leaned forward like conspirators in a small, clandestine basement as the screen flared and a few paragraphs of text
appeared:

> *This is all I can provide you, Dechert. It came from the
> surveillance camera of a Chinese Intelligence safe house
> near Guangzhou, October 2066—a safe house that had a
> cache of polymeric nitrogen in its stores.*
>
> *Our government spreads the word internally that
> this is an American conspiracy, planned years ago and
> designed to foment war. But others say more quietly it
> is a Secretariat operation, a double-switch by our own
> intelligence services. I don't know the truth. I only know
> that I trust no one, and neither should you. Both parties
> appear to want what is coming.*
>
> *Do with it what you can. I think the next time we
> communicate it will be with warnings of a solar flare. Luna
> has been a kind mistress, but like all kept women, she is
> having her revenge.*

Warnings of a solar flare. Their coded alert that an attack
was imminent. If Dechert took any solace from the cryptic message, it was in the fact that he wasn't the only sane person on
the Moon who had lost hope. Tzu was probably a stronger man
than he, and certainly a smarter one. His despair made Dechert
less angry at himself for similar feelings of helplessness.

The text disappeared and a grainy video filled the screen, distorted and backwashed with overexposure. They huddled closer in the center of the cockpit, Lane peering over Dechert's back, her hand absently on his shoulder. It was the feed from a fixed video camera showing an empty, nondescript hallway. Tan painted walls. Dirty linoleum floors. A time stamp in the bottom right flashed the seconds away, but there was nothing to indicate the year, and there was no sound or movement. Dechert saw a wisp of blue smoke at the bottom of the screen—and then another. Not much smoke, not enough to be a breaching charge. Must be muzzle fire. Then he saw it again. Tracers. Unmistakable. Quick orange lines of lead, lit up by tiny pyrotechnic charges in the bases of the bullets, lancing down the hallway.

Dechert squinted. The smoke in the nameless corridor grew. And then at the far end, the end under attack, a man appeared low to the ground, leaning his body from around a corner to fire. But he was doing it wrong, leaving himself exposed for too long. Shooting wildly instead of taking a quick glance and fixing his weapon on a planned axis to enfilade the corridor and block the intruder's assault, as they teach you in close quarters training. No skilled soldier, that one. A panicked man. And then, as if to confirm Dechert's silent opinion of the defender's war-fighting skills, he was down. A clean shot to the head, judging from how his neck snapped backward and his body relaxed.

Five seconds passed. No one in the cockpit of the *Aerosmith* moved. They stared at the video as the sound of the overhead heating vents grew louder. And then the second man appeared at the bottom of the screen. *The attacker.* Dechert grunted when he saw him. This was a warrior. Even through the veil of smoke and the distortion of the old video, it took only two of his metered strides for Dechert to recognize the man for what he was: a predator. He moved with purpose and a near-nonchalance, his weapon rotating to cover all of his threat points. A big man, wide-shouldered and thick at the center. Unusual for a special operator. Typically the best killers are small. And there was something in the way this barrel-shaped man moved that unsettled Dechert, causing him to shift in his seat and lean even closer. Graceful. Efficient for his size, even for a trained soldier.

The man made it to the end of the hallway—obviously an L-shaped accessway—focusing only on his left flank. He reached the corner, crouched low, and peered over the person he had just killed, using his unmoving legs as a makeshift barricade. And then, just as quickly, after firing a few more shots, he was gone. Up and around the corner, closer to his objective. A large shadow moving with purpose, his face and head covered by a balaclava. The screen popped with static and then went blank.

All three of them breathed and sat back, and Dechert looked out the cockpit window to see that Thatch and Waters had cleared half of the washout from the Monolauo Road. Moondust sparkled in the torchlight around them like falling silver.

"Well," Lane said, looking at no one in particular. "Can someone tell me exactly what we just saw?"

"I can give it a try," said Quarles. "Someone in China obviously wants us—or at least Tzu—to believe the stuff that blew up the *Molly Hatchet* was stolen from them by the guy in our poorly shot matinee. Only there's no time stamp or date, no proof of location, and no direct evidence that it's anything other than a taped training exercise."

Dechert rubbed the stubble on his chin and shook his head. "No, for whatever else it's worth, that was no training exercise. The one who went down was definitely shot. I'm more concerned about how Tzu got his hands on that video, or *why* he was able to get his hands on it."

"Someone within the Chinese Lunar Authority is trying to convince him the Chinese are being set up," Lane said. "But judging from his message, the video didn't seem to do the job for him, and it sure as hell won't convince anyone on our side of the mare." She leaned forward and rubbed her knees, closing her eyes as she always did when she wanted to think something through.

"So," she continued, "according to Lin Tzu, some of his people are saying this whole thing is an American setup that has its roots in a weapons raid six years ago, while some in the CLA also suspect their own government is behind it. And on our side, we have Mr. Standard painting the U.S. as an innocent victim, while at least one SMA official, whom I happen to trust more than anyone else down there, isn't so sure of our purity. And we've got about twelve hours to untie this Gordian knot, with a blurry video and the few bits of circumstantial evidence I collected in the Bullpen?"

Dechert closed his eyes, hoping Lane's mental exercise would work as well for him. There was something about that attacker. He moved like . . . an American. It seemed ridiculous, and he didn't want to say it out loud, but Dechert had seen special operators from dozens of countries in action. This one looked as though he had been trained at Bragg or Little Creek, not in the sheep hills of Hereford or the steppes at Balashikha 2. To the layperson, a SEAL in tiger stripes may look identical to an SAS trooper or a Spetsnaz, but to Dechert they were as different as the London Symphony Orchestra and the Boston Pops. Or was he just projecting his own suspicions and bias into the moment? Did he believe it was an American because it confirmed the doubts he had about the actions of his own government? The video didn't show anything that could allow them to make a definitive identification or to prove that Lin's representation of it had any validity. But something about it left him unsettled. The attacker's face could never be seen, but Dechert could almost picture it in his mind's eye. *A big man, and fast.* Whom had he known in Special Ops who reminded him of this killer?

"Lane, I hope your bits of evidence are more substantial." He looked up at her, and he knew in that instant that she saw the uncertainty in his eyes. They stared at each other for a few seconds, forgetting Quarles was there. She was surprised at the hesitation she had seen, and he wondered if he had always hidden his self-doubt from her so well.

"More interesting than revealing, I'm afraid," she said, biting a finger between her white teeth and looking away from Dechert. "I don't have any visual aids, so my presentation will be quicker than Jonathan's. Bottom line, I found no traces of polymeric nitrogen in Serenity 1. No decaying atomic particles, nothing to suggest the presence of a hyperexplosive anywhere near the base."

"Can you say without doubt there was never any polymeric nitrogen on the station?"

She shifted in her seat. "No, and that's the problem. If the material was properly stored in an inert containment device, protected by a pressurized chamber filled with xenon or halocarbon, it's doubtful there'd be anything to find."

"But?"

She looked at both of them. "But I did find something I can't explain on the floor of the Bullpen—screw shavings from the hull of the *Molly Hatchet*."

Quarles, who had been storing his briefcase under his seat, craned his neck to look up at her. "Screw shavings? Are you sure?"

"The molecular signature was unmistakable. I'm guessing it was a one millimeter drill bit, and the titanium shavings are a perfect match for the specs of the *Molly*."

That is interesting, Dechert thought. Nothing is ever screwed onto the hull of a mobile habitation unit—too much danger of stress fracture. Everything is plate-welded on. But if someone were going to stick a bomb on the side of a crawler, why not use bonding magnets? Were they worried they'd be detected by the sensors, or maybe that the magnets could be disabled by solar radiation or the Moon's fluctuating magnetic fields?

"Can you tell what part of the ship the shavings came from?"

"No. Only that they came from the outer hull."

"Did you check the maintenance logs? Have we ever screwed anything onto the outside of the *Hatchet*?"

"Of course not, and I did check the logs. No one's crazy enough to drill into the hull of a pressurized EVA craft after it's been commissioned. Even boy wonder over here isn't that strapped for brain cells."

For once, Quarles ignored the dig. "She's right. No way Thatch or Vernon or Cole would take a drill to the side of the *Hatchet*. Hell, maybe the shavings came from inside the ship somewhere, from drilling a hard-point onto the interior side panels or something."

Lane shook her hand. "I told you, I checked the molecular signature. Radiation, ionization. Everything. The shavings came from the *outer* hull of the *Molly Hatchet*."

Nobody spoke. Dechert looked out at the Menelaus Road again; Thatch and Waters were almost done now. Just a few more sweeps of the plow and the road would be ready for the descent.

"All right. So what do we have on recent visitors to Serenity? Last resupply, for example?"

"That's also interesting," Lane said. "The last shuttle run

from Peary Crater was forty-two days ago, more than a month before the explosion. It was a one-man resupply, which isn't unheard of, but it isn't standard protocol. I dug up the logs. An Ensign Kale Foerrster flew the mission; he stayed here for a quick hot-bunk and went back to Peary Crater twelve hours later."

Dechert nodded. Crews that made the thousand-kilometer run from Peary to Serenity 1 were required to take a nap before the return leg. Twelve hours was a bit of a long stay, but not unheard of. Dechert vaguely remembered the resupply. It had been a routine mission, nothing unusual to recall, and he never ran into Foerrster while he was on-station.

"One other thing," Lane said. "I got access to the current Peary Crater manifest. Ensign Foerrster is no longer on the Moon. He was here for only three months, and then he was reassigned to LEO-1. And his flight to Serenity forty-two days ago was his only long-hop run while he was up here."

"That's right," Quarles said. "I remember it. I was pissed Cverko wasn't doing that run."

He didn't have to elaborate that Cverko was the biggest black-market smuggler on the Moon, a pack rat who would barter anything from a lobster tail to a quart of homemade vodka, and get the better of his own mother in the deal if he got the chance. Dechert recalled thinking at the time that his crew would be most upset to hear that their sideways supplier of contraband wasn't coming to the station with his monthly treats.

"I met Foerrster when he got out of quarantine," Quarles added. "He seemed normal enough. Liked the Stones, if I recall."

Dechert didn't care about his musical taste, though. *Twelve hours on the station*, he thought. Enough time to slip into a pressure suit, sneak into the Bullpen, and drill a bomb onto the side of the *Molly Hatchet*, which just happened to be off-regolith at the time. One hell of a risky maneuver with six other souls on the station, but maybe it could be done.

"Is there any way Foerrster could have made an EVA into the Bullpen without any of us knowing about it?"

Lane shook her head, her lower lip bitten between teeth again. "I've run through it a dozen times. It wouldn't have been easy. Whoever was on duty in the CORE would have seen the pressure door open, unless Foerrster disarmed the sensors somehow. He would have had to rig the tunnel cameras and the quarantine alarm as well. Vernon was on duty for the first half of Foerrster's stay; I was on for the second half. Neither of us would have missed any of those alerts."

Dechert looked at Lane and Quarles, but neither of them spoke. A possible scenario had taken shape inside of all their heads for the first time, a scenario for what had killed their friend. It felt cold with age and implausible, but real nonetheless. Dechert bored his mind for alternate possibilities but found none. There's just no way a man in an EVA suit could sneak up to a mobile habitation unit out on the lunar surface and strap a bomb onto its belly while two crew members were inside or nearby working the mines. That theory never made sense. This one, unlikely as it may sound, did, but he still couldn't wrap his head around the idea of Foerrster accessing a depressurized part of the station without being noticed. Of course, there was another possibility: What if Lane or Waters were lying about what they did or didn't see while on duty that day? Dechert didn't even want to think about that possibility, but it couldn't be eliminated. *I'm missing something*, he thought.

"Well, can anyone think of a more likely solution?" Dechert finally asked, deciding for now to focus on the theory that

Foerrster had somehow pulled off the improbable. "This is a pretty big leap we're taking."

They looked at one another and shook their heads.

"Okay. It sure as hell isn't conclusive, but maybe I can take the screw shavings to Standard, or better yet to Hale." He picked up his helmet and popped the seals open. "Lane, get me your forensics data when we get back to the station. But not a word to anyone about the safe house video. There's no way to explain how it got into our hands. We'll rely on the evidence we collected ourselves. And I'll try to find a way to get my hands on the full employment dossier of Ensign Foerrster."

Quarles fumbled with his own helmet as they turned back to their stations and looked out at the Menelaus Road, each automatically going through their silent checklist for the final run to Hawking's Rim as they watched Thatch run the rover over the washout to smooth out the passage.

"You think it'll be enough to convince them that something crazy is going on?" Quarles asked.

Lane and Dechert stole a look at each other, and Dechert snapped his helmet onto his head, the seals reassuringly locking into place.

"I doubt it."

17

"So, are you prepared to cross the Rubicon?"

Dechert asked the question as Hale came in through the quarantine hatch from the hangar. The captain had just given the final prep to his Air & Space Marines and watched them buckle into their seats in the long-hop shuttle, which was retrofitted with missiles, EMP shielding domes, and redundant thrusters. It now had the look of an angry wasp. And it was definitely just as capable of delivering a sting—but also could easily be swatted out of the sky.

Hale's face was luminous with tension. He tried to smile. Dechert felt compassion for him and a nagging sense of envy at the same time; he remembered the soberness of sending men into dangerous places, but he also recalled the rush it provided.

"Unlike Caesar, I plan to make a quiet entrance," Hale said. "Hopefully they'll be shadows in the night."

Dechert nodded and they turned to walk back toward the CORE. "Maybe our Chinese friends are just digging for ilmenite up there in the hills."

Neither of them spoke for a few moments as they digested the unlikeliness of that scenario. They walked side by side down the narrow corridor, listening to the heating fluid flowing through the pipes around them and feeling the harmonic throb of the fusion reactor as its distributed energy came up through the flooring and into their legs. The living pulse of the station felt good, and Dechert hated what he was about to do; Hale had a mission to run that would put his men in harm's way, and he was wrapped up in it like an artist in the throes of creation. He didn't need to be distracted with the conspiracy theories of a Level-1 mining chief. Dechert was a former soldier and maybe Hale would respect that, but he wouldn't appreciate the intrusion into his focus on the task ahead. Especially now, when the mission was an electric current running through his head.

But what choice do I have?

"Captain, look, I know this is the wrong time, but we need to talk," Dechert said.

Hale glanced at him, surprised, but still only half aware of his presence. "What's on your mind?"

"I think I've got evidence that the Chinese weren't responsible for the sabotage of the *Molly Hatchet*."

Hale's pace slowed, just for a moment. He drew his lips back into his mouth and his jaws clenched and unclenched but then he continued walking, as if moving forward would help him escape the consideration of Dechert's words.

"Evidence?"

"Circumstantial, maybe, but it suggests that someone screwed something to the *Molly Hatchet*'s hull while she was sitting out in the Bullpen—our cold-soak hangar—more than a month ago." He paused. "I think it might have been the bomb."

A vein in Hale's temple pulsed and his voice grew quiet.

"What makes you think that?"

"Because you don't drill into the outer hull of a pressurized spacecraft. Ever. It's about as smart as opening a window on a submarine. Nobody on my crew would do that, for any reason."

"And?"

"And an ensign from Peary Crater apparently had the opportunity to do it on the last resupply that came in to Serenity, an ensign who left the Moon three days after he came here."

Hale continued to walk toward the CORE, but he wouldn't look at Dechert. He spoke almost in a whisper, his lips barely moving, his eyes lidded almost shut. "Are you telling me an American blew up your crawler, Dechert? Is that what you're telling me?"

They were close to the inner station hatch now, just thirty seconds or so from the command center, and Dechert knew that once he got into the CORE, Hale would think of nothing other than his crew skimming a shuttle through lunar canyons in blackout conditions, with Chinese commandos lurking nearby. He took the chance and grabbed Hale's arm to stop him, turning him around until they faced each other.

"Yes," he said. "Look, off the record, I found out this ensign used to work for the Office of Environmental Analysis. You remember those guys? Half spooks, half assassins. They ran so much crazy shit during the height of the Max that the president had to shut them down. And this ensign flew only one mission on the Moon. Think about that—an SMA pilot who used to be a special operator, who showed up here on a resupply, and then bolted back to Earth? And it's been suggested to me that the polymeric nitrogen used in the bomb was stolen from a Chinese safe house back in '66. I don't know who the hell stole it, but I think Standard's claim that the Chinese were the last ones with their hands on the stuff might be wrong."

The two stared at each other for several seconds and Hale glanced down for the briefest of moments at Dechert's hand on his arm, as if it were a piece of dust that might blow away if he didn't bother with it. His gray eyes didn't blink, but the lids continued to narrow into even tighter slits.

"Do you know how many times you said the word 'might' in the last thirty seconds, Commander? You're bringing this . . . this *story* to me right now, and you expect me to do what with it, exactly?"

"Tell Standard to request a delay of the mission. He's SMA Commissioner; he can go to Trayborr."

Dechert thought Hale might punch him in the mouth; he thought he might laugh out loud. But he remained stock-still. "Why don't you?"

"He won't believe me. He's incapable of believing anything other than Administration gospel. I could bring it up the chain of command, maybe to Yates, but he won't do anything unless I've got a signed confession. Right now you're the only one who can delay the recon, or at least convince Standard that the case against the Chinese has holes in it. Just let me show you what I . . ."

But Hale was already shaking his head and looking down at his watch, his body wrapped in cords of tension. "Dechert, you know that's not going to happen, and I can't believe you would bother to ask. I've got orders from a four-star to begin a recon of the Apennine Mountains in exactly sixty minutes, and his orders came directly from Cheyenne Mountain. If you have actionable intelligence," he paused and stuck two fingers into Dechert's chest, hard enough so that it stung, "*action-able* intelligence—then I'll send it up the chain of command.

Screw shavings from the floor of your hangar and hearsay from one of your Chinese friends in the Mare Imbrium doesn't fit that profile. The OEA guy is interesting, but it sure as hell isn't enough to call off a mission that just may save our asses from a missile strike."

Hale was right and they both knew it, and Dechert was surprised that the marine hadn't knocked him unconscious or walked right past him without listening. This wasn't Hale's problem. He had four thousand problems right now, but this wasn't one of them. And yet, even then . . .

"I know, look, I know. But you get how this will go down. If something happens out there in the badlands today, the whole damned thing will spin out of control. And it won't turn back."

He locked eyes with Hale one last time; the two of them only inches apart in the narrow accessway. "We don't know the truth, Captain. We don't know why this is happening."

"Really? I know why it's happening, Commander. It's happening for the oldest reasons there are. But when were we put in charge of assessing reasons?"

Dechert didn't know what else to say. "Maybe now is the perfect time to start assessing the reasons. When was the last time the people in charge got it right?"

But the conviction had left his voice. *There is a moment*, he thought, *when all soldiers forget about the underlying reasons for war and just take the damned job*. And Hale was past that moment.

The captain smiled from one side of his mouth and put his hand on Dechert's shoulder in a strong grip. "You're absolutely right, Dechert, but I've got my orders." He turned and started walking, and spoke again without looking back. "Do you recall those words?"

"What words?"

"'I've got my orders'? That's you talking, Commander.

That's you talking not so many years ago, as a captain in the Bekaa Valley, when you were given a mission that you knew was an absolute clusterfuck and you still took it."

"I didn't always take the mission," Dechert said to Hale's back. "And sometimes I was wrong when I did."

Hale popped the hatch open and waited for the sound of escaping gas to move beyond them down the tunnel. "Allow me the same mistakes of youth," he said, and disappeared through the entrance.

The shuttle flew on the deck, lights out, and low enough to kick up a line of leaden dust in its wake as it skimmed across the Sea of Serenity with the velocity of a rifle shot. The view from its nose cone filled the large quantum-dot display screen in the CORE, showing an eerie landscape of infrared green, passing by at speed. They watched from their chairs in the command center as the craft flew over the eastern rim of Crater Sulpicius Gallus, all of them except Waters, who was on the flying deck in the hangar in case a rescue mission had to be launched.

"Specter, Home 1 actual. Initiate Ballgame in one-zero seconds," Hale said into the comlink.

"Roger, Home 1 actual, heading three-three-seven degrees on my mark, dropping to one hundred meters."

Lieutenant Cabrera's voice projected calm even through the magnetic distortion of the signal. A few seconds later, she called her mark and the craft banked, heading north-northwest over the Serenity basin and descending even lower to the surface of the Moon. Cabrera found a deep lunar rille, and when she dropped into it, Dechert saw Lane wince. The canyon was steep walled and uneven, and from their vantage in the CORE, it looked as wide as an air-conditioning duct, but Cabrera flew with a light stick, weaving the craft with graceful nudges through the crumbling flutes of ancient lava and rock as she assessed its maneuverability. Dechert and Thatch looked at each other.

"The kid can fly," Thatch said.

"Yes she can," Hale replied from the center of the room, not looking over, his eyes fixed to the data that streamed into the bank of touchscreens and holo-displays on the operations console in front of him.

Dechert recalled the first time he had flown a high-maneuver profile on the Moon, through the Rima Hyginus just south of the Sea of Vapors. He had made the run in the simulator a hundred times and had practiced rapid banks and rolls on the Serenity plain, but nothing prepared him for that first drop into the chute, as lunar pilots call it when they fly into two-sided vertical terrain. As a marine aviator on Earth, Dechert had learned to muscle the stick of his fighter jet, heaving it back and forth and up and down to force his aircraft into high-g turns and ballistic climbs as the forces of gravity fought against him. But on the Moon flight controls had to be handled with a soft touch, like a stick of old dynamite ready to explode in your hands if you failed to treat it with respect. A bit too much pull to the left or the right, and the dozens of microthrusters affixed to all corners of the hull would have you into the canyon wall before you could call out a Mayday.

Flying in low gravity violates every human instinct to react with vigor when facing an imminent collision; you don't tiptoe out of the way of a truck that's bearing down on you. But that's the trick in one-sixth g—little inputs on the stick and rudder with the touch of a pianist. Dechert remembered when he had pulled out of that hundred-kilometer run through the Hyginus back in '67. He had wiped his wet palms on his thighs and put the shuttle on autopilot . . . and then he had thrown up into a gravity bag.

If Cabrera felt the same queasiness, she wasn't showing it. The additional plasma and HEDM thrusters Quarles had welded onto the shuttle's titanium skin and plugged into its fly-by-wire network had obviously added nimbleness, because the lieutenant darted the craft through the crumbling ravine in ways that even Waters wouldn't have tried.

As if to confirm Dechert's thoughts, Cabrera came on the com: "Home 1 actual, tell your propulsion guy he did well." There was an enjoyment in her voice, a pure pleasure in the flying that cut through the tension in the room. Quarles smiled, but kept his eyes on his screens.

"Roger that, Specter," Hale said. "Shake her out for a few more seconds then get back up on the basin. You're about four hundred and fifty klicks from leg two, ten minutes and counting."

"Roger, one-zero minutes to leg two."

Dechert looked around the CORE as the com popped and hissed and retreated into the background, a whisper of static. In ten minutes the shuttle would begin its run into the Montes Apenninus. For the first time in the history of the Moon two groups of people would be staked out across an unmarked boundary, looking for each other through the sights of a gun. Maybe the Chinese crewmen weren't even armed; maybe they didn't have radar domes set up to watch the northern approaches of Crater Conon, no missile launchers seeking an electromagnetic warble to lock onto. But maybe they did. Dechert cursed his decision to wait until after the mission to confront Yates with the evidence they had found. Knowing Yates, it wouldn't have done any good, but at least he could have tried.

He sat back in his chair in the half-light, watching the

blinking consoles splash the gunmetal walls of the CORE with diffuse blotches of red and green, yellow and blue. The room had an air of grim, professional morbidity. The focus on the protocol of their jobs kept each of them from thinking about the consequences of what might happen out on the lunar surface. Dechert and Standard were the only two in the CORE without a mission-critical duty. This was Hale's operation and he was utilizing Quarles, Lane, and Thatch as his own. Each one's head was frozen in place before a monitor, only occasionally glancing up at the thermal image of the shuttle thundering across the left flank of the Serenity basin.

Standard kept his focus on the main monitor, engrossed by the nose-cone video being fed in real time back to Serenity 1 and by the altitude and velocity numbers that scrolled like a stock ticker along the bottom of the screen. His dark eyes were alight with energy, and his body looked as if it wanted to twitch every muscle. He sat up in his seat, his hands gripping the armrests, and it occurred to Dechert that he had never seen the commissioner so alive.

What is it about the potential for battle, Dechert wondered, *that so enraptures people who have never taken part in it?* He plumbed the depths of his memory to see if he'd felt that same flare of excitement at the first sniff of war before he had become a marine, and the image that unexpectedly came to mind was of the snowball battles he used to have with his friends back in Maryland when they were children, after the first winter storms had blown in from the Allegheny Mountains. Ironhorse Lane against Five Logs Way, with two teams of kids spread out in equal numbers. It was a game of Capture the Flag with hardpacked slush balls as weapons, running all morning and afternoon and into the dusk until their mothers called them home for dinner. He recalled that surge of excitement, that sense that something important was about to happen as he pulled on his snow boots and picked a pair of climate gloves that weren't too thick to impede his ability to throw. Death wasn't a danger or even a distant thought in those days, but there was a recognition that a conflict was about to take place, and to their young minds, the results of that conflict meant everything.

Had it been any different years later when he went into actual combat? He had learned to transfer that same surge of adrenaline into pure awareness, to be at the polestar of mental focus as bullets flew by with ballistic cracks and rockets tore up the bricks around him. And wasn't it that same rush, that same feeling of being alive and engaged, that had stayed with him even after the first man went down? As he looked at the nervous energy pouring from Standard's body, Dechert knew exactly what the young commissioner was feeling. *We are war-lovers,* he thought. *It's written in the code that runs through our systems. Nobody remembers Gaia, the goddess of the Earth. But who forgets Mars, the god of war?*

"Are you sure our communications can't be picked up?" Standard asked into the silence. His voice sounded too high in the stadium-seated room, and it gave Dechert a start.

Hale barely looked up from the operations table. "Unlikely."

Standard knew not to ask Hale for clarification, so he looked to Dechert, who tried to ignore him as he pulled back from his memories and returned his focus to the screen in the middle of the CORE. But Standard continued to stare, and Dechert finally leaned over and said, "They're using multidirectional maskers and voice-and-data dampers. If the Chinese pick anything up, it'll sound like background noise from the rest of the communications bouncing around the Moon at any given moment. It won't have any structure for them to decrypt."

"Of course," said Standard. "Thank you, Commander."

The shuttle skimmed over a featureless and constant terrain; Dechert couldn't see anything he recognized. The Sea of Serenity is a caldera almost seven hundred kilometers wide, and within its annular borders are great stretches of volcanic cinder unmarred by craters and the brilliant white filaments of their ejecta. But Dechert somehow sensed that the marines were getting close to their first objective, the left turn toward Mons Hadley and the Apennine Mountains. After that, they would be following the profile Thatch had navigated for them down to the northern rim of Crater Conon. Dechert looked over at his EVA specialist and saw that he was sweating. Thatch had lobbied hard to be a part of the reconnaissance mission. He had been agitating for action ever since Cole's death, and maybe being out there with the marines would have been a catharsis for him, but Hale had refused to allow any nonmilitary personnel on the mission. Thatch's wide body barely fit into the microsuede chair he was sitting in, and his unkempt curls of brown hair hung down to his eyebrows as he squirmed—a caged bear in a tiny room, wanting to be let loose.

"One hundred klicks and they're in the pipe," he murmured, his eyes darting over to Dechert.

Dechert nodded and looked away. He swiveled his chair to the left, toward Lane, and watched as she ran threat variables through the Quantum. She sat with a straight lower spine, leaning forward in her chair. So small, but she was the largest person in the room. Standard had shrunk when Lane chastised him in the mess hall a few days ago, as though he had been scolded by a general. Thatch followed her orders without complaint, even if he disagreed with them, and even Hale gave her a wide berth, wise enough perhaps to know when to avoid conflicts that couldn't be won. She was a woman on a man's Moon, outnumbered fifty to one, but that was never a consideration for Lane. People were either weak or strong in her reckoning—which coincided well with the Moon's own reckoning, he supposed—and somewhere deep within herself, below any insecurities she might have, Lane *knew* she was strong. It projected out of her in unexplainable ways.

Her approach to the job was simple, similar to his own: You do your job, I do my job, and everything else is just noise up here. Even Waters, a man Dechert trusted as much as anyone, didn't always seem to grasp that. Lane, of all of them, knew that respect and competence were all that mattered on the Moon. Maybe it was because she had fought her entire career to remind others of her worth. Either way, she could rest assured that if Dechert was looking at her, the only thing she saw in his eyes was respect.

He couldn't imagine Lane working for a boss who *didn't* give her that.

"All right people, one minute and counting to Ballgame," Hale said. "Let's go through our checks."

"Propulsion is looking good," Quarles said.

"Passive radar is active and forward-scanning," Lane said. "Countermeasures online."

"They're in the socket for leg two," said Thatch. "Change of heading, two-zero-four degrees in fifty-one seconds on pilot's mark."

Hale nodded. "Specter? Do you concur?"

"Um, roger that, Home 1," Cabrera said over the com a few seconds later. "All systems nominal, initiating Ballgame on my mark."

Dechert switched his headset to a discrete channel and spoke in a low voice to Waters down on the flying deck. "Vernon, this is Dechert—are we prepped for SAR launch?"

"Roger, Commander. Shuttle Two warming up, three jet-suits on board, flight plan Beta-1 loaded into the system."

He nodded, said "Copy," and looked around the CORE to see if others had heard him. If they did, they didn't look up. It had been decided that Hale, Dechert, and Thatch would launch a rescue attempt if something went wrong on the mission, and Waters would take command of the station. Waters didn't like it, but Dechert knew he couldn't leave Thatch behind on yet another mission, and he needed Vernon and Lane at Serenity 1 in case things went completely off their axis. Quarles had rigged up the jetsuits per his instructions, sneaking them down into the Hole to avoid being noticed while he made a few mission-specific modifications. Antimissile arrays, lasers, and EMP shielding had been placed around the perimeter of the station by the marines; it bristled now like a Viking fortress on the dead surface of the Moon. Everything was ready, and Dechert prayed to God that none of it would have to be used. If he took any comfort, it was in the utter calm that filtered through Cabrera's voice as she radioed back to the station.

"Ballgame in three, two, one, mark."

The shuttle nosed down and dropped to the dust-top, banking left and continuing the turn until it had almost reversed its course.

"Slowing to 1300 knots, flying the wire on route Alpha-1," Cabrera said. "Hundred and forty klicks to Crater Aratus."

They could see the rocky flanks of the Montes Apenninus now, the thermal imaging revealing the large, mounded humps of the mountains as diffusions of green light in the background. The scarred bulk of Mons Hadley lay just ahead. Dechert wondered where in its shadows the abandoned rover and lander from Apollo 15 sat. Apollo. What had Armstrong declared when he first stepped on the Moon? One giant leap for mankind?

Now we're stepping backward, he thought.

"Looking good, Specter," Hale said, his voice clipped and short. Dechert looked around the room. They all hoped that it was true.

18

The alarm rang two minutes into their run through the mountains, and it sounded just as it had in Dechert's nightmares. Not the baritone chimes of Serenity's master alert. This one warbled, as if it couldn't put a finger on the danger it was trying to expose. It warbled again, and for a long, agonizing second, it was the only sound that anybody heard. Then the com exploded with chatter.

"Threat alert, Home 1. We're being painted," Cabrera said.

"Starboard side," said another voice on the shuttle.

"Confirmed," Lane said. "Fire-control radar. High PRF. Active infrared, high probability of detection."

Adrenaline poured into Dechert's veins, squeezing his chest. He looked at Hale, who locked and unlocked his jaw as he stood up over his console, gripping the sides of the tabletop until his knuckles went white.

"Go to active radar," Hale said. "Big bulge, wide-spectrum burst."

"Roger," Cabrera said, and they could hear her copilot amid the background static of the com, calling out numbers. The shuttle's sensors flared to active mode, firing out electromagnetic tendrils across the Montes Apenninus to find the source of the hostile radar. It didn't take long.

"Missile sites confirmed, mark one at two o'clock, bearing two-three-zero; mark two at two-thirty, bearing two-four-one. Confirmed high PRF."

Hale nodded. Only one country still used pulse-recurrence frequency in its surface-to-air missile targeting systems. The country that had warned them not to get too close to its territory on the Earth or the Moon. The People's Republic of China.

"Lock onto signal and go weapons hot," Hale said. "Change course to one-three-five degrees, increase EMP shielding to full, confirm."

"Roger, weapons hot. Changing course to one-three-five degrees, accelerating to two thousand knots. EMP to full."

Dechert and Thatch glanced at each other and then back at the main monitor. Hale was getting them out of there, ordering Cabrera to turn to port, away from the fire-control radars hammering the shuttle's hull. Cabrera banked left and skimmed into a broad, broken column of lunar foothills. It was a passive move, aimed to show the Chinese that she didn't intend to start a fight. But the shuttle was only 180 kilometers away from New Beijing 2, well within the range that Standard had said could prompt the Chinese to attack.

"You're pulling them out?" Standard asked. "Captain, I'm not sure you . . ."

Hale looked at Standard with a quick, menacing glare but

didn't take the time to say anything. The warbling alarm from the shuttle suddenly went shrill, like the flatline of a heart monitor. Then the forward-looking camera fuzzed over and the craft yawed violently to the right and rolled as if it had been punched, pitching the Moon's horizon over on its side on the display screen.

"Shit. EMP burst," someone on the shuttle yelled through a sea of static. "Focused EMP."

"Shit."

"Power spike," Cabrera said, still calm, working to correct the shuttle's lurch to the side. She rolled to the left, too far, and then back again, stabilizing the ship. "Mains are down, going for restart."

"Restart."

"Got 'em back."

Quarles looked over at Hale. "They took a full burst, Captain, at least fifty kV/m," he said. "Thrusters are up but spotty. I can't guarantee they'll stay online, and I don't think the EMP domes will absorb another hit."

"Go suborbital, Lieutenant," Hale said into the com, not waiting for any additional information. "Climb to thirty thousand meters and egress at one-one-zero degrees. Expedite." He turned to Dechert and Thatch, the look on his face asking for agreement as much as telling them what he was doing. "Getting some altitude in case the thrusters go. A SAR team can pick them up in orbit if they have to."

"Good," Dechert said, and Thatch nodded as well. If the shuttle's thrusters flamed out at low altitude because of the electrical burst, the marines would probably crash into the mountains. But if Cabrera could somehow get them into low orbit and away from the Apennines, it wouldn't matter if the engines shut down. A team from Low Lunar Orbit 1 or even Peary Crater could rescue them. Dechert watched the shuttle's altimeter numbers rise as they ran across the bottom of the screen, and he silently willed them higher.

But another alarm went off as Cabrera clawed for altitude. This one piped in a clear, universal language, loud enough to bring up everyone's head. Multiple, high-toned pips, a sound so shrill that the human ear had been trained to pay attention to it.

Missiles.

"SAM launch!" Lane shouted, and Cabrera acknowledged her a second later in a voice that somehow held its composure.

"Specter defending. Tracking two missiles, six o'clock low, range fifteen kilometers," she said. The young lieutenant didn't wait for orders from Hale this time. "Going to the deck, going to the deck."

She pitched the shuttle over and shot back down to the Moon's surface, increasing power and bolting into a broad valley, the craft rocketing downward like a bird with its wings tucked in. Dechert felt the nausea in the pit of his stomach climb into his throat as he watched them descend. No pilot liked to go to ground when suffering a power spike, but Cabrera had no choice. It would have been suicidal to stay at altitude with SAMs boring in on them. Dechert remembered what his air wing commander had once told him about flying against missiles that were locked on to you: "Hug the Earth like she's your mother, because your daddy's the air, and he ain't gonna help you."

"Missiles now at five o'clock low, range six kilometers, speed twenty-four hundred meters per second," Lane said.

"They're EM-guided," Cabrera said. "Maybe HQ-40s."

"Go weapons free," Hale said, and his voice held a controlled fury as he pulled an old-fashioned stopwatch out of his pocket and clicked on it. "Launch countermeasures and fire back down the threat points."

"You're locked onto ground targets one and two, weapons free," Lane said.

"Roger, Home 1," said Cabrera. "Weapons free, missiles locked. Fox three. Fox three."

"Launching antimissile spread," said another voice on the shuttle. Dechert assumed it was the copilot. He sounded more nervous than Cabrera.

They could see the bright flashes of light on the nose-cone camera as the shuttle fired two missiles toward the Chinese launch sites and dropped an antiballistic cluster, which began tracking the incoming missiles so it could launch its own spread of miniature, bullet-size smart rockets. The miniature rockets were supposed to enclose over the missiles like folding umbrellas in an effort to detonate them short of their target, but the Chinese missiles also were smart, able to detect and avoid the little buzz bombs and remain focused on their quarry. It then became a contest of whose programming was stronger.

Numbers ran through Dechert's mind in a runaway jumble—missiles at 4700 knots, shuttle at no more than 2600 knots—a little more than five kilometers and closing. How much time did that give them? Five seconds? Maybe less?

The shuttle descended to the Moon's surface with the nose pitched down at a severe angle, and it looked for a sickening moment like the speeding craft was going to slam into the surface. Cabrera pulled up just as the nose camera filled up with Moon.

"Jesus," Thatch said, "I can't even read how low she is."

Hale looked over at him, his face enflamed with the warning lights blinking in the room. "She's trying to throw off the missiles with moondust," he said, and everyone in the room understood. Dechert closed his eyes and imagined the picture: the shuttle at no more than twenty meters above the ground, flying faster than a sniper's bullet and spitting up in its wake the ankle-deep, microfine regolith that had formed at the foothills of the Montes Apenninus over millions of years. It would be like flying a Galaxy-class cargo plane over a sandy beach in Florida, at full power. Maybe the tons of rock and moondust being spit up in the shuttle's wake would throw off the missiles, or at least confuse them enough to let the countermeasures bore in and destroy them.

And it was working. Cabrera pulled the ship hard to the right and the threat tone still piping through the com seemed to lose some of its potency, as if the projectiles closing in on the shuttle had become less certain of their intentions.

"Firing secondary countermeasures," Cabrera said, and the camera fuzzed over white again as chaff flared out of the shuttle's belly and exploded behind the craft.

"I'm reading hits on ground targets one and two," someone in the back of the shuttle said into the com. "Confirm, Home 1. We have no visual."

"Roger that, Specter," Lane said. "Confirmed hits on targets one and two. Tracking remained strong right up to detonation."

Standard banged his open hand on the console in front of him and whispered something between his teeth. Hale and Dechert stole a quick look at each other; regardless of what happened to the marines in the next few seconds, blood had been drawn on the Moon. Several Chinese commandos had surely died at the end of those radar-guided, five-hundred-pound projectiles.

The room went silent. Everyone looked up, wondering what was missing. It took them a full second to realize that the threat radar on the shuttle was no longer whining.

"Home 1, Specter," Cabrera said. "Incoming missiles have lost lock. Maintaining speed and course at two-seven-five."

Was it over? The adrenaline thudding through Dechert's temples and pouring heat into his ears left a ringing echo in his head. He looked up and saw everyone in the room frozen, not yet exhaling. After a few seconds, Thatch rubbed his hand through his curly mop of wet hair. Lane's spine lost some of its straight precision, and Dechert could hear Quarles mumble "Jesus Christ" into his chest. Other than Dechert and Hale, none of them had ever been in combat before or even seen it from afar in real time. They all looked pale and sick with relief.

Then the alarm came back. A quick, persistent beeping, repeating much faster this time. Dechert's head snapped up. *What the hell?*

"Specter defending!" For the first time in the mission, Cabrera's voice was too loud.

"Snapshot," her copilot yelled. "Three thousand meters and closing."

Three thousand meters? How the hell could that be? Dechert looked over and saw the blackness in Hale's eyes, his pupils blown open, as it became clear to both of them at the same time: The shuttle had been drawn into an ambush. A kill-box set up by the Chinese.

"Banking right," someone on the shuttle said. "Launch . . ."

The missile detonated behind them a second later, its explosive charge pushing the shuttle forward in space as if it had been swatted by a bat. The craft's rear end yawed to the left, and now the alerts and sirens filtering into the CORE droned together in a continuous, discordant symphony. Cabrera tried to right the sideways lurch. Too far. The ship spun counterclockwise. Slowly at first and then faster. The horizon blurred on the viewscreen as the shuttle began to spin out of control.

"Starboard and aft thrusters down," Cabrera said over the panic of electronic noise. "Go for restart."

"Restart. No fire."

"Try again."

"Restart. Negative on restart."

"All thrusters down."

Quarles looked over at Hale and spoke in a quiet, measured tone. "Mains and secondaries are off-line, Captain. Everything's down. I think we should . . ."

But Dechert didn't hear the rest, because it didn't matter. He looked around the CORE, which had spun into slow motion like the shuttle out on the Serenity basin. He could see Standard trying to make sense of the picture being beamed back to their monitor. He had never witnessed a spacecraft in a flat spin. His mind was trying to figure out how the camera had malfunctioned. Dechert almost yelled at him that if you fire enough missiles or EMPs at something, it's sure to fail, but held his tongue. The CORE felt silent even with the mass of beeping alarms. The lights blinked less often. The sounds distorted in Dechert's ears and then became artificially clear. Thatch clicking his teeth together. Quarles sucking in his breath. Hale, a statue, standing over his console, palms out on the gunmetal table, pulling his thumbs across the polished surface in a dull, desperate rasp.

"Flameout, Home 1 actual, I've got nothing," Cabrera said. Her voice was calm again, and she waited for a long second before she spoke her next words in the professional monotone of a pilot. "Mayday, Mayday, Mayday."

Hale remained still except for his thumbs, which were trying to punch through the tabletop. "Copy your Mayday, Specter."

The shuttle spun horizontally, nose to tail, a few hundred meters above the Moon's surface and slowly descending. Not high enough. In the blur of the infrared display, Dechert could see a low massif approaching in front of them. It inched closer with every spin until it began to fill the monitor. There was no way they could clear it. The alarms continued to drone.

"Mayday, Mayday, Mayday," Cabrera said again. "Angels below one. Terrain in front. Going in, seventeen-point-two degrees north, four-point-six east."

"We're tracking you, Specter," Hale said, and it was the calmness, the steadiness of his tone that cut through the transmission and reached his team on the Moon. "Launching SAR team to your location."

"Roger that, Home 1 actual," Cabrera replied. "Beacon lit."

It was all just talk. The picture on the viewscreen continued to spin, faster now. The alarms on the CORE's main console continued to pipe. Then the screen went black and all the noise stopped.

19

Dechert breathed in deep and felt the hot air expand his lungs. It was the air you inhale when you open the door of an oven to check what's cooking inside. Dry and roasting. The sky to the west flamed orange as dust rose over the desert. Beams of heat hit his face and then passed by, and looking up, Dechert saw that he was sitting under the fat fronds of a date palm, which moved in the shimmering heat and cast the ground below in parallel lines of daylight and shadow. A helicopter's rotors thwopped in the dead air somewhere nearby.

"Pocket cowboys. Kiss my left nut, Matchstick, you are the luckiest sonofabitch in the Bake."

They were sitting in the sand around a sawed-off oil barrel, playing poker as the day ground itself down and the

Muslim call to prayer echoed through the limestone jum-bles of the Bekaa Valley. Matchstick—the skinny kid from Scranton whose helmet bounced on his head like a paint can whenever he broke into a run. B-Dog—the machine gunner from Memphis who had "Recidivist Soul" tattooed across his back. Dawes—the pensive corporal who frowned with his eyes and never told anyone where he was from. Snook—the trailer-born Florida cracker who had been an expert at fishing the saltwater flats of Cockroach Bay long before he became an expert at killing men.

"It ain't luck, Snooky," Matchstick said, pulling a pile of spent cartridge shells toward his stack. "It's called playing tight-aggressive."

"Shit. The boy thinks he's Johnny Chan Jr."

The afternoon slipped away grudgingly, as it always did in the desert. Billows of heat created distant rivers in the air as the sand began to cool. Helicopters buzzed in and out of the base, the great insects of war. Artillery fire thundered along the river basin. The *thunk* of mortar rounds echoed now and again as they came into the wire. Indirect fire, they called it. There was nothing indirect about it when a round landed close enough to rattle your teeth.

The day had gone well; the week, badly. Two mornings ago, they had lost Jimenez, the radioman from Texas whom everyone called Habanero because he ate hot peppers by the dozen. He could squirt the damned things into his eyes, and occasionally did, when some poor bastard from D Company laid down a big enough bet. Nobody thought Habs would ever die. Not a guy who could pour juice from the hottest natural substance on the planet over his baby browns like it was so much eyewash. Not a guy who had never looked scared, even when the fire was coming in fast and heavy. His death had hit the squad hard—had hit Dechert hard—and nobody had said a word about it since they lined up his boots in the makeshift boneyard behind the mess hall.

But this was when they thought about death. Right about now, when there was no ambush scheduled for the coming night and no ingress to plan over a map table in a stifling tent, and they could sit in the dirt and play poker and let the adrenaline settle in their veins like blood pooling at the bottom of a corpse.

"You keepin' count, Snook?" B-Dog drawled. "Your ass has gotta be two grand in the hole this week."

"Fuck you. My dead ass'll pay its markers before your live one ever will."

That got a chuckle, even from Dechert. B-Dog did anything to avoid paying cash on a poker debt. He'd trade his last plug of chewing tobacco, his precious virtual porn minutes, or even the twice-distilled white lightning he brewed in an arms depot at the far end of the firebase. He'd even take another grunt's foot patrol if the debt was large enough, and word got around quickly through the brigade that B-Dog found paying a bet much more difficult than losing one.

"Yeah, well your dead ass may have to if we go back into Aanjar tomorrow," B-Dog said, and the laughter dissolved. No one spoke at the mention of Aanjar. The name itself held sinister energy. The Muslim call to prayer had died away on the glowing air, and a rare eastern breeze came in off the Litani River. It carried the smell of burning oil and rotting fruit with it.

"Yeah, boss," Matchstick said, the enjoyment drained from his voice. "When they gonna bring some real armor in here, maybe even a hover-tank or two? Humpin' through that Haji-ville without any tin cans behind us is getting old."

"Maybe they'll do it the tenth time I ask," Dechert replied. He flicked away a camel spider with the tip of his boot and took a sip of warm water from his canteen. They had lost fourteen men in Aanjar in the last month, most of them to homemade rattler mines. Even the children in that mud-bricked town looked dangerous. A year ago, the U.S. government had talked about winning hearts and minds in the Bekaa Valley. A week ago, when a reporter asked a corporal on his third tour whether the "hearts and minds" campaign was still operative, he had replied, "Yeah, but now it's two in the heart and one in the mind."

The corporal caught hell from Political Reengineering, but he got free cigarettes for a week from every marine in the company when his quote was picked up by the stream.

"If I gotta get it in Aanjar, I'll take it like Habs," B-Dog said. "One round in the thumper. Through and through, nice and clean."

"Yeah, that goddamn Mexican was dead falling down."

Matchstick shuffled the deck, his pupils fixed on the cards. "Not me, man. I'll take mine between the eyes. High velocity round, nonexplosive tip. Then you don't even hear the shot before the whole damn game shuts off."

Snook spat a small fleck of leaf tobacco through the gap in his front teeth and wiped his face with the back of his sleeve. "Are you shitting me? You don't even want a second to know you've bought it?"

"A second for what?"

"I don't know. Repent of your sins, whatever the hell."

Matchstick snorted. "Jesus, Snooky, you'd need a lot longer to do that."

Dechert smiled again as the rest of them laughed. *This was the low-desert version of catharsis,* he thought. Figuring out how you wanted to die in some godforsaken, sandblasted guerrilla hamlet while playing poker behind a latrine. But even in the closeness of the death cult, he felt detached from the rest of them, almost wishing that he'd be the next casualty or at least that he'd catch some kind of evacuating wound before his tour was up. Then he wouldn't be abandoning them.

The platoon didn't know it yet, but Dechert would be rotating out in less than three months. His second tour was done, and he had asked to be transferred to the Air Corps. They needed pilots, and he had flown the Alaska hop before the war, and the logistics boys figured that was good enough. The air is arctic at forty thousand feet, which suited Dechert just fine. He was done with the desert. Done with the heat and the spiders and the political reengineering bullshit—done with thinking that his tactical skills could keep his men alive in a place where everyone hated everyone else and no one stayed alive for long. Dechert looked over the oil can at his troopers, at their dirty faces in the gloaming, and had a strong premonition that all of them would be gone before the war was over. They'd all be dead or too fucked up to know otherwise, and he'd be alive. That was the sick kind of luck that he had.

"What about you, Dawes?" B-Dog asked. "When it's your time, you gonna go as quietly as you've walked the Earth?"

Dawes looked up from his hole cards as if startled from deep thought. "Huh?" He gave his best impression of a smile as the rest of them laughed and he continued to digest the question, a single eye open and the other half squinted at his cards.

"I guess it all depends on how I go."

A marine could only nod at logic like that. Every infantryman in the Bake wanted to take a round through and through if they had to die. Something clean, so their parents could put them in an open casket and know that their little boy or girl was going into the ground intact and ready for corporeal resurrection when the trumpets blared. No one wanted to get hit by a bomb or a seeker slug or, even worse, a sonic charge, which ripped you apart from the inside and left you collapsed like a suit of skin. Some deaths were too gruesome to consider. At least a clean kill provided an acceptable ticket to the theme park in the sky that the chaplain kept telling them about.

"Commander, are you ready? Commander?"

Dechert looked up. Lane was standing over him, a slim, blurred figure in a dark blue heavysuit. He came back to the room and saw that he was sitting in front of an equipment locker near the main hangar, and that he had one boot locked down and sealed onto the padded leg of his pressure suit. The other remained on the changing table, its clamps extended.

"Yeah. Yes. How much time?"

"Two minutes until takeoff. Are you okay?"

He nodded and grabbed the other hard-shelled boot and began to cram his foot into it.

"Yes, I'm fine. How are we looking?"

She got down on one knee and grabbed the bottom of the boot, helping to push his heel into the tight opening. "Thatch and Hale are in prelaunch. Vernon's working on a flight plan. I think it's to drop into Crater Yangel', and then you take the jetsuits from there. Hopefully their radar can't track a hopping astronaut. The shuttle's last coordinates were about fourteen kilometers north of the crater, in the Lacus Felicitatis."

The shuttle's last coordinates. Lane didn't want to say "crash site." She kept her eyes down as she locked the seals on his footgear. Dechert thought of his snap daydream from a moment ago—how vivid it had been. He had smelled the Bekaa Valley, that unctuous mix of sewage, roasting meat, and decaying fruit. *How much our memories are meshed to smell*, he thought, and he wondered how that fact would affect his future recollection of their time on the Moon. The things you smelled the most up here were gunpowder out on the regolith and the hydraulic grease that kept everything lubricated on the inside of the station.

And then, of course, there was Lane. She didn't wear perfume but she smelled like the lavender his mother used to keep on the kitchen windowsill. Better than Quarles's weed-infused clothes and Thatch's . . . well, Thatch pretty much stank. Still, if he could remember those human essences from his time on the Moon, it would be better than the stench of cordite and machine oil.

"Does Jonathan have the jetsuits rigged for direct video feed?"

"Yes, we can look at each other as we witness the end of all things on the Moon."

Dechert stood up and stomped his feet, pushing his toes toward the front of the boots. He caught Lane's eyes and held her gaze.

"Listen, I want you bugging out at the first sign of trouble. You hear me? No heroic bullshit if an alarm goes off, just trigger the AMD and get the hell out of here. And I want everybody in pressure suits, as soon as you get us launched."

"What about you? I'm trying my best not to fall off the edge here, but if you and Thatch don't come back, I can't make any promises."

"We'll be fine."

Lane grabbed his helmet and they walked together toward the hangar hatch. They were silent, even though they should have been talking about contingency plans, message encrypting, SAR operations, jetsuit configurations . . . something.

Dechert stopped and put his hand on Lane's shoulder. He didn't have his gloves on yet and she felt solid but small under his fingers as he squeezed. "I'm serious, Lane. I'm telling you to stay alive." He paused. "And please keep Quarles and Vernon in a similar condition."

She looked at him and flashed a meager smile, one side of her mouth turning up slightly and the other descending. "Finally an order I can take without complaint." Her anger at Dechert seemed washed away as she turned her eyes from his face. "I'm heading up to the CORE. I'll be monitoring you from there."

"Okay."

Dechert pulled the hatch open and put a foot inside the circular opening. "Lane?"

She turned around. "Yes?"

"I thought you should know. Nietzsche was wrong. God isn't dead."

"He isn't?"

"No. He just has shitty representation back on Earth."

She smiled, enough this time so that a few of her teeth flashed white. "So that's it. Just in case you're right, I'll be praying for you."

20

They talked in pilot-speak because there was little else to say. Being encapsulated in their pressure suits and helmets heightened the sense of isolation within the tiny shuttle cockpit. Three men alone in the same cramped space, taking brief moments to call out technical bits of information.

"Turning to two-nine-five."

"Turning two-nine-five."

"Eighteen hundred knots, altitude five hundred meters."

"Okay, let's keep it there."

"Negative feedback on passive radars."

"Keep an eye on them and I'll watch for EM spikes."

"Okay."

The Moon slipped away under the shuttle, every kilometer

a blur of regret. *It had happened so fast,* Dechert thought, and he realized how much better it was to show up in the middle of a war than to be there at the beginning. Now that he was experiencing one this way, he could say without a doubt that the beginning is worse. He wanted to yell into his helmet, yell for them all to stop. To dial up Peary Crater and tell them the whole thing was a setup, that someone other than the Chinese had drilled a bomb onto the hull of the *Molly Hatchet.* That some other force had caused Cole to die alone in the vacuum. That the theft of the helium-3 casks and the crippling of the water mine at DS-7 were little more than political pranks. That an American strike on China's spiral mine in the Mare Imbrium could be apologized for. That all of it was a bunch of bullshit cooked up on Earth, by men who have their coffee brought to them while they draft papers in oak-paneled rooms for institutions connected at their roots to the Ivy Fucking League or some exclusive Chinese think tank. *Dulce bellum inexpertis,* Sheldon Starks had said. War is sweet to those with no experience of it.

That's about damned right.

But it was too late for that. There were four dead marines somewhere in the barrenlands of the suddenly poorly named Lake of Happiness, and nothing else mattered now. There was no way to unring the bell. Peary Crater was in crimson red war mode. Dechert could picture General Trayborr rallying his troops for the coming assault, telling them that he regretted what was to come even as he inhaled the intoxicant of war that every field commander privately indulges in. How can you despise the genesis of your profession?

And Commodore Yates, leaning back in his prefect's chair and watching the marshaling with eyes gleaming from under a pair of white-piled eyebrows. He might not have wanted things to degrade to the point where Peary Crater would be in jeopardy, but he sure as hell wasn't going to do anything to stop it now. He was the SMA's man and enough of a gambler to realize that going for the whole pot of gold was a value bet at this point. He might take some hits that would damage short-term productivity, but he could end up with half of the Moon if the battle went America's way.

All U.S. lunar stations had gone to DEFCON-1. Full war-time footing, expectation of an imminent attack. Someone up there at the North Pole was waiting for word to launch the big AI seeker missiles—the ones that would fly like sentient things, outsmarting their stupid antimissile cousins as they cruised toward New Beijing 1 on the opposite pole of the Moon with algorithmic precision. And somewhere in the Chinese main base someone was tickling their finger across a similar red button. Neither side was supposed to have a stockpile of the big cruise rockets on the Moon, but Dechert was certain that by now both of them did. Weapons-grade lasers still weren't powerful enough to take out an entire station. Missiles certainly were.

He pictured every coming event in his mind's eye with a soldier's clarity, as if it had already happened and he was reliving the whole thing in a dream. One side would decide that waiting was no longer a viable option and would target the other's Level-1 and Level-2 mining stations. If they went to full-scale war—if no shred of sanity seeped through on Earth—the low-hanging fruit would be the first to go. Sea of Tranquility 1. Eastern Sea 2. Sea of Serenity 1. New Beijing 2. A bunch of miners and astro-scientists would become small green icons in the midpoint of a radar screen, with fast-moving dots blinking toward them through narrowing sets of concentric circles.

Dechert wanted to close his eyes and keep them closed. In their rush to launch he had asked Yates once again to pull his crew off the station, to let them bug out to the impact ridges of Menelaus Crater. But Yates couldn't let mining stations be abandoned. There was $90 billion of SMA hardware scattered across the Moon's equatorial bulge, and an effort had to be made to protect it. Dechert took two deep, calming breaths. *What the hell was there to say?* And how the hell could he say anything to Hale after his men had just been killed by a Chinese missile? Yet, just as Hale had his obligations, Dechert had his own.

"Hale, maybe we should . . ."

Hale turned his helmet toward Dechert as soon as he spoke, and the look in the captain's eyes was empty and complete in its amorality. There was no right or wrong in the black of his pupils, no anger or sorrow. There was only a will to take the next action because that was what nature had intended.

"Never mind," Dechert said.

The entropy was complete. Dechert felt as though he were spinning around the rim of a black hole, being sucked toward the singularity. No force in the universe, maybe not even God himself, could resist the pull of so much gravity.

"One hundred eighty klicks from Crater Yangel'," Thatch said. "ETA five minutes."

Hale nodded and spoke, a man on autopilot. "Why don't you go in the back and work up your jetsuit, Thatcher? You can help us gear up when we land."

"Will do," Thatch said, looking at Dechert before unbuckling his harness and crawling into the rear of the cabin.

They flew the ship together in silence for several minutes, the thermal image on the windscreen casting a dark green glow to the cockpit. The eerie flatness of the Serenity basin gave way to a series of rounded bumps and ridges as they reached the outer approaches to the Apennine Mountains. Hale brought them lower to the lunar surface, dodging outcrops with light nudges on the controls.

"We're going for a quick in-and-out, Commander," he finally said. "Just a confirmation of the crash. No retrieval of bodies if there aren't any survivors. How long of a trip in the jetsuits will it be from Yangel' to the shuttle's beacon?"

"I figure four hops each way, maybe fifty minutes total EVA time." Dechert looked at him. "You understand there's very little . . . ?"

"Yes, I do."

"Okay."

"Two minutes to Yangel'."

"What do you think is going to happen?"

Hale breathed and the sound comforted Dechert. It was the first sign that the captain still retained some human qualities.

"Best guess is we'll launch on their substations soon after we get confirmation of the shuttle loss. Trayborr is pushing it right now."

"And they'll launch on us. Probably on Serenity."

"Good chance. I don't think either side will go after a main base yet. Too much risk of losing it all. But who knows? If a shooting war starts on Earth as well, all the gloves will come off."

So it would be Vernon, Lane, and Quarles in the crosshairs, with Standard tagging along for the death ride. Three miners and a bureaucrat manning antimissile defenses and electromagnetic pulse domes, hundreds of kilometers from any help. *God help them.*

"My people aren't soldiers, Hale."

"They're going to have to be."

Dechert shook his head, his jaw clenched. "No, the first whiff I get of a launch, they're bugging out. They can set the auto defenses, but I'll be damned if I'll leave them there to die."

"You make that call, Commander. It's not my station, and they're not my people. But you'll have to answer for it."

"I'm sure I will."

They could see Crater Yangel's blast wall now, a nine kilometer lip reaching up from the monolithic expanse of the lunar desert. Hale slowed the shuttle and pulled it up from the surface of the Moon, and Dechert felt his stomach lurch as the craft climbed over the looming cliffs and began its rapid drop into the crater's mouth.

"Thirty seconds," Dechert said.

"Roger that."

"I'm sorry about your men, Captain."

"Thank you. So am I."

The three men rocketed up from the Moon's surface in a staggered line, fifty meters apart. Dechert could feel the push of the high-energy thrusters on his back as they ascended from inside the crater rim, their helmet visors set to infrared so they could see one another in the darkness. The hop felt even more disorienting than his first jetsuit leap into Dionysius because of the blackout conditions. They couldn't risk lamps or beacons this close to the Chinese, and without them it was impossible to get any sense of spatial orientation.

Their visors provided an artificial grid view, like a scene in a virtual reality game, but the image wasn't real enough for Dechert to feel as if he were taking part in the scenario unfolding in front of his eyes. He had to trust the telemetry numbers and the false horizon on his heads-up display, never mind the feeling of extreme nausea that threatened to climb up from the back of his throat and take over the upper reaches of his brain. The positive g's made it feel like all of his organs were being pushed down into his pelvis, giving him an almost uncontrollable desire to squirm. He resisted because he learned from his flight in Dionysius to remain as motionless as possible, so the thrusters on his shoulders and backpack and boots would remain in sync. Dechert imagined being encased in the middle of a giant lake of tar as he looked around the artificial grid-world he was in, and he began to drum up other analogies to keep his mind off the nausea. A mosquito caught in black amber. A diver trapped in the inky midwater of the ocean, with bioluminescent creatures scattered like stars all around him . . .

"Is this going to start feeling normal?" Thatch asked, breaking the silence. His voice sounded a note higher than usual and he was breathing heavily. The intrusion of sudden noise into Dechert's helmet made him lurch inside his suit.

"No."

"Great. What happens if you puke in your helmet?"

"Don't." Dechert looked to his right and saw Hale, a glowing silhouette in the deep gray-green of the infrared and the amplified light of the surrounding stars. "How you doing, Captain?"

"I'm fine."

He hadn't really expected a different answer. "Okay. Two-zero seconds to apogee; two minutes, ten seconds to first hop."

"Remind me what to do when we get there," Thatch said between breaths.

"Take two steps like you're dunking a basketball and punch REENGAGE. It's fly-by-wire from there."

Neither of them answered. Maybe they were worried about talking this close to the Chinese, or maybe they were trying not to get sick. Dechert knew it was a bit of both for him. He waited a few seconds and then switched the com to a private channel, using blinks of his eyes to cue the retinal sensors that Quarles had installed in his EVA helmet. It was a modification that allowed him to control the walk-profile computer on his chestplate, which regulated everything from his propulsion systems to his communications, without moving his hands. He hoped that the rest of the modifications Quarles had made would work just as well.

"Lane, are you there?"

"Yes."

"Go secure."

Static popped on the line for a few seconds. "Secure."

"What's your status?"

"We're all in pressure suits, ready to bug out and waiting for orders. Radar screens are empty so far."

"Roger that. Patch in the video feed and get out of the CORE. Go down and do the same in the main hangar. If we have to go back to secure, find a reason to leave the room. I don't want Standard hearing anything he doesn't have to."

"Okay. How is it out there?"

"Dark."

They rose out of the crater to the Moon's surface and Dechert could see the gray silhouette of the Lake of Happiness before them. Its ancient lava flow ran through the Apennine Mountains like a river valley cutting between looming peaks. A blackened smear on the Moon in the full light of the sun, but in infrared it was a patch of absolute nothingness. Thatch had them locked onto the emergency beacon marking the spot where the shuttle had crashed. Hale made futile calls to his doomed team of marines every twenty seconds.

"Specter, search-and-rescue, actual. Specter, SAR."

Nothing came back but static, and after the fifth call, they all knew it was a search-and-rescue mission in name only.

"You sure the Chinese didn't pick up the shuttle's communications last time?" Thatch asked. "Maybe we should be quiet."

"They were sitting there waiting for them, Thatch," Dechert said, recalling his training on how to set up a kill-box and realizing that someone with serious military skills was now operating on the Chinese side of the mare. "And you heard Quarles in preflight. There's probably too much commo flying around the Moon right now for us to be detected."

"Yeah, so says Quarles. But what if they *do* pick us up?"

Hale answered this time. "Well, they wouldn't waste a missile on us. If we're in line of sight, they'd just kill us with a HELS or a rail gun like the one you have strapped to your suit."

"What the hell is a HELS?"

"High-energy laser system. But it's better if you don't know what they can do to a man."

"That's not exactly encouraging."

"Didn't mean for it to be."

The three astronauts descended; the thrusters on their jetsuits flipping over to shoot a few bursts of plasma spaceward and then turning back toward the ground and releasing smaller bursts to slow them down. Positive g's turned to negative as they dipped from the apogee of their hop, and Dechert's organs began to float up into his rib cage. He reached for the harness at his midsection, for the matted grip of the gun that Hale had just reminded them of. It felt strange in his gloved hand. He was a man used to weapons, but he never thought he would have one tucked into his spacesuit on the surface of the Moon. Hale had insisted that all three of them take one from the weapons locker the marines had brought with them to Serenity. They were curious devices—handheld rail guns with twin-mounted conducting bars welded to either side of a dark blue tungsten barrel. They looked more like science experiments than weapons to Dechert, with their bulbous magnetic accelerators, long, slim barrels, and gas ejection ports. But he had read enough about them to not be scornful; the projectile that these guns fired came out with enough energy to go through a man's head and continue unabated into orbit—with almost no recoil.

Dechert had never considered himself an intelligent man, but he had enough self-awareness to know from an early age that he possessed a keen sense of irony. How could he do anything now but shake his head at the situation he was in? Three men flying from the Sea of Serenity toward the Lake of Happiness, with guns strapped to their guts and an almost certainly dead crew somewhere in front of them? He decided to think of all lunar features from that point forward in their Latin names. Mare Serenitatis. Lacus Felicitatis. The classical language made them sound less optimistic.

"Forty seconds to first hop," Dechert said. "Check your LZ for terrain."

"Looks clear."

"I'm good."

"Copy."

Their speed seemed to grow as the surface came closer, but Dechert knew they were decelerating. He exhaled in relief that they wouldn't have to change their landing areas as he watched the heads-up display pinpoint his touchdown with four inwardly pointing red arrows. The arrows started to blink. He could see the regolith in greater definition now, even in the infrared. What had looked like a polished lunar floor from above became a field of rocky scree on a shallow slope. Would he slip and take off on the wrong trajectory? His computer beeped a warning. The machine sound of their breathing echoed in their helmets.

"Five seconds, four, three, two, one . . . mark . . . step, and step, and engage."

All three of them lit their thrusters at the same time, bouncing twice on the lunar soil and then rocketing spaceward. Dechert stole a look to his left and his right to see that they were still in formation. He felt sweat stinging his eyes and he wished he could wipe them.

"Attitude is eighty-two degrees and nominal," the computer said into his helmet in an anodyne voice. "Climbing to four thousand meters in one-five-zero seconds."

"Good God," Thatch said into the open com, gulping in air with rapid breaths.

"Get used to it," Dechert replied. "You've got three more hops to go before we get there."

21

When they were halfway to the crash site, Hale stopped calling to his dead crew. He left the channel open but only static came back across the dark lunar valley. The talk between the three men was limited to quick commands and affirmations. Every kilometer they flew took them closer to the spot where a Chinese launch crew had fired a surface-to-air missile at the marine shuttle. Could the attackers have stayed in anticipation of a rescue to shoot down the next team as well, or could they have moved forward to the crash site to lay a second ambush? Did the three of them provide enough of a radar profile to be fired at with an automated gun or a laser, or enough of an infrared signature to even be detected?

Dechert shook the questions away. He had learned long

ago not to linger on the unknown avenues of death. In Lebanon, where half the windows held a sniper, that path led to a rapid mental breakdown. He closed his mind to the dangers ahead and tried to focus on the events leading up to the bombing of the *Molly Hatchet*, as though a sudden epiphany to the mystery could stop the scenario that was unfolding before them. But every thought ended with a question.

How could Kale Foerrster have put a bomb on the crawler? Dechert had checked the ensign's dossier during his last sleepless evening before the marine mission, calling in some hard-won markers at Peary Crater to get access to the blue-tabbed sections of the lunar pilot's employment file. Foerrster's background only reinforced him as a suspect. He had joined the 3MA after three years with the Office of Environmental Analysis, a benign-sounding agency that had been formed after the Thermal Maximum with the stated mission of mitigating future environmental disasters. In reality, it was a clandestine wing of Military Intelligence set up to combat the insurrectionists and militias roaming the North and South American post–Thermal Maximum badlands.

Word of the OEA's tactics had trickled to Dechert over the years through his military contacts. They were like the "Studies and Observations Group" of old—the SOG operators of the Vietnam War who were so far off the grid that they took orders mostly from themselves. Two months in the triple-canopied jungle alone, stalking the enemy like jaguars hunting food. *What the hell would that do to a man?* If Foerrster had done more than paperwork for that crew, he could be capable of anything.

But as logical as it seemed to blame Foerrster for the bombing, especially in light of his background, one thread in the story refused to hold the weave. *There was just no way he could have gotten into the Bullpen without Lane or Vernon noticing it.* When a pressure door is opened on the Moon, there are a lot of alerts. Something was pricking Dechert's mind like a burr, some instinct, and it had burned there since the very beginning. He had sensed the same hesitation in Lin Tzu. *I only know that I trust no one, and neither should you,* Tzu had said. *Both parties appear to want what is coming.* If that were true, it led to a grim question: How do you stop a war that both sides have deemed inevitable, maybe even necessary?

Dechert refocused on the black and green virtual landscape around him, telling himself that musings were pointless. Only one thing was certain: The Chinese had just shot down an American shuttle. They had killed four marines patrolling neutral territory. Dechert reached down again for his weapon. If commandos were waiting for them in the Lacus Felicitatis, Dechert was more than willing to fire back. At least the ones he killed wouldn't be his friends from New Beijing 2.

"Strong beacon signal two klicks ahead," Thatch said. "We'll be landing three hundred meters short of it."

They touched down a minute later, each of them stumbling forward for a few meters as their legs got used to the sensation of remaining on the ground. They looked at one another. Any other time, what they had just done would have been an incredible thing, something to celebrate with the colorful adjectives of test pilots. The first formation jetsuit flight on the Moon, in total blackout conditions. But there was nothing here to gloat about. They turned toward the beacon's signal and began to shuffle in its direction.

They were in a low valley; a sheer cliff loomed in the distance. They bounced forward, their feet hitting the regolith every two or three meters, and when they got to within a few hundred meters of the cliff's decaying walls, they saw what they had come to see. How could it be missed? A crater the size of a small office building several stories up the face, gap-

ing at them like an open mouth. A crater on the vertical axis
rather than the horizontal, where a crater had no business
being. They continued to make their way forward in silence,
moving slower now, looking up at the deep rounded hole in
the rock face. As they got close enough to have to crane their
necks upward, they began to see debris on the ground, small
pieces of metal and wiring and carbon fiber strewn across the
cinereous lava flow of the valley, mostly unscorched by an explosion that had occurred in the vacuum. Nothing larger than
a filing cabinet was left of the shuttle and most of the pieces
were smaller than Dechert's gloved hand. They stopped in the
midst of the debris field, within a stone's throw of the wall.
Thatch tilted his helmet down to read the Lunar Positioning
Satellite pad strapped to his wrist, and then he shuffled a few
yards to the right, scanning the regolith beneath his boots. He
leaned over and picked up a small white tube and dusted the
ashen lunar soil off with a gloved hand, turning to show it to
Hale and Dechert. A red light blinked at its rounded edge.

The emergency beacon.

Dechert stared at the thing as if it could tell him the final
story of the young marines, the last seconds of their short lives.
He cursed the SMA for not putting an escape pod or ejection
seats on their long-hop lunar shuttles. The miners had fought
for catastrophic survival modules after John Ross Fletcher's
crash near Tycho, but the Administration had already received
its contingent of shuttles under a subsidized contract, and it
didn't want to go back to drink from Washington's trough one
time too many. Just another goddamned way of making the
margins and keeping their federal minders happy. If Cabrera
and her men had had a way to get out of that shuttle before it
spun into the cliff wall, they might all be standing here now,
waiting for rescue.

Hale looked at the beacon in Thatch's hand for a long moment and then turned away, nudging a piece of unmarred metal on the valley floor with the toe of his boot. He opened a flap on his EVA suit and pulled out an Air & Space Marine patch and laid it on the piece of wreckage, where it would remain untouched for a million years if another human hand didn't move it. Then he straightened up and looked at the marker for several seconds.

"All right," he said, and switched channels on the com. "Peary Crater, this is Cherokee."

"Go ahead, Cherokee."

"Confirmed shuttle down. All souls lost."

"Copy, Cherokee. Shuttle down. All souls lost. Return to Serenity and remain at Condition 1. Wait for further instructions. Copy?"

"Copy."

Dechert looked out across the shadowed plain and saw what must have been a helmet sitting near a small impact crater, glowing in the infrared. Its heat signature was dying as it froze in the supercold vacuum, fading its rounded margins from dark green to black. He took a step toward the helmet and then stopped. What additional nightmares lay over there that he didn't need to see? *This isn't a recovery mission*, he thought. *It's a tally.* He turned away to prepare for the return hop to Crater Yangel'. Let the bastards at Peary Crater come out here and collect the remains once all the shooting stops.

22

John Ross Fletcher picked up a rock and threw it at the vaulted cavern ceiling. It ricocheted off the wall in silence, knocking down a few chunks of petrified lava that floated to the ground in slow motion. He warmed up a handheld radar and blasted the roof and side walls with microwaves to check the structural integrity of the mammoth grotto.

"Always good to make sure the ceiling won't fall down on you," Fletcher said. "These lava tubes aren't young."

"You're joking, right?"

Fletcher looked back at Dechert and grinned. "Yeah, I'm joking. Mostly."

He went to the wall and flipped a switch and a horizontal bank of lights on either side of the cavern flickered and flared, illuminating the length of the passageway in the flat blue xenon glow of a subway tunnel. A three-story pyramid of boulders and broken rocks loomed before them, blocking the way to the mining pit.

"The catwalk's over here," Fletcher said, turning to his right. "Watch your step."

They shuffled through the most celebrated lava tube on the Moon, an underground pipe that stretched for three kilometers beneath the southern spine of the Dorsa Lista. Dechert had read about these tubes and how much bigger they were than their geologic cousins back on Earth, but he had never imagined the full scale. The tunnel was bigger than the nave of Westminster Abbey. He recalled a John Christopher novel about just such a cavern, inhabited by an intelligent being that spread its plantlike tendrils through the underbelly of the Moon, and he could almost envision such a creature living in a place like this.

"Why didn't they just build Serenity 1 in here?" he asked, his head swiveling to take in the scope of the place. "Looks pretty comfortable."

"Not enough titanium in the regolith around here. Too far away from the He-3 fields north of Menelaus, and they couldn't convince some of the selenologists that a Moonquake wouldn't bring down the roof, no matter how much they did to reinforce it."

"So . . . no good reason?"

"Welcome to the Moon, son."

They found the catwalk, which rose over the rock pile in an arch that came close to the lava tube's rounded ceiling. Dechert fell into line behind his mentor for the steep climb. He made an effort to keep his focus on the alien world in front of him; this was his first extended Moonwalk with Fletcher, and he wanted to leave a good impression. A twenty-centimeter pipe ran along the base of the catwalk and out to the tube's entrance, looking like an artery pumping the lifeblood of the American lunar colonies straight from the heart of the Moon. At its end, three hundred meters down the tunnel, lay Peary Crater and Serenity 1's frozen manna—the greatest deposit of ice found to date on Luna.

Fletcher leaped up the narrow catwalk two steps at a time, reaching the top and stopping to wait for his pupil. He leaned back against the railing and folded his arms, looking down at Dechert with his helmet tilted back.

"You never run out of energy, do you?" Dechert asked between breaths. He felt light-headed and wondered if the walk-profile computer had somehow screwed up his gas mix.

"This is the Moon, kid, not some low-orbit getaway for wannabes. There's no time for half-assing it up here."

"Well, that's the first time I've been called a kid in about a decade," Dechert replied, "so I'll forgive the part about half-assing it."

He made it to the top of the catwalk and took a few long, deep pulls of air. They looked down the other side to see an even larger rubble field than the one they had just climbed over. Massifs of anorthosite and troctolite lay strewn along two sides of a deep, angled depression. It looked as if a giant child had punched through one of the cavern walls hundreds of thousands of years ago, collapsing the roof and leaving a large oblong dent in the floor, which grew deeper and more elongated at its western edge. The pipe running along the catwalk snaked through the boulder field and disappeared into the cigar-shaped hole, and as they began to descend the stairs, Dechert could see what they had come for: ice. Small deposits of it frozen into the lunar bedrock, dirty-gray but flecked with slivers of white that gleamed in the fluorescent lighting. Ice that would never melt, hidden away from the sun that now broiled the Serenity plain a few hundred meters above them.

"The cosmic mother lode," Fletcher said. "The day we found this was the day that we knew we could live on the Moon without having to squeeze water from miles of polar rock. The day we knew we could survive in situ, straight off the land."

"Minus the occasional imported beefsteak," Dechert said.

"Mmm. For now. But one day we'll overcome that deficiency as well."

Dechert looked over at his boss. He spoke with the fervor of a man who had just found God and wanted to share him with the rest of the world. But Fletcher's religion wasn't theistic, Dechert knew; it was a worship of space. The SMA's chief lunar explorer hadn't been back on Earth in six years, the longest off-planet stretch ever for any human being. And he wasn't going back any time soon—in six months the greatest pioneer the Moon had ever seen would be heading to Mars to set up a way station at its icy south pole.

"As you can see, the comet fragment came in at just the right angle of attack to not completely collapse the tube," Fletcher said, drawing his arm in an arc across the width of the tunnel. "It was large enough to leave a viable deposit of volatiles, and just small enough to not annihilate them when it exploded."

"The Goldilocks comet," Dechert said.

"Exactly. Four times larger than any other known water deposit on the Moon, and much easier to extract than perma-ice."

They stepped down from the base of the stairwell and made their way through the narrow path cut into the boulder field. Dechert reached the edge of the impact crater and looked down into the pit, where a robotic sifter scraped at the ice and rock, heating it up and then sucking the water into the processing pipe for export back to the silos.

"How much is left?"

"At least nine hundred thousand cubic meters. Enough to supply a good chunk of our lunar operations for ten years, if you include recycling. And by then we'll find more."

Dechert peered down into the pit again, making sure he had a strong grip on a reinforced metal stanchion that had been spiked into an overhanging ledge.

"Must have been a bitch getting the sifters set up down there."

"Yeah, it was."

Dechert looked over at him. "And after all this work, you're going to Mars to start all over again?"

"That's right."

"You still haven't told me why."

Fletcher leaned back from the hole and looked at the man who would be taking over his command at Sea of Serenity 1.

"Because it's farther out and it's running its own circle around the sun, free of the Earth. A new world altogether."

Dechert shook his head. He knew the excitement of exploring alien worlds, but he would never feel it like Fletcher. Dechert had come to the Moon for escape more than illumination, and he wondered if his boss had already figured that out. Joining the SMA wasn't the typical career path for a dust-broken marine and ex-pilot who had been shot at too many times.

"Yeah, but Mars?"

"Why not? Jupiter's at least six years away. They're not even sure the He-3 scoops will survive the Jovian atmosphere, and the last plans I saw for an ice-shielded base on Europa were a disaster waiting to happen." He patted the large pipe coming up from the comet's crater. "Mars is the best thing we've got going right now. I'll think of Jupiter once the god of war starts to bore me."

Good Lord, Dechert thought, *the Christopher Columbus of space. How do you replace a man like this?*

"Do you think I can hack it up here, John?" he asked.

They stood in silence for a few seconds, both of them looking down into the deep hollow as the sifter sniffed and crawled for water, and life.

"Yeah, I think you'll be fine," Fletcher said. "Just remember two things."

"Okay?"

"One: Keep your crew alive. No one needs to be a hero up here." He patted Dechert on the shoulder and headed toward the tunnel's exit.

"And two?"

Fletcher held up a second finger as he reached the catwalk and began the long climb back to the lunar surface, his back still turned to Dechert. "Don't let anything happen to my station."

"Commander, it's Lane. Go secure."

Her voice cut into Dechert's daydream at the midpoint of their second hop back to the shuttle, as the three astronauts descended from four thousand meters over the outer washes of the Lake of Happiness. She didn't yell, but the tension in her voice unloosed the ghosts that had lingered in Dechert's mind for years, snapping him back to the present.

"Yes—okay, hold on. I'm secure."

"Dechert, we just got a solar-flare warning from NB-2. I repeat: We just got a solar-flare warning from NB-2."

Dechert felt like he'd been punched in the throat. His eyes watered, and he swallowed what moisture was left in his mouth to make sure his voice would sound even and in pitch when he replied.

"Confirm, Lane, you have a solar-flare warning from Lin Tzu."

"That's confirmed."

He waited for another second, but she didn't say anything else, and then he realized that she didn't have to say anything else.

"All right. Get everyone out of the CORE and down into the main hangar, right now. Get ready for immediate evacuation. I repeat, immediate departure from the station."

"Copy. We'll be there in one minute." She hesitated for a second. "Standard will want to know why."

"Tell him whatever the hell you have to. Tell him you can run the autodefenses from the flying deck, but on my orders I want you thirty seconds from bugout at the first sign of incoming. Just don't let him know about our trip wire."

"Okay. I'm on my way."

So here it was. Weeks of slow burn coming to real fire. His station was about to be hit by the Chinese. The station Fletcher had hacked out of the ground in the frontier days of the Moon, working sixteen hours a shift on the regolith before collapsing for a few hours of rest in an inflatable bubble-tent. The station Dechert had made his own through more than three long years of careful stewardship. And his people—Lane and Quarles and Vernon—were still stuck inside. Still vulnerable.

Have to get them the hell out of there.

Have to get them into Menelaus Crater.

The rebreathers in Dechert's suit grew loud once again. He felt blood rushing into his ears and the pounding sound of flowing liquid that it carried with it. What was his obligation to Peary Crater and the military men who now ran it? He wasn't a soldier anymore. Did he have to warn them that an attack on Serenity 1 was imminent? He had pledged to Lin Tzu that any warning between them would remain that way, at least until something showed up on radar. Let the sons of bitches at Peary Crater and New Beijing 1 fend for themselves.

But could he do that—hold back information from his own people at the North Pole? A strike was about to be launched on a U.S. mining station, and the next one could be aimed at Peary Crater. Telling Trayborr about it now would give him a tactical advantage, a chance to go on the offensive before being hit himself. Dechert thought of his friendship with Lin Tzu and how alike they were—two men who had seen too much in life and had escaped to a quiet, frozen world devoid of the heat of war. But they weren't friends anymore, and the heat of war had followed them up from Earth. As of two minutes ago, they couldn't even say they were the same people who had set up the warning in the first place. Lin might have made a last gesture by sending the signal to Serenity, but now he would be preparing for battle. And knowing Lin, Dechert realized that his Chinese counterpart had warned him knowing full well that Dechert would have to break his pledge.

"Peary Crater, Cherokee," Dechert said between closed teeth onto an open channel on the com, and as he prepared to break a promise to his friend, he saw a streak of brilliant white on the peripheral edge of his field of vision. He turned his head and saw a sight he could never have envisioned on the Moon: three missiles flying overhead, overtaking the astronauts as they sped to the east—straight toward the Sea of Serenity.

23

"Hale, two-thirty high. Missiles."

Hale and Thatch snapped their heads to the right, and the three of them watched in silence as the missiles flew over the lunar surface on a direct course to Sea of Serenity 1.

"Mother of God," Thatch whispered.

Hale clicked his com. "Peary Crater, Cherokee."

"Cherokee, Peary Crater, go ahead."

"Peary Crater, we have Vampires. I repeat, Vampires. Eyes on a hostile package inbound to Serenity. Three missiles tracking southeast out of the Mare Imbrium, heading approximately one hundred and ten degrees."

"Please confirm, Cherokee, you have visual on hostile missiles, outbound from the Mare Imbrium toward Serenity 1."

"Confirmed, headed for Serenity. We're a few klicks away. They look like large hypervelocities."

"Copy, Cherokee. Give me a range please, and confirm they're of cruise variety."

"Confirmed cruise missiles. Not SAMs. Repeat, not SAMs. Maybe six hundred klicks from Serenity 1. I repeat, roughly six-zero-zero klicks from the station."

"Roger that. Stand by," the voice said, and the line went dead.

As the conversation between Hale and Peary Crater went on in the foggy background, Dechert switched channels with a blink of his eyes and yelled into his com, keeping sight of the receding missiles as he fought to maintain his composure.

"Serenity, this is Dechert. You have incoming missiles, six hundred klicks out. I repeat, you have three missiles inbound. Confirm last and reply."

Quarles came on the line. "Serenity here. Shit, are you serious?"

"Dead serious, Jonathan. You've got maybe five minutes. Put the defenses on auto and get the hell out of there. I repeat: Bug out as soon as antimissile defenses are online. I'm patching Hale and Thatch into our coms."

"Roger, we're ten seconds from the flying deck, preparing to turn AMD and pulse shielding over to the computer. Estimate bugout in three minutes."

"Make it two. And switch on the video feed in the hangar. I want to watch the prep. Are Lane and Vernon on com?"

"Getting their helmets on now."

"Vernon?"

"I'm here."

"Fire up the rover while Lane and Quarles handle the defenses. Don't worry about system checks. I want you out of there in no more than two minutes. You need to be at least a klick away when those things hit the defense grid. Confirm, please."

"Confirmed. We're out of here in two."

Standard's voice cut into their clipped discussion. "Commander, listen, believe me I want to evacuate the station as much as anyone, but I need authorization from Peary Crater for us to bug out during a . . ."

"You've got authorization, Commissioner, from me," Dechert said. "Now get off the line."

Dechert, Thatch, and Hale were a thousand meters over the Lake of Happiness and descending. Just one more hop to the shuttle. Then ten minutes to Menelaus Crater to pick up his crew. Dechert seethed in frustration, trapped by the auto-sequence of their leaps along the northern rim of the Mare Vaporum. A jetsuit hop couldn't be sped up. He couldn't outrun a cruise missile. He couldn't get to the station in time to do anything. All he could do was listen and watch.

The walk-profile computers on their chestplates beeped out the final descent sequences, and Dechert could see on his heads-up display that the landing beacon had overridden an incoming video transmission from Serenity. The feed wouldn't cut in on a priority operation. "Five, four, three, two, one, mark, step, and step, and firing."

Dechert, Hale, and Thatch rocketed up from the lunar basin one last time. Four kilometers from the shuttle now. Getting closer. Radio traffic flew across the Moon in a dizzying flurry of opposing voices. Someone was calling Dechert's name from Peary Crater. He ignored them.

The direct video feed Quarles had set up flared to life in the lower left corner of Dechert's heads-up display, and he used his visual cues to increase its size until it took up the bottom half of his field of vision. The camera provided a 180-degree view of the main hangar. Lane was at the flying deck, suited up, punching in commands for the CORE to take over the defense of the station. Quarles was checking the back of Standard's pressure suit, making sure of the gas mixes. Waters was nowhere to be seen. *Must already be in the Bullpen heating up the rover.*

"We're all green on personal life support," Lane said on the com. "Depressurizing main hangar and opening Bullpen door now. Vernon, you can open the outer hatch in ten seconds from my mark. Mark."

"Opening outer hatch in ten seconds. Rover warmed and ready."

Hale's voice cut in. "Briggs, set the AMD to account for multiple incoming targets; algorithmic random maneuvering. Those are spore missiles coming at you. They're going to open up and launch a spread of projectiles, and they're all gonna be smart."

"Copy," Lane said. "AMD and lasers set to intelligent defense. Electromagnetic pulse shielding at a hundred percent, fusion reactor encased in second shield."

Dechert went through a mental checklist of their evacuation procedure. Station secured. Shield doors down. Power grid at minimum sustaining. Reactor encased in liquid metal. Defenses engaged.

"Lane, confirm evacuation sequence is complete and bug out."

"Confirmed complete."

"Quarles, verify."

"I agree, Commander. We're ready to go."

Dechert checked the chronometer on his heads-up display. They had three minutes. Maybe four. He could hear the outer hatch opening through the background hiss of the com, its door beeping a muted alert that the vacuum of space was about to be let into the station. They were going to make it, with a decent margin for error.

"Okay, let's . . ."

His helmet erupted with alarms before he could finish speaking. Fast-beeping shutdown alarms from Serenity 1's fusion reactor. Slower, deeper pressure-door alarms. Chimes for a computer master alert. A symphony of alarms. More alarms than he could register.

Dechert looked at the video on his heads-up display, confused by the sudden flurry of noise. The video blurred and slowed down. The main hangar went red, its emergency lighting on full. A white and yellow strobe flashed on top of the pressure door leading to the Bullpen. The two-ton door began to shut. *The exit from the station began to shut.*

"Quarles, what the hell?"

The wailing sirens continued.

"Shit, I don't know. We're on automatic lockdown. Shit, everything's locking down!"

"Override."

"Trying now." Quarles leaped up to the flying deck. He punched the touchscreens on the plasma banks, his fingers thick and unwieldy in the pressure gloves. The sirens kept going. The Bullpen pressure door—now a third of the way shut.

"Quarles, override!" Dechert yelled. "Vernon!"

"Yeah. Outer doors just shut and sealed," Vernon said. "I can't get them back open."

"Get the Bullpen door," Dechert yelled. "Vernon, Bullpen hatch is closing!"

He saw Lane and Quarles look up from the flying deck's control bank at the hatch that was sealing them into the station. They froze for a fraction of a second, and then returned their focus to the control bank. Standard stood in the background, unmoving except for his helmet, which swiveled from right to left in uncertainty.

"Sonofabitch!" Vernon yelled, still outside of the camera's view.

Lane and Quarles ran through recovery sequences, yelling at each other in bits and pieces of short, staccato jargon.

"Main buses A, B, C, and D, off line. E through H nominal."

"I'm locked out of the system. CORE is not responding."

"Reactor undervolt. Liquid-metal sphere stable, but fusion first-wall is unresponsive. It's gonna shut down from lack of inner containment."

"Jesus."

After five seconds of listening, Dechert realized with a jolt that his station was being put to sleep. It was in emergency lockdown/shutdown, the type of quick-freeze that would be initiated only in a full-scale solar storm. And there was no solar storm—only a fleet of missiles flying more than seven thousand kilometers per hour toward his entrapped crew.

"Dechert," Thatch yelled into the com. "What the hell is going on?"

"Station's on emergency shutdown," Dechert managed. "Crew's still inside."

"What the hell?"

Dechert ignored him. *Think. Slow down.* The infrared Moon view above the video display in his helmet began to blur, the interlocking grids becoming a haze of glowing green. Could the Chinese have sent a command directly into the CORE, ordering it to lock down and turn off its defenses? Impossible. Only hardwired code could shut down the station, and the CORE was completely protected from wireless signals. Could they have snaked a line into the station itself? No, it had to come from within.

"Quarles, run command override Dechert two-one-one-two. Repeat, Dechert two-one-one-two."

"Roger. Dechert twenty-one twelve."

Quarles punched in the command. The sirens still wailed. The Bullpen door continued to close—now half shut. Thirty seconds more, and they'd be sealed inside the station.

"Negative on command override."

"Can you run a bypass into the CORE?"

Vernon appeared in the video's background, outside the Bullpen door. He was trying to wedge one of the crawler's thick hydraulic tire chucks into the portal in an effort to keep it open. It had only a few meters to go before shutting them in completely.

"Negative on bypass. Takes too long. I'm shit out of ideas."

How much time left before missile impact? Three minutes? Dechert's mind flashed through alternatives. Quarles and Lane had to keep trying to regain control of the station's servers so they could get the outer pressure door open and keep the defensive systems on. Waters had to keep the Bullpen hatch ajar so they could all make it to the rover and escape the station—if they could find a way to pry open the outer doors.

"Standard, help Waters!" Dechert yelled. The commissioner's head snapped up when he heard his name, and he turned and shuffled toward Waters, unused to the bulk of his pressure suit and to the need for immediate action.

"I can keep the mains online, Commander, and I should be able to sequence the autodefenses, because they're off the CORE's operating system," Lane said, "but we're locked out of the pressure-door controls. We can't open the outer hatch."

"I count three minutes to impact," Hale said.

"Lane, can you blow the outer doors?"

"Negative. Explosives are in the shed."

"Acetylene torch?"

"Negative. Takes at least ten minutes."

No one spoke for a few seconds as they all went through the alternatives again. The tire chuck Vernon had wedged into the Bullpen door began to bend from the thousands of pounds of pressure being exerted on it. Should they get into the Bullpen and take their chances, or retreat deeper into the station?

"Lane, what about sealing yourselves into the Hole?" Dechert asked. "Can you get down there in time?"

"Maybe, but I don't know if we can open and close the roof."

"What about the observatory?" Thatch asked. "Blow the glass."

"Shield doors are reading down in Observatory."

Dechert, Hale, and Thatch began their descent over the open mouth of Crater Yangel'. They could see the shuttle now, parked on a small ledge just inside the impact wall about a kilometer below them. Just a few seconds more, and they could begin the run back to Serenity. Maybe the autodefenses would stay online and knock the incoming missiles out of space. Maybe things could still be salvaged.

Maybe . . .

The crack of a rifle shot went off in the station. Dechert's ears rang with the sound. He saw Lane and Quarles flinch and look up, saw Standard stumble back from the Bullpen door, and saw Waters's head snap back and turn, the visor on his helmet cracking into spider webs.

The titanium tire chuck had snapped in two and hit Waters in the head, smashing his helmet with machine force.

"Vernon!" Lane screamed.

They went to him. Standard turned him over. The Bullpen door—now a little more than four feet from closing them in. Waters didn't move.

"He's venting," Quarles said. "Jesus Christ, man, he's losing pressure."

"Seal his helmet," Dechert yelled. "You're almost out of atmosphere. And get him into the Bullpen. Quarles! Do you hear me? Quarles? Get in the Bullpen!"

A few random pops of static disrupted the signal. The video feed distorted in waves, first horizontally and then vertically. It fuzzed over completely. It came back again long enough for Dechert to see a horrific scene: Lane running to snatch a bottle of emergency sealant off the bulkhead wall. Quarles leaning over Vernon and yelling his name. Standard, now trying to hold the Bullpen door open with only his thin legs and arms as leverage, a weakling Sisyphus, fighting a losing battle against a rock that was about to roll over him.

"Lane!" Dechert yelled into the com. He got no response.

The video fuzzed over again. Dechert tried to increase the signal strength. The picture came back and then died. The screen was black now, the hum of a dead transmission filling Dechert's ears.

"Lane, Jonathan, report. Lane! Jonathan!"

The signal disappeared. Dechert cued his computer to reset. There was nothing but black space in a small rectangular border.

"Dechert, I've lost all communications with Peary Crater as well," Hale said, his voice coming in as if from a great distance. "We're being jammed."

A muted alarm rang in Dechert's helmet. He looked down and saw that they were only a few hundred meters from the surface. The touchdown beacon flared to life, illuminating a landing area about twenty meters east of the shuttle, just a few feet in front of the sheer edge of the cliff. Dechert paid the treacherous landing sequence little notice.

"Lane, Jonathan, report."

"What the hell's happening?" Thatch asked.

Dechert ignored him, continually trying to punch reset on the frequency button with blinks of his eyes. They landed on the narrow promontory, close enough to the edge to look down into the night-shaded abyss of Crater Yangel'. Dechert stumbled twice and came to a halt near the drop-off, breathing in gasps, his hands on his knees and his temples throbbing.

The final tally had been set. His team at Serenity would most likely be dead in two minutes. Images of the video feed filled his head as his mind raced through the odds of what would happen next. What were the chances of surviving a missile strike? Were they able to at least keep the autodefenses online? Could the system intercept the smart projectiles before they hit?

Dechert straightened. He turned to walk back to the shuttle, but he had little energy left. Hale turned toward the shuttle, too, without saying a word, keeping a comfortable distance from Dechert. Thatch stood ten meters away, glowing infrared near the lip of the crater wall, a halo of moondust falling around where he had just landed. The gray dust on his legs and boots stood out as cold spots on the IR signature.

Fleeting images came together in Dechert's mind and snapped into place like a dead bolt, stopping time. A white spacesuit staring back at him from the broken innards of the *Molly Hatchet*, its legs covered in dust. A thick fringe of grime on the control panel at Spiral 6. Groombridge treads at the water mine—old boots from the back of a storage locker. The assassin in the safe house video: *A big man, and fast . . .*

Dechert put a hand on the shuttle's hull near the hatch controls, as if he were taking a rest. He locked his knees so that he wouldn't fall down. His face burned as a drop of sweat ran down the center of his nose from the bridge to the tip, and fell below his neckline. *It had to come from within.* He reached for the rail gun at his midsection with his concealed right arm, trying to peer to his left without turning his helmet.

Thatch already had his gun in his hands.

"Hale!" Dechert yelled.

Somehow Hale saw it coming, some instinct moving him into action at the tone in Dechert's voice. A warrior's alertness, or maybe he had suspected Thatch all along. He moved with improbable grace in the bulky spacesuit, bending low on a knee, spinning his body, and pulling his own rail gun from the holster on his belly.

He pointed the gun at Thatch. Thatch fired first. The tiny projectile came out in silence, unimpressively. Just a small puff of plasma and a blue arc of electricity. But it hit Hale's chest at ten thousand kilometers per hour, making the size of the round inconsequential. Hale's body flexed inward as if hit by a cannon shot. His shoulder blades snapped with the force. He flipped up and backward over the ledge of the promontory, gas venting from his open chestplate as he fell into Crater Yangel'.

Dechert had his own gun out and fired at Thatch. Nothing happened. He pulled the trigger again. Nothing. Then he remembered that Thatch was the one who had loaded the rail guns onto the shuttle. Thatch stood unmoving in the dark of the cliff wall, his weapon recharging.

Dechert dropped the useless gun and turned and walked to the drop-off, expecting Thatch to shoot him in the back. He looked over the edge and saw Hale falling, a smudge of heat in a frozen abyss. His body bounced once on a ledge five hundred meters below them and then spun into the blackness until it was a green dot in the infrared. In ten seconds there was nothing.

Thatch walked to the edge and looked down as well, his gun still pointed at Dechert's guts. They stood there for what seemed like a minute, looking down in silence, and then they turned to each other.

Thatch. The assassin in the video. Cole's killer. The man who sabotaged the station. The one who started it all—the one who brought war to the Moon.

"How did you figure it out?"

"You said you never took a walk at Posidonius, Thatch. But I looked inside the *Hatchet* before they took her away, and I saw your spacesuit. You did the first EVA to set a timer on the bomb, didn't you? The satellite trigger never made sense."

Thatch grunted. "Moondust on the suit."

"And you logged a flight to Spiral 6 two weeks ago, but the control panel was too dirty for you to have been there. I'm guessing you were busy crippling the water mine."

"Dust again. I swear I'm going to live in a rain forest if I get off this rock alive."

"One thing I still can't figure out," Dechert said. "How'd you land at DS-7 and leave no trace?"

Thatch tilted his head. "Rigged the outflow valves to brush over the LZ." He looked at Dechert. "You're smarter than I thought."

"No, I'm pretty damned stupid. There was other stuff, Thatch. I don't know how I didn't see it before now."

"Give yourself some credit. No one else did."

"You killed Cole."

Thatch stepped back from the ledge, his gun still pointed at Dechert. "I didn't like it. He was a good kid."

Dechert edged back from the ledge as well. "You killed us all, Thatch. For what? Money?"

Thatch stiffened and Dechert could see anger in the movement.

"It's like you to think that, Dechert, always playing the

innocent. You can't imagine the idea that I'm taking orders. That I'm doing my job, just like you."

Thatch turned on his headlamps, blinding Dechert. The burst of light automatically shut down the infrared viewscreen in his helmet, returning the autofilters to visible light. He blinked the spots out of his eyes and opened them, turning on his own lamps. He could see Thatch's face now in the pale illumination. The big man was frowning as if angry at himself for not having fired yet.

"You're OEA, aren't you?"

"I was."

Dechert looked down at the heads-up display in his helmet. A single dot, blinking red.

"So that's it, Thatch? You take orders from some lunatics who were kicked out of special forces on the back end of the Max, and that makes it all okay? You killed your own crew, for Christ's sake. You started a *war*."

Thatch looked at the shuttle, then at Dechert. "You have no idea where my orders come from. You still don't get it, do you, Dechert? You think you can run away from Earth and hide up here, and everything will be okay, because the Moon is just kumbaya?"

Dechert braced himself, waiting to be shot. "Why don't you enlighten me?"

"I'll give you one minute, mostly because I'm sick of your bullshit. You run around the Moon defending your buddies at NB-2. You're a sucker, Dechert. The Chinese have been lying about their He-3 production for years. They're converting fifty metric tons a month, and the dipshits at The Hague and the ISA won't do a thing about it."

"Bullshit."

"No, Dechert. It's real shit. The Chinese have won the

Moon. And they're about to win the solar system. And we're going to continue being what we've been since the day the Max hit: a third-rate nation. Unless we do something about it."

Dechert kept his hands away from his chestplate, palms extending outward in submission, knowing that a man like Thatch, who had lived among them for three years while waiting to kill them, would pull the trigger on instinct.

"Let's say you're right, Thatch. How the hell is a war on the Moon going to change anything? Or do they want this thing to spread to Earth as well?"

Thatch shifted his feet, impatient, his eyes getting smaller.

"I don't do strategy, Dechert. I follow my orders. But I can tell you one thing, I'm not going to sit around and wait for America to slide back to what she was five years ago. I was out there in the wastelands while you were cruising at fifty thousand feet. I saw kids getting raped. I saw them getting eaten, after they were fucking raped. I'm never going to see that again. I'll expend you and Waters and Briggs and anyone else so that never happens again. I'll expend myself if I have to."

"Is that why you sealed the station? You could have let them escape."

"Like I said. Orders. There had to be enough casualties."

The blinking light at the bottom of Dechert's helmet turned green. He turned his head toward Yangel', as if to scan the blackness one last time for Hale. He looked up and to the right and blinked twice into his optical cue. The heads-up display in his helmet keyed into sequence.

"We're all expendable, aren't we, Thatch?"

He turned back, and they looked at each other, standing together on the inside of the rim wall. *No one knows what it means to be alone until they've been in space*, Dechert thought.

"I regret it, Dechert," Thatch said, and he raised the gun

barrel. "You're a self-righteous sonofabitch, but you're a good man."

"You're not," Dechert said.

He closed his right eye and opened it again. The green dot flashed and he heard a shrill warble in his headset as the computer accepted his command.

The minijets on Thatch's suit flared to life. The two locked eyes and he thought that Thatch flashed him a grin, this time in recognition. He blasted from the Moon's surface a millisecond later.

Dechert watched Thatch ascend into space. He could see the big man struggle at first, trying to hit the kill switch on the minijets. Then his body steadied and Dechert saw him aim the rail gun. Dechert jumped to his left as Thatch fired—an impossible shot—the angles all wrong and no chance for sight alignment. But Dechert felt a pull on the back of his shoulder and two sounds rushed into his ears, the hiss of escaping air and the low chime of a pressure alarm. He went to the ground in disbelief, rolling in slow motion onto his back, desperately feeling for the tear in his suit. His eyes caught Thatch through a haze of falling moondust, still climbing into space, a blue arc once again spitting from his rail gun. The second bullet punched into the regolith an inch from Dechert's faceplate. The concussion knocked him onto his side. He rolled over again, in a panic now, blinded by the ring of dust kicked up by the bullets. He pushed the air from his lungs and tried to focus on not breathing as he felt the warmth of the suit escaping and the coldness of space closing in. He pulled a bottle of quick-seal from a leg pocket, but then realized he couldn't find the tear on his back anyways.

Dechert's world spun around in snapshots and distorted sounds:

The heads-up display showing pressure at 0.6 atm.

Oxygen at 20 percent.

The hissing of air.

The alarm even louder.

He crawled to his feet and stumbled toward the shuttle, remembering at the last second to look up. Thatch was a white dot in space, but he fired yet again, the projectile whomping into the Moon a few yards to Dechert's right. Blackness closed in on the margins of Dechert's vision. He reached the shuttle and punched at the hatch, his sight reduced to two small circles directly in front of him. The door opened. Dechert lurched in, his hand reaching for the pressure controls. He was blind now. He scrabbled at his helmet as he heard the pressurization sequence kick in. It sounded miles away. He tried again to pop the seals on his helmet, but it was too late. He collapsed on the shuttle floor and everything went away.

24

He heard an alarm clock and tried to punch snooze, but the button didn't work. He kept trying, but the beeping wouldn't stop. The sound clawed at his dreams, twisting them until he realized they weren't real at all. He felt cold and opened his eyes. Dechert was lying on a rubberized floor, his cheek pressed against the matting, a temperature warning still ringing in the distance. It took him a few seconds to realize he was alive—that somehow he had engaged the pressure button and managed to pull off his helmet before passing out. He didn't remember doing either.

He wouldn't have moved if it weren't for the impossible cold . . . and the memory of Thatch firing at him from space. *How in God's name had he managed to hit me while being launched like a cruise missile?* That was his first thought. Then he wondered where Thatch was now. Dechert got to his knees and crawled to the shuttle cockpit, his breath steaming and his nostrils frozen. He turned on the heaters and then slipped into the pilot's seat, firing up the computer to search for Thatch's beacon, all the while craning his neck to look out the window into space. The locater numbers came back. Thatch was six hundred kilometers from the Moon and traveling faster than a bullet. His thrusters were drained, but that didn't matter anymore. He was heading toward Arkab in the constellation Sagittarius. Arkab. Almost four hundred light-years from Earth. Dechert imagined Thatch arriving there in a few hundred million years or so—a frozen man, crossing the void alone. It was almost enough to make him smile. But then he remembered what Thatch had done and knew there was nothing to smile about.

Dechert rotated the shuttle's satellite dish toward Peary Crater, its cold motor struggling to warm in the nightside freeze, and in a few moments he was no longer alone. The com popped and fizzled and became awash in cross-traffic. Human voices yelling orders and ticking off targeting telemetry. They were the voices of war, terse and urgent.

"Peary Crater, this is Cherokee," Dechert said into the clamor. "Put Yates on the line."

After a few seconds, a voice came back to him. "Cherokee? Confirm status and repeat."

"Put Yates on the goddamned line."

He sat in the pilot's seat and waited for an answer. The heaters blew warm air down on him. He had the top of his EVA suit off, and he started to spray quick-seal on the two-inch gash caused by Thatch's bullet. His back felt sore, but it wasn't bleeding. There was comfort in the task of fixing something, a few seconds of monotony before he had to fly back to the

station and look for the bodies of his last three friends on the
Moon.

The old man came on the line, his voice electric. "Cherokee, where the hell have you been?"

"Yates, it was Thatch. Shut it down."

"What the hell are you talking about?"

"It was Thatch," Dechert said, his voice flat. "He killed
Hale. I've got it on tape. I'm sending it over. Shut it down, the
whole damned thing, or I'm punching an open transmission
to Earth."

"What do you mean it was Thatch? Dechert, have you lost
your mind?"

"He blew up the *Molly Hatchet*. He sabotaged the station.
He just killed Hale. Do you hear me, Yates? *It was our own
fucking guy.* He started the whole thing. Now shut it down or
everyone's gonna know."

The line went silent.

"Hold on, I'm receiving your transmission," Yates said after
a few seconds. "I'll get back to you on a secure channel, for
Christ's sake."

"Tell your minders they have two minutes, and let them
know it's too late to try anything clever, like sending a fake
SAR team to check on my well-being," Dechert said. "I've already dumped the video to a server and they aren't going to
find it. If I don't stop it at a set time the whole story gets pushed
out into the open."

"Dechert, we've got missiles en route right now, and so do
the Chinese. We can't just turn this thing off."

"Yes you can, Yates. Of course you can. Get it done." He
hesitated then, taking a long breath, not wanting to ask the
question. "Do you have any word from Serenity?"

The line went back to static, and Yates finally answered.
"They've gone dark. We have no word."

"Copy. I'm heading over there now."

"Dechert?"

"You have ninety seconds, Yates. Do it, or the ticker in Times Square is going to say we started a war on the Moon by killing our own people."

Dechert put the top half of his suit and his helmet back on, fired the shuttle's engines, and flew out of the crater's mouth. In the distance over the Apennine Mountains, the Earth hung in aquamarine splendor over a crumbling slope of gray rocks.

He saw the first pieces of debris scattered a few kilometers west of the station. The sensors picked them up and plotted them on a plasma screen and the data unfroze Dechert's blood. It was a missile, shot down just short of Serenity 1, its resin composite hull strewn in a disjointed line across the dark mare. The autodefenses had stayed on long enough to shoot down one of them. Dechert thought for a moment that the system had been smart enough to save his crippled station.

But reality came thundering back thirty seconds later, draining the adrenaline from his body and leaving him empty. The infrared cameras told the tale when he was still a few thousand meters from Menelaus Crater. The station was emanating too much latent heat. It had been hit.

Dechert flew the shuttle over the broken remains of Sea of Serenity 1, his hands and feet moving the flight controls on instinct. A jagged hole stood out on the Moon below him illuminated by the infrared cameras—a hole where his station used to be. The observatory was gone, blown away, and moondust hung over the impact crater like a shroud. The southwestern corner of the station, where the Bullpen had been, was missing, caved in by tons of regolith and moon rocks. Dechert checked his gauges; there was no power coming from the sta-

tion. He flew in a tight circle over the wreckage and landed
the shuttle a few meters outside of the dust cloud. He tried
raising Lane on the com and got background noise and the
sputtering radio sounds of space in reply.

He unbuckled himself from the pilot's seat, moving slowly,
his thoughts broken and scattered. The memory of an inter-
view he had read years ago back on Earth entered his mind
like an unwanted ghost. It was of a U.S. Navy lieutenant who
had survived the sinking of the USS Florida in 2046. The frig-
ate had been struck by an aerial drone loaded with HIEX, and
the lieutenant had abandoned ship with the few dozen sailors
who were still alive as it sank from the stern, leaving his captain behind on the tilting bridge.

The lieutenant had pleaded with his captain to leave with
the rest of them: "Sir, we need to get out of here."

"I'm staying with the ship," the captain had said.

The young lieutenant pressed his boss, telling him there
was no reason to die a pointless death for an empty naval tradi-
tion dreamed up centuries before. "Sir, it's a ship."

But the lieutenant said the captain sat back in his chair on
the bridge and grunted: "Yeah. But it's my ship, and those are
my men down there dying in the fo'c'sle. And I'll be damned
if I leave them."

Dechert found his way through the shuttle's outer hatch
and began the long walk toward his station, entering the dust
cloud which now stretched for more than a kilometer across
the Mare Serenitatis. Why can't I be that guy? he asked himself. Why do I always watch my people die around me, then
walk away?

The wreckage of four years of his life appeared through the
shroud of moondust, everywhere beneath his feet. A saucepan
from the galley, somehow unharmed. Pieces of red insulation
from the air condensers. Shards of moon-baked clay from the

3-D printer. And wiring, miles of wiring, flung out across the regolith, the expelled entrails of the dead station. Dechert checked the bioscanner on his wrist. It should be able to pick up any living soul within a kilometer of the station. It was flat-lined and dark.

He came to a high mound of rubble that had been heaved upward from the center of Serenity 1. He climbed it using his hands and knees to gain traction in the unstable pile, oblivi-ous to the sharp pieces of metal and fiber that threatened to slash open the legs of his pressure suit. After a short struggle, he made it to the top and looked down with his lamps on full, into the crater that had been formed at the heart of the station. There was no fire in the vacuum, only a few live wires spitting into the darkness. He could see that the missile had reached far down into Serenity's sublevels, deep into its guts. *Must have been a ground penetrator*, he thought, realizing that even the confines of the Hole had likely been obliterated by the blast. He looked to his right, and a wall of collapsed rock lay where the Bullpen had stood.

He sat down on top of the pile, small amid the wreckage. Where to begin looking, where to scrabble with gloved hands in a field of debris that stretched for hundreds of yards? He felt like a man trapped on a cliff wall. Rimrocked. Exposed.

"Peary Crater, this is Serenity," he said into the com.

Yates answered this time. "Go ahead, Serenity."

"Station's destroyed. I need a rescue team out here with heavy equipment, expedited."

"Okay, but we're still fully defensive, Dechert. They've asked the Chinese for a cease-fire and your transmission has gone to the White House, but there are missiles still in the air. I'll have to get permission to launch anything from Peary right now. I repeat, we are fully defensive and trying to pull back to DEFCON-2, but there are no launches authorized."

"Get authorization, Yates," he snapped. "My crew's buried."

"Okay. I'll talk to Trayborr. Do you have anything on bioscan?"

"Negative."

"Okay."

Dechert pulled his knees as close to his chest as he could and put his head in his hands, letting the quiet of the mare embrace him. He stared at a circuit board near his boot, following the crisscrossing lines as they ran from diode to resistor. How random their order appeared to be. Intersecting lines cut by a machine laser.

He stood up, suddenly angry at himself, and began to climb down the rubble field as fast as he could. Even if they were dead, he had to find them. Static hissed on the open com. A heavily distorted voice broke into his fevered mind.

"Peary Crater, this is Low Lunar Orbit 1. We caught your last transmission with Serenity. Uh, I've got a signal up here that I'm trying to figure out, sir. Do you copy?"

No one responded.

"Peary this is LLO-1. Are you reading?"

"This is Serenity, LLO," Dechert finally said. "What's your signal?"

The voice came back. "It's an emergency beacon on an He-3 cask, sir, but it's well below the orbital ejection flight grid. Flying on a southeast trajectory, but it's too shallow and too slow. Can you confirm?"

An emergency beacon on a helium-3 cask. *What the hell?* Dechert's mind stirred back to life as he pondered the absurd timing of it. Then his muscles tensed and he stopped climbing down the rubble heap.

"LLO, can you confirm it's a canister beacon?"

"Yes, Serenity. That's what I can't figure out. It should be heading to Lagrange Point Three, but it's not even in a stable orbit. And we obviously didn't have any ejections scheduled for today."

Holy shit. The rail launcher. Dechert's heart fluttered in his chest. Could they have done that? Could they have been crazy enough to do that?

"LLO, launch your barge on a search-and-rescue to that beacon," Dechert said, turning around and scuffling back up the wall toward his shuttle. "I repeat, launch SAR immediately to that beacon. There may be souls aboard."

"What, aboard an He-3 cask?"

"Yes."

"Jesus. We're scrambling now, Serenity."

"I'm back in the shuttle in thirty seconds," Dechert said. "Send coordinates to my craft. Peary Crater, are you hearing this? They may have escaped the station in an He-3 cask. I repeat: Crew may have jettisoned from the Bullpen in an He-3 cask. I'm taking the shuttle into low orbit. Tell whoever needs to know that my launch is not hostile."

Dechert bounded from the dust cloud, his heart thumping, crossing the distance to the shuttle in five-meter hops. He waited for Yates to come back to him in protest, to tell him that he couldn't violate the stand-down with a launch. He got ready to tell Yates he could screw himself because nothing was going to keep him on the surface of the Moon.

Yates came back. "Serenity, we've made a direct call to the South Pole to let them know you're not hostile. You're a go for launch. Good luck to you."

25

The technobabble of a propulsion geek from Peary Crater ran through Dechert's mind in a loop as he rocketed up from the lunar surface, his hands turning the insides of his gloves wet with perspiration.

The engineer had been overseeing the installation of Serenity 1's rail launcher just as Dechert was taking over the station in early 2069, a few months after John Ross Fletcher had died in the shuttle crash near Tycho. The electromagnetic gun, which rose from the Bullpen like a five-story howitzer, was built to shoot two-ton casks of helium-3 into orbit like so many spitballs, out to a Lagrange point for pickup and delivery to Earth. The engineer had looked up at the launcher's giant dual conducting bars as if they were his newborn twins.

"Amazing, aren't they?" he asked Dechert. "This baby will spit out sixty megajoules per ejection and accelerate a four-thousand-pound projectile from zero to three kilometers-per-second in the time it takes your heart to skip a beat."

"As long as it works right," Dechert said, not wanting to prompt an additional stream of physics from the man.

"Oh, it'll work right," the engineer replied. "Just make sure no one's inside when one of those babies gets launched. They'd be pulling enough g's to shoot their eyeballs straight out of their assholes."

"I'll remember that."

"Yeah," the engineer said, his eyes glassing over. "What a ride that would be."

What a ride that would be.

Dechert was no mathematician. He couldn't pinpoint the amount of g-forces involved in an orbital ejection by rail launcher, but he figured a standard shot had to be at least forty. Forty g's. Enough force to make a two-hundred-pound man suddenly weigh four tons. Enough force to rip the pulmonary artery right out of the heart muscle or rupture every organ. But the com-jockey at LLO-1 had said the cask was well below the flight grid and moving below escape velocity, so Quarles or Waters must have rigged the launcher for a slow, shallow shot. How many g's would that have cut from the launch, maybe ten or fifteen?

And how long would the high-g acceleration have lasted? That was the critical question. Just five seconds of that force would kill them all, but what about two seconds, or three? Could their bodies have survived that? An air force doctor had endured over 40 g's in a rocket sled back in the twentieth century, Dechert recalled, and some lunatic test pilot had taken 80 g's in a similar experiment a few decades later, but those were controlled tests of horizontal force—for a very brief amount of time. Vertical force was worse, wasn't it? *And helium-3 casks don't have any seats or five-point harnesses.*

Dechert pushed the shuttle to its operational edge, keeping the thrusters on maximum as he climbed into a low orbit over the Sea of Serenity and felt the force of acceleration pushing against his chest. LLO-1 had already sent him the coordinates. The emergency beacon was now over Copernicus, in sector D-3, so the cask must have nearly made an entire orbit around the Moon. He turned southeast over the equator and punched numbers into the shuttle's navigation system. His closing speed had him less than four minutes from intercept, somewhere in the northern Mare Nectaris. Four minutes from an answer to the most important question of his life: *Would he ever command a crew that remained alive?*

How had B-Dog died back in the Bake? Was it a roadside bomb? No, a sniper in Aanjar had taken him out. And Snook? Brought down when he stormed a mud-brick house with a cherry private covering his ass. Dawes had killed himself. And Matchstick? Didn't he make it? Yes, he was alive the last Dechert had heard. But he'd probably never be able to eat without someone feeding him.

And Cole. *Can't forget Cole.* He spent the last few seconds of his life feeling the water in his body boil under his skin, not knowing he was killed by a man who had been his friend for more than three years.

"LLO, this is Serenity shuttle," Dechert said, brushing aside the image of his young mining specialist. "I'm just crossing Sinus Honoris, about three minutes from intercept. Report, please."

The transmission bounced and warbled a few times, and Dechert could hear nervous cross-chatter on the open channel.

"Serenity, LLO-1. I'm patching you over to collection barge *Xerxes.* They're heading almost due east over Albategnius, less than two minutes from capture. Be advised the cask is only four kilometers above the surface and slipping, so they're pushing safety protocols for a quick grapple. Terrain ahead is a concern."

Dechert's grip on the stick tightened. *Terrain ahead.* He plumbed his memory for the lunar topography in front of the He-3 cask. There wasn't much in the way of vertical relief. The Montes Pyrenaeus was about it, but those peaks weren't high enough to be an immediate concern . . . were they?

"*Xerxes*, this is Commander Dechert in Serenity shuttle. Report please."

"We read you, Commander. This is *Xerxes*' pilot. We have eyes on your He-3 cask; velocity about two thousand meters per second, altitude about three-point-seven kilometers. It's in a precession of about eleven degrees, probably from irregular weight distribution. We project it's gonna hit terrain in four minutes or less. We're one minute to intercept. This is going to be close."

"What terrain, *Xerxes*?"

"Mons Penck. They're heading right for it."

Dechert felt sick. Mons Penck is a wide promontory that rises four kilometers above the lunar flatlands. "Copy, *Xerxes*. What's your plan?"

"Expedited capture and then a quick burn to get over the hump—if we don't abort. I've got an EVA team waiting at the storage rack. I'm not sure I can pull a g-maneuver with them out there, and I don't have time to bring them back in."

"We're locked into our suitports and holding on, lieutenant," said another voice on the com, obviously one of the three astronauts strapped to the back of the collection rail. "We'll live if you don't plow us into a mountain."

Dechert wanted to plead with the barge pilot not to abort, but he had done the math and knew how close it would be.

His mind raced with convincing words, but the pilot spoke first.

"Are you sure there are souls on board, Commander?"

"I am," Dechert said.

There was a short silence. "Okay. Going for capture. Twenty seconds. Tran, you got one shot at this."

"Copy. I'm going for the drogues on the middle of the barrel."

Dechert could see them now, a flash of light in the darkness ahead as the barge lit its forward search lamps. They were flying toward the terminator of the waxing crescent Moon, just a few minutes from sunlight. The He-3 cask would go from freezing to broiling in a few minutes. And it kept getting lower.

"Terrain ahead," the barge's navigation system announced in an anodyne voice. *Xerxes* extended its grappling arm, and Dechert saw the cask, wobbling on its axis as it plummeted toward the Sea of Nectar. The mechanical arm moved slowly, like a robotic mother reaching for her child. A band of searchlights illuminated the cask, and Dechert could see the astronauts locked on to the collection rail, waiting to be sucked into the back of their suits by an orbital burn.

Slow motion. A few meters per second, as his crew flew in a dying orbit toward one of the Moon's tallest mountains. Dechert cursed the slowness of space.

"Closing speed down to one meter per second. How we looking, Tran?"

"Just fifty meters more. Give me some room on the low side to work with; this thing's got a shimmy."

"Okay. Two minutes to abort."

"Roger, one minute to capture."

The ship's computer continued its warning: "Terrain ahead. Pull up. Terrain ahead."

Dechert's shuttle gave him the same alert, but he ignored

it, staying a few hundred yards behind the barge and the tumbling cask, willing the mechanical arm to move faster.

"Ten meters."

"That's good. Keep it there."

"One minute to abort."

Dechert blinked the sweat out of his eyes. The grappling arm reached around the middle of the barrel. Probes on each side of the arm tried to connect with small drogues built into the cask. . . .

They missed.

Dechert could see them scrape down the metal skin, peeling paint.

"Final report, Tran. We gotta move."

"Give me ten seconds."

"*Warning. Terrain ahead. Pull up. Pull up.*"

The probes inched back toward the sockets. Dechert looked forward; he could see Mons Penck looming in front of them. They were going to lose them.

"Capture," Tran said. "We have soft capture."

"Retract."

"Retracting. How much time?"

"No time. Get it in."

Slowly—way too slowly for Dechert—the mechanical arm retracted, bringing the cask into the metal folds of the ship and locking it into a secure umbilical.

Dechert's cockpit filled with Moon.

"Uhh, boys," one of the astronauts said.

"Hard capture. Go for burn."

"OMS burn," the lieutenant said. "Hold on."

The barge pitched up and clawed for altitude. Dechert lit his own thrusters as warning alarms from both ships rang in his ears. He could see the *Xerxes* shudder. It wasn't built for hard orbital maneuvers. Mons Penck filled Dechert's viewscreen.

The *Xerxes* stayed below the mountain's sloping peak, trying to climb as thrusters on its belly pushed spaceward. But it wasn't happening fast enough. Dechert saw Moon and ship getting closer, and braced for the image of destruction that had been racing through his mind. Moon and ship getting closer . . .

And then his viewscreen filled with the emptiness of space. Dechert sucked in a breath. The barge was ahead of him. There was nothing solid in its path. The alarms went silent.

"OMS shutdown," the *Xerxes'* pilot said, and you could hear relief in his voice. "Angels at fourteen and climbing. You guys okay out there?"

"We're alive, lieutenant. That was a ride."

"How close did we get?"

"I could have reached down and grabbed some dirt for you."

"Roger. Let's see if it was worth it."

"Commencing rescue, lieutenant."

The astronauts began working to unseal the maintenance door on the cask. Dechert pulled in close to the barge; he could see the spits of light as they torched the hatch, which must have been jammed from the inside. He squinted and leaned forward, blood rushing into his forehead. A warning beeped on the console and he looked at the heads-up display. He was coming in too fast. He hit reverse thrust and nosed the shuttle up.

"*Xerxes*, shuttle," Dechert said. "You boys are some stone-cold astronauts."

"We do it for the glory, shuttle."

"Well, I know you don't do it for the pay. Requesting docking clearance."

"You're a go to dock. Port side, soft seals engaged."

In his mind's eye, he saw Lane's face as he made the final approach, her short, straight, dark copper hair, her upturned

nose and small chin. He saw Vernon's wild hair and lidded
eyes, and Quarles's shaved head and sagging heavysuit.

"What's the status out there, EVA?" the *Xerxes'* pilot asked.

"Give me a second."

The cockpit boards lit green and Dechert docked the
shuttle, taking his clenched fists off the controls, his fingers
twitching with cramps. Still the rescue team remained silent.
Vernon's dead, he thought. *He has to be dead. They all have to
be dead.*

"Damn, we have four souls in here," someone finally said,
and Dechert could see one of the astronauts sticking his head
into the open maintenance door as he shined a lantern into
the cask's dark interior, his feet hanging into space like a clown
looking into a rodeo barrel. The astronaut began throwing
what looked like pieces of packing foam out of the container.

"What's their condition, EVA?" he asked, unable to re-
strain himself.

"Hold on."

Another thirty seconds ticked by.

"What's their status, John?" the *Xerxes'* pilot asked.

"Get medical ready," the spacewalker said. "I think some
of them are alive."

26

Dechert slouched in a chair, half asleep, in a corner of the medical pod, his head on his chest and his feet on an overbed table. He heard Lane rustle and looked up in time to see her eyes open and wander around the small room. He saw the puzzlement in her face as she slowly digested the fact that she wasn't in Sea of Serenity 1. Her eyes continued to roam until they found him. He had stubble on his face and hadn't showered in a week, but she clearly recognized him. She stirred and coughed, and he stood up.

"Hey."

"Hmmm," she said, trying to move her legs and wincing in pain at the effort. She looked down and saw a bioscanner attached to her right arm and a fluid drip inserted into the left.

A machine beeped in the background, a much less intrusive noise than the alarms that had filled her dreams.

"So, I guess I'm alive?"

"Yeah."

He came over to her, sat on a stool by the bed, and looked into her eyes, which were still run through with spiders of red from the g-load that had burst most of her capillaries. Her face was swollen from the trauma, and her lips were cracked and dry.

"How do I look?"

"Like shit."

She grunted and tried to smile, but it hurt. He watched her drift in and out. She opened and closed her hands for a few minutes without speaking, making fists to determine the strength that remained in her arms. Then she turned her head and opened her eyes and looked at him again, more focused this time.

"The others. Are they okay? Is Vernon okay?"

He put his hand on her shoulder. "Yeah, they're all gonna make it. Even Standard. Vernon's messed up bad, but you know him. Couldn't kill him with a tank."

"Or a missile, I guess." She tried again to smile. "He saved our asses. I thought he was freakin' dead, and all of a sudden he's grabbing epoxy foam and throwing it into the cask. Probably kept us all from snapping in two. And he couldn't even see—he was blinded by the deco sickness and the seal on his helmet."

"Sounds like Vernon."

"Yeah. And Quarles rigged the launcher for auto-eject and found a way to override the safeties for trajectory and escape velocity. Little creep finally did something right."

Dechert laughed. "Vernon Waters, the best man on the Moon. And Jonathan Quarles, a little better than you'll ever want to accept. But you're the one who saved them, Lane. It was your insane idea to climb into the business end of a rail launcher."

She grimaced. "I thought I was killing us, but I couldn't come up with anything else. I mean, I was trying to guess what you'd do, but you were running around out on the mare."

"I'll tell you what I would have done," Dechert said, "I probably would have died, along with everyone else. I sure as hell wouldn't have thought of that."

"Well, don't start handing out ribbons. It was a selfish thing, really. I just figured I'd rather die moving than standing still."

Lane closed her eyes. It would be at least a week before she'd be able to stand on her feet, the doctors had told Dechert. And another two weeks before her body started to feel like it hadn't been squeezed in a vise. *She might never be able to have children, but we don't think there's any brain damage. Has she been known to have seizures?* Questions and possible side effects tumbled out. One of the neurosurgeons had asked Dechert if they could keep her in an observation dome for three months since she had broken the known g-force survival load for a woman, and the tests could result in a groundbreaking medical study for deep-space exploration. Dechert was too tired to break the man's nose, so he had just cursed and walked away.

She tugged at Dechert's sleeve.

"Is it over?"

"Yeah, it's over. The station's a total loss and a lot of people are dead, but it's over. The assholes down on Earth are trying to wiggle out of it, and I think they want to see us disappear, but I've got a little leverage."

"What leverage?" she asked, trying to arch an eyebrow. She was always alert to a scheme. Then she looked up and around the room again. "Where's Thatch?"

Dechert put his hand on her shoulder. How to tell her that Thatcher, her crew member and friend, was an assassin—a killer that had been sizing her up for death every time he had looked her in the eyes? How to tell her that Thatch had betrayed her, just as he once did?

"Thatch is off the Moon, too. Stop worrying so much," he said. "We've got all the time in the world to go through the details."

If she sensed something was wrong, she didn't let him know it, closing her eyes and letting the drugs take hold of her again. "All right," she whispered, and she was in between the room and someplace else.

"How do you feel?"

"Ever get shot out of a cannon?"

"No."

"Lucky you."

Dechert grinned. "Well, the doctors say you just might heal up, even though you pulled somewhere north of twenty-five g's. I'm thinking you'll be flipping off bureaucrats in no time."

She coughed. Dechert sat back and wiped a dry eye with his index finger. He had cried when he first heard they were alive, cried for the first time in thirty years, and it was an incredible feeling, both liberating and revolting. He was glad they were all unconscious at the time, but now he felt the emotions welling back up and he fought to suppress them. All he wanted to do was pull them out of their hospital beds and take them to a bar and get them drunk. *Really, really drunk.* They were alive—all of them except Thatch, who deserved to be dead anyways. A freakin' miracle—for the first time in his life.

"So what's next for us?" she asked, just when he thought she had fallen back asleep. "A few years in the brig? A burrito stand at Las Cruces?"

"Probably a long debriefing in a cold room, and then a little R&R. After that, I don't know. Are you done with space?"

She tried to get up on her elbows. "Hell no. Like I said, I want to die moving."

"Then how does Jupiter sound?"

She raised both eyebrows this time. "Europa Station?"

"Why not? They'll be launching the *Magellan* next year, and I think the government wants us to be out of the neighborhood for a while. You wanna check out the only permanent colony beyond the Asteroid Belt?"

"Maybe." Her hands moved across her hips as if she were checking to make sure the bones were still there. She licked her lips, and Dechert wet a cloth and put it to her mouth.

"I feel like my tongue's wrapped in sandpaper."

"Yeah I know. They don't want you to drink yet; your guts are all messed up. Just let me know when you need some moisture. Nursing's my new specialty. I got Quarles an electrolyte Popsicle a few hours ago, for Christ's sake."

She opened her eyes again, and this time they were focused.

"You know, I read the specs for the Europa base. Looks pretty dicey."

"Oh yeah. Fletcher thought the same thing. Radiation. Gravity wells. Geysers. Moonquakes. Wind up to four hundred knots on Jupiter. At least a ten percent chance of catastrophic failure, last I heard."

She laughed. "You're a pretty terrible salesman. If you want me to be safety officer at the gates of hell, you could at least make up a few positives."

Dechert remained silent for a long moment. Finally he spoke again.

"There aren't too many positives, but I wasn't thinking safety officer." He dabbed her mouth with the cloth again. "I was thinking station chief."

She looked at him. "Station chief? That's your gig."

"Here, maybe. But there—no, I think it should be yours. I'll run the mining ops on Jupiter, but this is a two-track mission. Half the station will be devoted to the science team running subs into Europa's ocean, and someone needs to manage the whole show."

Lane's eyes focused and he thought he saw a flash of anger. "I'm not one for handouts, Dechert. Don't try throwing me a promotion because you feel guilty that you almost got us killed on the Moon. I know you're a masochist when it comes to self-blame."

It was Dechert's turn to be angry—or at least pretend that he was. "I don't throw promotions around, Officer Briggs. I'd can your ass tomorrow if I didn't think you could get things done anymore. But you've been working your way to command for two years now, even if you didn't realize it."

"I didn't realize it."

"Well then, work on your self-awareness. It's an important command attribute."

She digested his words for a few moments. "You'd report to me? You know how crazy that sounds?"

"Don't get too far ahead of yourself. I intend to have plenty of autonomy running the helium-3 ops. But yeah, if a decision has to be made concerning the entire station, it will be your call."

"I would have thought they already had a crew in line for the mission," Lane said, almost like it was a final protest to his offer.

"They did. It was the guys at Sea of Tranquility 1, but the commander and XO got killed in the same missile strike that took down Serenity. Don't think we're the second string, though. You earned this, Lane, and I can get it for you. Do you want it, or not?"

She smiled, and this time it was full. "Yeah, I want it. Especially if Quarles is coming. I'll run that little shit into the ground."

Dechert laughed. "Don't go Ahab on me."

"Only when it comes to Quarles."

And they both laughed.

27

Yates poured scotch into a pair of cut-glass tumblers with a precise hand, as though the two drinks were the most important thing in the universe. Dechert wondered if he got the stuff from the same smuggler that Lane and Quarles used or if his rank allowed him to openly break the Administration's prohibition of alcohol on the Moon. *Hell*, he thought, *what's a little booze when you weren't supposed to have weapons up here?*

"We're working under the theory that Foerrster brought the bomb to Thatch when he visited Serenity in November," Yates said as he stood at the beverage cart. "Military Intelligence believes it's unlikely that Thatch was sitting on a vial of polymeric nitrogen for the last three years. Much more plausible that Foerrster brought it up to the Moon after the op was green-lighted. Thatch probably screwed it to the crawler right before they went out to Posidonius."

He turned to look at Dechert. "He's gone, by the way. Foerrster, I mean. Disappeared like a dust cloud on the terminator. Probably went to ground somewhere in Africa or the South Pacific."

"I'll find him if they don't."

The old man sighed. He was in full uniform, pressed and white, with a gold Space Mining Administration insignia on the chest, and he had no gravity-inducing weights on his body. Legend had it that Yates refused to wear his 1-g heavysuit, arguing that he planned to die on the Moon and wouldn't need the extra bone mass to get around back on Earth. He looked tired, but was clearly trying not to show it.

"Have you ever read von Clausewitz, Dechert?" Yates asked as he finished measuring a few drops of water into the whiskey. "'War is the continuation of politics through other means?'"

"I remember the quote."

"Well, you've pretty much subverted those other means. And a lot of people on Earth are pissed about it."

"I'm just a dirt digger, Yates. What exactly are you trying to say?"

Yates gave the drinks a quick stir with a silver bar spoon, letting the alcohol chill into the ice. He turned to hand one of the glasses to Dechert.

"I'm trying to say that I'm a little amazed someone hasn't come up to the Moon yet to toss you into a black bag."

"They already tried, remember? And I'm right here. Tell the next one to look me up."

Yates shook his head. He glided around his large circular desk, which appeared to be made of organic wood and obsidian and must have cost a fortune to ship up from Earth. He sat down in his high-backed black leather chair.

"Such brio," he said. "I don't understand it. There was a time when business was strictly business on the Moon. Now everyone wants to get personal. It's . . . so unprofessional."

"I'm not in the mood to talk business or political theory with you, Yates. And I'm not here to listen to excuses. I'm here to set my terms and find out when there's going to be a reckoning."

Yates sat back in his chair and took a tiny sip of the scotch. His white eyebrows hung over the glass like a condor's wings as he studied Dechert's face. "A reckoning," he whispered. "All right, Commander. What are your terms?"

Dechert stood up and walked over to the panoramic window, which ran from one end of Yates's cylindrical corner office to the other and gave a spectacular view of the sunlit reaches of the lunar North Pole. An astronaut appeared below, bounding along the surface toward a storage silo at the far corner of the station. Dechert could see the small plumes of moondust he kicked up in his wake.

"Pretty simple. A bilateral weapons ban in space. And the Jupiter mission for my team." He took a sip of the scotch. "I want Briggs for station chief, and I want full control of the mining operation."

Yates coughed into a closed fist. "Well, you don't come cheap. Do you really think you can blackmail them, Dechert? At some point new leaders will take over in D.C., and they won't care if you expose the dirty little secrets of their predecessors."

Dechert turned. "I'm sure that's true, Yates. But for now I think they *do* care, and that's all that matters. Let the ones who remain standing know that if any of my crew conveniently dies in the next few years, my little montage of Thatch doing bad things will be all over the stream, with a lot of appending information."

"But a weapons ban in space?" Yates said, chuckling. He

put his glass down on a stone coaster and rubbed the wrinkled seam of his forehead with an index finger. "Isn't that like asking for world peace?"

Dechert shrugged and returned to his seat. "It's like a one-night stand in Vegas. It might not matter a month after it happens, but it feels pretty damned good at the moment. I just want to buy some time so my crew isn't running from missiles again anytime soon. Once we're dead and gone, you assholes can start all the inner-system wars you want."

Yates considered him. Dechert had heard enough through side channels to know the predicament the government was in. Parrish and the rest of the Earth media had been banging down doors in Washington and Beijing to figure out what had happened on the Moon over the last few days, and despite the news embargo, word was trickling down to the home planet about the destruction that had been wrought on U.S. and Chinese mining stations. The main bases were still intact but Sea of Serenity 1 and New Beijing 2 had been wiped from the lunar surface, as well as a few smaller Chinese and American mining stations. His friend Lin Tzu was dead, as were twelve other Chinese miners and soldiers. Tzu had stayed at his post until a U.S. missile bored in and ended his life, and even though Dechert knew the Chinese government would never have allowed him to evacuate the station, he felt a slight twinge of envy at the bravery of his last act. Who was the better man? Once again Tzu had proven that he was, by a significant margin.

Nine U.S. crew members had also been killed, including Hale, Thatch, and the shuttle team led by Cabrera. Billions of dollars of mining infrastructure had been destroyed, tourism and sys-ex and terra-energy franchises had been put in jeopardy, and Chinese and American production of helium-3 had been set back by months.

And then it all stopped, like the shutter on a camera being closed.

The fallout had begun to disperse behind a lot of important doors on Earth. The previous head of the Office of Environmental Analysis—currently the chief of naval operations and a candidate for president—had been quietly relieved of his duties. Word had it that he was going to claim ill health and retire from the presidential race. Other heads had been lopped off completely, mostly two-star generals and a few cabinet-level bureaucrats.

But why had the Chinese agreed to stand down? Why had they been so quiet about a one-day war that apparently had been launched by the other side? That was the one thing that Dechert couldn't figure out, but he knew from the look on Yates's face that the Moon's American prefect was about to tell him.

"You know Thatch was right about the Chinese?" Yates finally asked. "They were grossly underreporting their He-3 production to the ISA, and working side deals in Holland and Peru to cut us out of some very large contracts. They also stole our specs for the magnetic drive on *Magellan*, maybe the biggest intelligence coup of the twenty-first century. Word has it they're launching the *Yang Liwei* to Uranus before next summer, and it will get there before we get to Jupiter. They've been playing the big new bully on the block to a tee. They were stomping their boot right on our neck, and they didn't seem to care that we knew it."

Dechert shook his head. "So we start a goddamned war?"

"You think I'm agreeing with this lunacy? I'm just painting the picture for you, Dechert, because you're not very good at looking at things from more than six feet above the ground."

"So paint away," Dechert said. "This crazy bastard who used to head up the OEA, Admiral Parks, he ran some kind of clandestine group that planted Thatch on the Moon three years ago, just in case they needed to drum up a war with the Chinese—by killing our own people? Do you know how insane that sounds?"

Yates nodded. "Of course it's insane, but I doubt everything was as preplanned as you suggest. And have you forgotten how insane things have been on Earth for the last ten years? Do you think all the fear, all the insecurity that came out of the Max just fades away? Did you think our leaders would react well to becoming a secondary power?"

Dechert shook his head. "So what did they get out of it? What could they possibly have gotten out of their own gold getting blown up on the Moon?"

"I don't know. A pause, maybe. A window for Europa to be based, and the mining operations in the Belt to start turning a profit. Probably, more than anything, they wanted to tell China they weren't going to go quietly."

"And if the whole thing blew up into a war on Earth?"

"Oh, I'm sure they had those chances calculated down to a percentage point. My guess is, they found the risk acceptable."

Dechert could feel his face getting hot. He took a drink and tried to keep his voice down. "Well, I don't find it acceptable. And I'm not going to sit by and watch Parks and Foerrster and whoever else ran this thing quietly retire to their mansions on the Chesapeake Bay or their safe houses in the Solomon Islands. I told you I want a reckoning. Those bastards killed Cole. They damned near killed my entire team."

Yates chuckled, then held up a hand when he saw Dechert was about to blow.

"Easy. I'm not laughing about Cole or anything else that happened up here. I lost people, too, and I won't soon get over it. I'm laughing at your naiveté. If Thatch was right about anything, it was that."

"What do you mean?"

"I mean this: Do you really think a three-star admiral was the last person to sign off on a plan to stage a lunar conflict with China?"

"Baby me, Yates. I'm still not getting you."

"Fine." Yates stared at Dechert as he ran a finger along the rim of his tumbler. "Did you know that Admiral Parks and the president are both ring knockers?"

"Come again?"

"Ring knockers, Dechert. Naval Academy graduates. They were in the same class. I understand they roomed together as plebes."

Dechert sat back and took it in. "What . . . you're saying the president of the United States did this?"

"Well, I doubt that he knew all the details, and I'm sure you won't find a written order anywhere, plausible deniability being what it is, but yes. It's a pretty safe bet that a lunar war wasn't initiated without his say-so." Yates leaned forward. "In other words, this is no conspiracy of middle managers, Dechert. And that's why I'm trying to get you to stop tilting at windmills."

"You've got to be kidding me."

"You're surprised?" Yates asked. He stared at Dechert again and took another sip of his whiskey. "We're not talking about some piddling oil field under the North Atlantic, Dechert. This is about the long-term rights to a power supply that could fuel the Earth for a thousand years, and perhaps beyond. We're talking about the gateway to Jupiter and Uranus and the Kuiper Belt. Who knows? Whoever wins this treasure could be the first to reach Epsilon Eridani fifty years from now, and colonize the stars a hundred years after that."

He stood up and stretched, putting his hands behind his back and strolling around the desk. "How many kingdoms fell in antiquity trying to win the Silk Road or the spice routes from Asia? Silk and salt? Those are trinkets compared to helium-3, Dechert, the childhood toys of feckless princes."

"That was thousands of years ago, Yates," Dechert said. He had heard this argument in a strikingly similar way from Lin Tzu, and it still irritated him. "I was hoping we could take into account some form of human evolution."

"Oh? Then you're a damned fool. Let me give you the real picture, Dechert. We are still the beast, and we always will be. And all this stuff that we fight over—power, money, territory, helium-3—it's little more than a carcass on an African plain. A more refined version of life and death in the animal kingdom."

Dechert finished his drink and put his glass down on Yates's desk, ignoring the nearby coaster. He wanted to say that settling space could have changed all of that, that people could have set a new order to things when they left Earth. *That they didn't have to bring all their shit up to the heavens with them.* But he only shrugged his shoulders.

"I'll let you fight for the scraps with the rest of the hyenas, Yates. I've done enough for those assholes, and I want out."

"Mmm," Yates purred. He returned to his desk and sat down. "Which brings us to our current business. You know the spooks will find your secret file on the stream, this blind runner account that you boast of. They'll find it and destroy it, and their current need to bow to your demands will be rendered obsolete."

Dechert laughed. "Are those the same guys who let China steal our plans for a deep-space drive?" He caught Yates's eyes and held them. "My guy is smarter than their guys, Yates. If he cared a little more about the spoils you speak of, Quarles would probably be running the entire show by now. They'll never find his program."

"You're wrong, Dechert. Governments may be stupid and

clumsy, but they have the advantage of brute force." Yates straightened his jacket. "Listen, I've gone to the mat for you on this thing. I've even threatened them with my own personal treason if anything happened to you or your team. I like the idea of you being alive out there beyond the Asteroid Belt—the last idealist in the solar system. But you have to follow my lead on this, or I'll cut you loose like a torn sail."

The two stared at each other for a few seconds, not speaking. Dechert relented. "Fine, what's the proposal?"

Yates sighed. "Simple. You hand over your little video of Thatch. You and your crew sign the mother of all nondisclosure agreements, and then you get Europa. Burling and Jenner are dead, so I can make the argument that you're the next team up. They'll like the idea of you being very far away, and it won't be hard to pitch the value of you running the mining operations on Jupiter. You've always been a hell of a digger."

He put his palms on the table. "I can't promise you much about the world peace thing, but if it helps, rumor has it we're already talking to China about a five-year ban on weapons on the Moon."

"And Cole? Lin Tzu? Who pays for the lives that were taken?"

Yates shrugged. "I don't know, Dechert. If I had to guess, I'd say no one. You hurt them, but this isn't a beast that you or I can bring down. Even if you went full disclosure with your video of what happened at Yangel', they'd come up with a way to wriggle out of it. When it comes down to it, most people on Earth are still too worried about food to give two nickels about what happens on the Moon."

They locked eyes again as Yates slurped a piece of ice into his mouth and rolled it around his tongue. Dechert nodded and stood up.

"I'll do it, Yates, but between you and me, this thing isn't over. Someday it will get out."

"Fine. Just take your scalps *after* I'm dead."

Dechert shook his head and turned to the door.

"And Dechert?" Yates asked to his back.

"What?"

"Make me some money when you get to Europa, or all deals are off. Business is business, you know."

28

"And I thought you loved the Moon," Quarles said.

They sat in the passenger hold of a freighter on the way to Low Earth Orbit 1. The station hung in space like a gleaming snowflake a few thousand kilometers away. Lane and Quarles were across from Dechert in folding jump seats, looking bruised and stiff but alive. They all stared out at the space station and the home planet below it. Earth took up half of the porthole. Its bright colors made it seem less than real.

"I did love the Moon," Dechert said, his eyes fixed on the Pacific Ocean. "It's just too damned close to Earth."

Lane began to laugh, but she stopped midway when she looked at Dechert and saw that he wasn't smiling.

"I wonder how long it will be before you think the same thing about Jupiter," she said.

Vernon wasn't with them. He was still in a medical pod in lunar orbit, getting treatment for his damaged lungs. Dechert had visited him every day for the last week, sick at the sight of a man who had been so strong, now stuck full of tubes and immersed in a nucleopeptide bath. The doctors said he would recover and could even make the trip to Jupiter if his lungs healed in time, but Dechert had never done well around the injured and was guiltily relieved that he wouldn't see his mission chief for a while. He hoped that the next time he entered his hospital room, Vernon would at least be lying in a regular bed and looking human.

The shuttle banked in its final approach to LEO-1, the spars of the station gleaming white and gray against the blue backdrop of Earth's oceans. *Six months of training if the deal holds up,* Dechert mused, *and then a one-year hop to Jupiter in the largest spaceship ever constructed.* He wondered if the deep-space medical tests they gave these days were more intrusive than the ones he had to undergo for lunar service. Hopefully, the instruments were smaller by now.

"I can't believe we're letting those bastards walk away from this," Lane said, breaking the silence. "It feels like we're leaving Cole behind."

Dechert's eyes strayed from the window to Lane's face. "Don't be so sure about that."

"What do you mean?"

"I mean you should look for a story about war and treachery on the Moon sometime next year, after we're long gone. A Reuters story, by a kid named Josh Parrish."

Quarles's eyes flared open. "You broke the NDA?"

"Hell no. I wouldn't do that."

"Then who did?"

"Standard—from the moment he walked into Serenity 1. He had me give Parrish access to our server the day after our first meeting, so he could file a story to his editors back on Earth. How was I supposed to know the little snoop would look up my personal passwords?"

"You mean . . . ?" Lane asked.

"I mean I'm pretty sure he found a stream address that can't be opened until the end of 2073. An address containing my updated personal logs. It might not have any videos, but you know how anal I am about writing down all the details."

"You're my hero," Quarles said.

"All I did was misread reporters. I thought they had better ethics."

They laughed, and Dechert returned to the view below, the Earth taking up the entire margin of the glass now, no blackness of space to be seen. Quarles punched a button on a miniature player he had strapped to his belt, and the faraway voice of a singer spilled from the tiny device. A man who was long dead, singing about something stirring and trying to climb toward the light.

"That's some depressing stuff," Lane said.

"It's deep, my princess of Jove," Quarles replied. "Someday I'll explain it to you."

"Call me Commander, and don't even try."

Quarles made a gagging gesture.

"Good Lord," Dechert grumbled.

The shuttle slowed as it neared an open landing bay on one of the station's rotating trusses. The Earth shone like a marker in the surrounding void, seductive and alive. Dechert stared at her oceans and continents and clouds, and thought of the Catoctin Mountains and their greenstone streams, brimming with trout.

Then he closed his eyes and dreamed of Jupiter's moons, the spell of the Earth broken.

ACKNOWLEDGMENTS

First and foremost, I'd like to thank my agent, David Fugate of LaunchBooks Literary Agency, and my editor, David Pomerico of Harper Voyager. They made this a much better book than it would have been and did so in true professional fashion. I'd also like to thank all of the people at Harper Voyager and HarperCollins who had a hand in bringing this book to life. A special shout-out to Dr. Mark Pedreira, professor of English literature and rhetoric, who took time away from the genius of Milton, Johnson, and Locke to read this story and provide valuable feedback; and to Madison Pedreira, budding young scientist, who helped with math and other thorny issues that exceeded my intellectual capabilities. Also, I'm indebted to all the reporters and editors I worked with over the years at

Capital News Service, *The Annapolis Capital*, the *Tampa Tribune*, and the *St. Petersburg Times*. They all made me a better writer, whether it's reflected here or not. Lastly, my deepest appreciation to my entire family, for their decades of patience and love.

ABOUT THE AUTHOR

A former reporter for newspapers including the *Tampa Tribune* and the *St. Petersburg Times*, David Pedreira has won awards for his writing from the Associated Press, the Society of Professional Journalists, the Maryland-Delaware-D.C. Press Association, and the American Society of Newspaper Editors. He lives in Tampa, Florida.